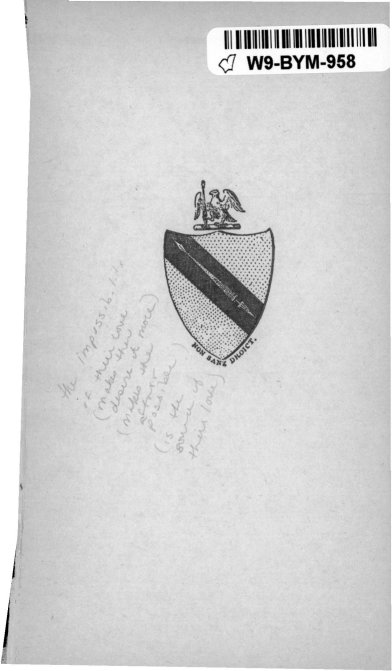

the impossibility
of their love
(makes their
desire the more)
(makes their
desire the more
possible)
(is the
source of
their love)

William Shakespeare

The Tragedy of
ROMEO AND JULIET

EDITED BY J. A. BRYANT, JR.

The Signet Classic Shakespeare
GENERAL EDITOR: SYLVAN BARNET

*Revised and Updated
Bibliography*

A SIGNET CLASSIC
NEW AMERICAN LIBRARY

New York and Scarborough, Ontario

Ⓒ

SIGNET CLASSIC TRADEMARK REG. U.S. PAT. OFF. AND FOREIGN COUNTRIES
REGISTERED TRADEMARK—MARCA REGISTRADA
IECHO EN CHICAGO, U.S.A.

SIGNET, SIGNET CLASSIC, MENTOR, PLUME, MERIDIAN AND NAL
BOOKS are published in the United States by
New American Library,
1633 Broadway, New York, New York 10019,
in Canada by New American Library of Canada Limited,
81 Mack Avenue, Scarborough, Ontario M1L 1M8

20   21   22   23   24   25   26   27   28

PRINTED IN THE UNITED STATES OF AMERICA

Contents

Shakespeare: Prefatory Remarks

Between the record of his baptism in Stratford on 26
April 1564 and the record of his burial in Stratford on
25 April 1616, some forty documents name Shakespeare,
and many others name his parents, his children, and his
grandchildren. More facts are known about William
Shakespeare than about any other playwright of the period
except Ben Jonson. The facts should, however, be distin-
guished from the legends. The latter, inevitably more
engaging and better known, tell us that the Stratford boy
killed a calf in high style, poached deer and rabbits, and
was forced to flee to London, where he held horses outside a playhouse. These traditions are only traditions; they
may be true, but no evidence supports them, and it is well
to stick to the facts.

Mary Arden, the dramatist's mother, was the daughter
of a substantial landowner; about 1557 she married John
Shakespeare, who was a glove-maker and trader in various farm commodities. In 1557 John Shakespeare was a
member of the Council (the governing body of Stratford),
in 1558 a constable of the borough, in 1561 one of the
two town chamberlains, in 1565 an alderman (entitling
him to the appellation "Mr."), in 1568 high bailiff—the
town's highest political office, equivalent to mayor. After
1577, for an unknown reason he drops out of local poli-
tics. The birthday of William Shakespeare, the eldest son of
this locally prominent man, is unrecorded; but the Stratford parish register records that the infant was baptized on
26 April 1564. (It is quite possible that he was born on

23 April, but this date has probably been assigned by tradition because it is the date on which, fifty-two years later, he died.) The attendance records of the Stratford grammar school of the period are not extant, but it is reasonable to assume that the son of a local official attended the school and received substantial training in Latin. The masters of the school from Shakespeare's seventh to fifteenth years held Oxford degrees; the Elizabethan curriculum excluded mathematics and the natural sciences but taught a good deal of Latin rhetoric, logic, and literature. On 27 November 1582 a marriage license was issued to Shakespeare and Anne Hathaway, eight years his senior. The couple had a child in May, 1583. Perhaps the marriage was necessary, but perhaps the couple had earlier engaged in a formal "troth plight" which would render their children legitimate even if no further ceremony were performed. In 1585 Anne Hathaway bore Shakespeare twins.

That Shakespeare was born is excellent; that he married and had children is pleasant; but that we know nothing about his departure from Stratford to London, or about the beginning of his theatrical career, is lamentable and must be admitted. We would gladly sacrifice details about his children's baptism for details about his earliest days on the stage. Perhaps the poaching episode is true (but it is first reported almost a century after Shakespeare's death), or perhaps he first left Stratford to be a schoolteacher, as another tradition holds; perhaps he was moved by

> Such wind as scatters young men through the world,
> To seek their fortunes further than at home
> Where small experience grows.

In 1592, thanks to the cantankerousness of Robert Greene, a rival playwright and a pamphleteer, we have our first reference, a snarling one, to Shakespeare as an actor and playwright. Greene warns those of his own educated friends who wrote for the theater against an actor who has presumed to turn playwright:

There is an upstart crow, beautified with our feathers, that with his *tiger's heart wrapped in a player's hide* supposes he is as well able to bombast out a blank verse as the best of you, and being an absolute Johannes-factotum is in his own conceit the only Shake-scene in a country.

The reference to the player, as well as the allusion to Aesop's crow (who strutted in borrowed plumage, as an actor struts in fine words not his own), makes it clear that by this date Shakespeare had both acted and written. That Shakespeare is meant is indicated not only by "Shake-scene" but by the parody of a line from one of Shakespeare's plays, *3 Henry VI:* "O, tiger's heart wrapped in a woman's hide." If Shakespeare in 1592 was prominent enough to be attacked by an envious dramatist, he probably had served an apprenticeship in the theater for at least a few years.

In any case, by 1592 Shakespeare had acted and written, and there are a number of subsequent references to him as an actor: documents indicate that in 1598 he is a "principal comedian," in 1603 a "principal tragedian," in 1608 he is one of the "men players." The profession of actor was not for a gentleman, and it occasionally drew the scorn of university men who resented writing speeches for persons less educated than themselves, but it was respectable enough: players, if prosperous, were in effect members of the bourgeoisie, and there is nothing to suggest that Stratford considered William Shakespeare less than a solid citizen. When, in 1596, the Shakespeares were granted a coat of arms, the grant was made to Shakespeare's father, but probably William Shakespeare (who the next year bought the second-largest house in town) had arranged the matter on his own behalf. In subsequent transactions he is occasionally styled a gentleman.

Although in 1593 and 1594 Shakespeare published two narrative poems dedicated to the Earl of Southampton, *Venus and Adonis* and *The Rape of Lucrece,* and may well have written most or all of his sonnets in the middle nineties, Shakespeare's literary activity seems to have been almost entirely devoted to the theater. (It may be significant that the two narrative poems were written in years when the plague closed the theaters for several months.) In 1594 he was a charter member of a theatrical company called the Chamberlain's Men (which in 1603 changed its name to the King's Men); until he retired to Stratford (about 1611, apparently), he was with this remarkably stable company. From 1599 the company acted primarily at the Globe Theatre, in which Shakespeare held a one-tenth interest. Other Elizabethan dramatists are known to have acted, but no other is known also to have been entitled to a share in the profits of the playhouse.

Shakespeare's first eight published plays did not have his name on them, but this is not remarkable; the most popular play of the sixteenth century, Thomas Kyd's *The Spanish Tragedy,* went through many editions without naming Kyd, and Kyd's authorship is known only because a book on the profession of acting happens to quote (and attribute to Kyd) some lines on the interest of Roman emperors in the drama. What is remarkable is that after 1598 Shakespeare's name commonly appears on printed plays—some of which are not his. Another indication of his popularity comes from Francis Meres, author of *Palladis Tamia: Wit's Treasury* (1598): in this anthology of snippets accompanied by an essay on literature, many playwrights are mentioned, but Shakespeare's name occurs more often than any other, and Shakespeare is the only playwright whose plays are listed.

From his acting, playwriting, and share in a theater, Shakespeare seems to have made considerable money. He put it to work, making substantial investments in Stratford real estate. When he made his will (less than a month before he died), he sought to leave his property intact to his descendants. Of small bequests to relatives and to friends (including three actors, Richard Burbage, John Heminges, and Henry Condell), that to his wife of the second-best bed has provoked the most comment; perhaps it was the bed the couple had slept in, the best being reserved for visitors. In any case, had Shakespeare not excepted it, the bed would have gone (with the rest of his household possessions) to his daughter and her husband. On 25 April 1616 he was buried within the chancel of the church at Stratford. An unattractive monument to his memory, placed on a wall near the grave, says he died on 23 April. Over the grave itself are the lines, perhaps by Shakespeare, that (more than his literary fame) have kept his bones undisturbed in the crowded burial ground where old bones were often dislodged to make way for new:

> Good friend, for Jesus' sake forbear
> To dig the dust enclosèd here.
> Blessed be the man that spares these stones
> And cursed be he that moves my bones.

Thirty-seven plays, as well as some nondramatic poems, are held to constitute the Shakespeare canon. The dates of composition of most of the works are highly uncertain, but there is often evidence of a *terminus a quo* (starting point) and/or a *terminus ad quem* (terminal point) that provides a framework for intelligent guessing. For example, *Richard II* cannot be earlier than 1595, the publication date of some material to which it is indebted; *The Merchant of Venice* cannot be later than 1598, the year Francis Meres mentioned it. Sometimes arguments for a date hang on an alleged topical allusion, such as the lines about the unseasonable weather in *A Midsummer Night's Dream,* II.i.81–117, but such an allusion (if indeed it is an allusion) can be variously interpreted, and in any case there is always the possibility that a topical allusion was inserted during a revision, years after the composition of a play. Dates are often attributed on the basis of style, and although conjectures about style usually rest on other conjectures, sooner or later one must rely on one's literary sense. There is no real proof, for example, that *Othello* is not as early as *Romeo and Juliet,* but one feels *Othello* is later, and because the first record of its performance is 1604, one is glad enough to set its composition at that date and not push it back into Shakespeare's early years. The following chronology, then, is as much indebted to informed guesswork and sensitivity as it is to fact. The dates, necessarily imprecise, indicate something like a scholarly consensus.

PLAYS

1588–93	*The Comedy of Errors*
1588–94	*Love's Labor's Lost*
1590–91	*2 Henry VI*
1590–91	*3 Henry VI*
1591–92	*1 Henry VI*
1592–93	*Richard III*
1592–94	*Titus Andronicus*
1593–94	*The Taming of the Shrew*
1593–95	*The Two Gentlemen of Verona*
1594–96	*Romeo and Juliet*
1595	*Richard II*
1594–96	*A Midsummer Night's Dream*
1596–97	*King John*
1596–97	*The Merchant of Venice*
1597	*1 Henry IV*
1597–98	*2 Henry IV*
1598–1600	*Much Ado About Nothing*
1598–99	*Henry V*
1599	*Julius Caesar*
1599–1600	*As You Like It*
1599–1600	*Twelfth Night*
1600–01	*Hamlet*
1597–1601	*The Merry Wives of Windsor*
1601–02	*Troilus and Cressida*
1602–04	*All's Well That Ends Well*
1603–04	*Othello*
1604	*Measure for Measure*
1605–06	*King Lear*
1605–06	*Macbeth*
1606–07	*Antony and Cleopatra*
1605–08	*Timon of Athens*
1607–09	*Coriolanus*
1608–09	*Pericles*

POEMS

Shakespeare's Theater

In Shakespeare's infancy, Elizabethan actors performed wherever they could—in great halls, at court, in the courtyards of inns. The innyards must have made rather unsatisfactory theaters: on some days they were unavailable because carters bringing goods to London used them as depots; when available, they had to be rented from the innkeeper; perhaps most important, London inns were subject to the Common Council of London, which was not well disposed toward theatricals. In 1574 the Common Council required that plays and playing places in London be licensed. It asserted that

> sundry great disorders and inconveniences have been found to ensue to this city by the inordinate haunting of great multitudes of people, specially youth, to plays, interludes, and shows, namely occasion of frays and quarrels, evil practices of incontinency in great inns having chambers and secret places adjoining to their open stages and galleries,

and ordered that innkeepers who wished licenses to hold performances put up a bond and make contributions to the poor.

The requirement that plays and innyard theaters be licensed, along with the other drawbacks of playing at inns, probably drove James Burbage (a carpenter-turned-actor) to rent in 1576 a plot of land northeast of the city walls and to build here—on property outside the jurisdiction of the city—England's first permanent construction designed for plays. He called it simply the Theatre. About all that is known of its construction is that it was wood. It soon had imitators, the most famous being the Globe (1599), built across the Thames (again outside the city's jurisdiction), out of timbers of the Theatre, which had been dismantled when Burbage's lease ran out.

There are three important sources of information about the structure of Elizabethan playhouses—drawings, a contract, and stage directions in plays. Of drawings, only the so-called De Witt drawing (c. 1596) of the Swan—really a friend's copy of De Witt's drawing—is of much significance. It shows a building of three tiers, with a stage jutting from a wall into the yard or center of the building. The tiers are roofed, and part of the stage is covered by a roof that projects from the rear and is supported at its front on two posts, but the groundlings, who paid a penny to stand in front of the stage, were exposed to the sky. (Performances in such a playhouse were held only in the daytime; artificial illumination was not used.) At the rear of the stage are two doors; above the stage is a gallery. The second major source of information, the contract for the Fortune, specifies that although the Globe is to be the model, the Fortune is to be square, eighty feet outside and fifty-five inside. The stage is to be forty-three feet broad, and is to extend into the middle of the yard (i.e., it is twenty-seven and a half feet deep). For patrons willing to pay more than the general admission charged of the groundlings, there were to be three galleries provided with seats. From the third chief source, stage directions, one learns that entrance to the stage was by doors, presumably spaced widely apart at the rear ("Enter one citizen at one door, and another at the other"), and that in addition to the platform stage there was occasionally some sort of curtained booth or alcove allowing for "discovery" scenes, and some sort of playing space "aloft" or "above" to represent (for example) the top of a city's walls or a room above the street. Doubtless each theater had its own peculiarities, but perhaps we can talk about a "typical" Elizabethan theater if we realize that no theater need exactly have fit the description, just as no father is the typical father with 3.7 children. This hypothetical theater is wooden, round or polygonal (in *Henry V* Shakespeare calls it a "wooden *O*"), capable of holding some eight hundred spectators standing in the yard around the projecting elevated stage and some fifteen hundred additional spectators seated in the three roofed galleries. The stage, protected by a "shadow" or "heavens" or roof, is entered by two doors; behind the doors is the "tiring house" (attiring house, i.e., dressing room), and above the doors is some sort of gallery that may sometimes hold spectators but that can be used (for example) as the bedroom from which Romeo—according to a stage direction in one text—"goeth down." Some evidence suggests that a throne can be lowered onto the platform stage, perhaps from the "shadow"; certainly characters can descend from the stage through a trap or traps into the cellar or "hell." Sometimes this space beneath the platform accommodates a sound-effects man or musician (in *Antony and Cleopatra* "music of the hautboys is under the stage") or an actor (in *Hamlet* the "Ghost cries under the stage"). Most characters simply walk on and off, but because there is no curtain in front of the platform, corpses will have to be carried off (Hamlet must lug Polonius' guts into the neighbor room), or will have to fall at the rear, where the curtain on the alcove or booth can be drawn to conceal them.

Such may have been the so-called "public theater." Another kind of theater, called the "private theater" because its much greater admission charge limited its audience to the wealthy or the prodigal, must be briefly mentioned. The private theater was basically a large room, entirely roofed and therefore artificially illuminated, with a stage at one end. In 1576 one such theater was established in Blackfriars, a Dominican priory in London that had been suppressed in 1538 and confiscated by the Crown and thus was not under the city's jurisdiction. All the actors in the Blackfriars theater were boys about eight to thirteen years old (in the public theaters similar boys played female parts; a boy Lady Macbeth played to a man Macbeth). This private theater had a precarious existence, and ceased operations in 1584. In 1596 James Burbage, who had already made theatrical history by building the Theatre, began to construct a second Blackfriars theater. He died in 1597, and for several years this second Blackfriars theater was used by a troupe of boys, but in 1608 two of Burbage's sons and five other actors (including Shakespeare) became joint operators of the theater, using it in the winter when the open-air Globe was unsuitable. Perhaps such a smaller theater, roofed, artificially illuminated, and with a tradition of a courtly audience, exerted an influence on Shakespeare's late plays.

Performances in the private theaters may well have had intermissions during which music was played, but in the public theaters the action was probably uninterrupted, flowing from scene to scene almost without a break. Actors would enter, speak, exit, and others would immediately enter and establish (if necessary) the new locale by a few properties and by words and gestures. Here are some samples of Shakespeare's scene painting:

> This is Illyria, lady.

> Well, this is the Forest of Arden.

> This castle hath a pleasant seat; the air
> Nimbly and sweetly recommends itself
> Unto our gentle senses.

On the other hand, it is a mistake to conceive of the Elizabethan stage as bare. Although Shakespeare's Chorus in *Henry V* calls the stage an "unworthy scaffold" and urges the spectators to "eke out our performance with your mind," there was considerable spectacle. The last act of *Macbeth,* for example, has five stage directions calling for "drum and colors," and another sort of appeal to the eye is indicated by the stage direction "Enter Macduff, with Macbeth's head." Some scenery and properties may have been substantial; doubtless a throne was used, and in one play of the period we encounter this direction: "Hector takes up a great piece of rock and casts at Ajax, who tears up a young tree by the roots and assails Hector." The matter is of some importance, and will be glanced at again in the next section.

The Texts of Shakespeare

Though eighteen of his plays were published during his lifetime, Shakespeare seems never to have supervised their publication. There is nothing unusual here; when a playwright sold a play to a theatrical company he surrendered his ownership of it. Normally a company would not publish the play, because to publish it meant to allow competitors to acquire the piece. Some plays, however, did get published: apparently treacherous actors sometimes pieced together a play for a publisher, sometimes a company in need of money sold a play, and sometimes a company allowed a play to be published that no longer drew audiences. That Shakespeare did not concern himself with publication, then, is scarcely remarkable; of his contemporaries only Ben Jonson carefully supervised the publication of his own plays. In 1623, seven years after Shakespeare's death, John Heminges and Henry Condell (two senior members of Shakespeare's company, who had performed with him for about twenty years) collected his plays—published and unpublished—into a large volume, commonly called the First Folio. (A folio is a volume consisting of sheets that have been folded once, each sheet thus making two leaves, or four pages. The eighteen plays published during Shakespeare's lifetime had been issued one play per volume in small books called quartos. Each sheet in a quarto has been folded twice, making four leaves, or eight pages.) The First Folio contains thirty-six plays; a thirty-seventh, *Pericles,* though not in the Folio is regarded as canonical. Heminges and Condell suggest in an address "To the great variety of readers" that the republished plays are presented in better form than in the quartos: "Before you were abused with diverse stolen and surreptitious copies, maimed and deformed by the frauds and stealths of injurious impostors that exposed them; even those, are now offered to your view cured and perfect of their limbs, and all the rest absolute in their numbers, as he [i.e., Shakespeare] conceived them."

Whoever was assigned to prepare the texts for publication in the First Folio seems to have taken his job seriously and yet not to have performed it with uniform care. The sources of the texts seem to have been, in general, good unpublished copies or the best published copies. The first play in the collection, *The Tempest,* is divided into acts and scenes, has unusually full stage directions and descriptions of spectacle, and concludes with a list of the characters, but the editor was not able (or willing) to present all of the succeeding texts so fully dressed. Later texts occasionally show signs of carelessness: in one scene of *Much Ado About Nothing* the names of actors, instead of characters, appear as speech prefixes, as they had in the quarto, which the Folio reprints; proofreading throughout the Folio is spotty and apparently was done without reference to the printer's copy; the pagination of *Hamlet* jumps from 156 to 257.

A modern editor of Shakespeare must first select his copy; no problem if the play exists only in the Folio, but a considerable problem if the relationship between a quarto and the Folio—or an early quarto and a later one—is unclear. When an editor has chosen what seems to him to be the most authoritative text or texts for his copy, he has not done with making decisions. First of all, he must reckon with Elizabethan spelling. If he is not producing a facsimile, he probably modernizes it, but ought he to preserve the old form of words that apparently were pronounced quite unlike their modern forms—"lanthorn," "alablaster"? If he preserves these forms, is he really preserving Shakespeare's forms or perhaps those of a compositor in the printing house? What is one to do when one finds "lanthorn" and "lantern" in adjacent lines? (The editors of this series in general, but not invariably, assume that words should be spelled in their modern form.) Elizabethan punctuation, too, presents problems. For example in the First Folio, the only text for the play, Macbeth rejects his wife's idea that he can wash the blood from his hand:

> no: this my Hand will rather
> The multitudinous Seas incarnardine,
> Making the Greene one, Red.

Obviously an editor will remove the superfluous capitals, and he will probably alter the spelling to "incarnadine," but will he leave the comma before "red," letting Macbeth speak of the sea as "the green one," or will he (like most modern editors) remove the comma and thus have Macbeth say that his hand will make the ocean *uniformly* red?

An editor will sometimes have to change more than spelling or punctuation. Macbeth says to his wife:

> I dare do all that may become a man,
> Who dares no more, is none.

For two centuries editors have agreed that the second line is unsatisfactory, and have emended "no" to "do": "Who dares do more is none." But when in the same play Ross says that fearful persons

> floate vpon a wilde and violent Sea
> Each way, and moue,

need "move" be emended to "none," as it often is, on the hunch that the compositor misread the manuscript? The editors of the Signet Classic Shakespeare have restrained themselves from making abundant emendations. In their minds they hear Dr. Johnson on the dangers of emending: "I have adopted the Roman sentiment, that it is more

honorable to save a citizen than to kill an enemy." Some
departures (in addition to spelling, punctuation, and
lineation) from the copy text have of course been made,
but the original readings are listed in a note following
the play, so that the reader can evaluate them for himself.

The editors of the Signet Classic Shakespeare, following tradition, have added line numbers and in many
cases act and scene divisions as well as indications of
locale at the beginning of scenes. The Folio divided
most of the plays into acts and some into scenes. Early
eighteenth-century editors increased the divisions. These
divisions, which provide a convenient way of referring
to passages in the plays, have been retained, but when
not in the text chosen as the basis for the Signet Classic
text they are enclosed in square brackets [ ] to indicate
that they are editorial additions. Similarly, although no
play of Shakespeare's published during his lifetime was
equipped with indications of locale at the heads of scene
divisions, locales have here been added in square brackets
for the convenience of the reader, who lacks the information afforded to spectators by costumes, properties, and
gestures. The spectator can tell at a glance he is in the
throne room, but without an editorial indication the
reader may be puzzled for a while. It should be mentioned,
incidentally, that there are a few authentic stage directions
—perhaps Shakespeare's, perhaps a prompter's—that suggest locales: for example, "Enter Brutus in his orchard,"
and "They go up into the Senate house." It is hoped that
the bracketed additions provide the reader with the sort
of help provided in these two authentic directions, but it
is equally hoped that the reader will remember that the
stage was not loaded with scenery.

No editor during the course of his work can fail to
recollect some words Heminges and Condell prefixed to
the Folio:

It had been a thing, we confess, worthy to have been
wished, that the author himself had lived to have set forth
and overseen his own writings. But since it hath been
ordained otherwise, and he by death departed from that

right, we pray you do not envy his friends the office of their care and pain to have collected and published them.

Nor can an editor, after he has done his best, forget Heminges and Condell's final words: "And so we leave you to other of his friends, whom if you need can be your guides. If you need them not, you can lead yourselves, and others. And such readers we wish him."

SYLVAN BARNET
Tufts University

Introduction

Romeo and Juliet, even in the mutilated versions that Restoration and eighteenth-century audiences knew, has always been one of Shakespeare's most popular plays. Since 1845, when Charlotte and Susan Cushman finally brought a version approaching Shakespeare's original back to the stage, it has been a coveted vehicle among actors and actresses alike, on both sides of the Atlantic; and some of the theater's greatest names have been associated with it. In recent years audiences have also been enjoying it in film versions and on television. Among professional scholars the play has sparked less enthusiasm. In this quarter one hears praise for the ingenuity of the language, for the brilliance of the characterizations, and for the portrayal of young love; but such praise is frequently qualified by the uneasy admission that *Romeo and Juliet* resists measurement by the rules conventionally applied to Shakespeare's later tragedies. More than one scholarly critic has expressed misgivings about the emphasis on pathos, the absence of ethical purpose, and what appears to be a capricious shifting of tone, particularly between the first two acts and the last three.

Such misgivings among modern readers are understandable, but one may question whether the Elizabethans would have felt or even understood them. Apparently most of Shakespeare's contemporaries still considered an ending in death the principal requirement for tragedy; and since *Romeo and Juliet* offered six deaths, five of them on stage and two of them the deaths of protagonists, audiences in those days probably thought it more tragic than many plays so labeled. Elizabethan audiences would have found equally strange the objection that the play lacks ethical purpose. They knew by training what to think of impetuous young lovers who deceived their parents and sought advice from friars. Arthur Brooke, whose *Tragicall Historye of Romeus and Juliet* (1562) was most likely Shakespeare's only source, had spelled it all out as follows:

> To this ende (good Reader) is this tragicall matter written, to describe unto thee a coople of unfortunate lovers, thralling themselves to unhonest desire, neglecting the authoritie and advise of parents and frendes, conferring their principall counsels with dronken gossyppes, and superstitious friers (the naturally fitte instrumentes of unchastitie) attemptyng all adventures of peryll, for thattaynyng of their wished lust, usyng auriculer confession (the kay of whoredome, and treason) for furtheraunce of theyre purpose, abusyng the honorable name of lawefull mariage, the cloke the shame of stolne contractes, finallye, by all means of unhonest lyfe, hastyng to most unhappy deathe.

In addition, Elizabethans also knew that suicide was the devil's business and usually meant damnation; in their view, therefore, *Romeo and Juliet* must have had automatically an abundance of ethical import. Shakespeare probably should be given some kind of credit for not challenging these deep-seated convictions of his contemporary auditors and readers; for, ironically, the modern feeling that his play is ethically deficient stems partly from the modern ability to see that Shakespeare has really approved the love of Romeo and Juliet, condoned their deceptions, and laid the blame for their deaths, even though by suicide, upon their elders.

A better explanation for the modern reader's uneasiness about ranking *Romeo and Juliet* with the so-called major tragedies lies in the widespread assumption that Shakespeare meant the play to be deterministic. Shakespeare seems to invite such a view when he promises in the Prologue to show the "misadventured piteous overthrows" of "a pair of star-crossed lovers" and thereafter lets the principals make references to fate and the stars and has them express various kinds of premonition. Romeo, for example, says in Act I that his "mind misgives/ Some consequence yet hanging in the stars" (I.iv.106–7); Friar Lawrence tries to reassure himself with uneasy prayers but soon observes that "violent delights have violent ends" (II.vi.9); and Juliet, on taking leave of her husband, cries, "O Fortune, Fortune! All men call thee fickle" (III.v.60). These and other references make it easy to argue that the characters are, as they themselves sometimes imply, little better than puppets, pitiful perhaps but ethically uninteresting and scarcely due the fearful respect that one gives to the heroes of Shakespeare's later tragedies. Actually, the text as a whole gives little justification for such a view. It is true that Romeo says, as he is about to enter the Capulet's great hall,

> . . . my mind misgives
> Some consequence yet hanging in the stars
> Shall bitterly begin his fearful date
> With this night's revels and expire the term
> Of a despisèd life, closed in my breast,
> By some vile forfeit of untimely death.
>
> (I.iv.106–111)

But he immediately adds, ". . . he that hath the steerage of my course/ Direct my sail!" The first part of this quotation is typical of what we find—and find not so often as some imagine—in *Romeo and Juliet:* premonitions, prayers, misgivings, references to Fortune, all uttered much as we ourselves utter such things, without necessarily implying real belief in astral influence. Sometimes the character's premonition is confirmed by later events; sometimes not, as is true of the auspicious part of Romeo's dream on the night before his suicide. The second part of the quotation is typical, too; for almost as often as these characters speak of fate they speak of a superior Providence, mysteriously directing but never absolutely determining human destiny. Moreover, accident-prone as Romeo and Juliet may occasionally seem, they are really no more so than Hamlet, who also has his share of premonitions; and their actions are no more clearly determined by supernatural influence than those of Macbeth. Like its successors, *Romeo and Juliet* takes place in a universe where there is a special providence in the fall of a sparrow and where what will be, assuredly will be. All that is asked of the inhabitants of this Shakespearean world of tragedy is that they achieve readiness or ripeness for what is to come, and in this tragedy as in the others they are allowed and expected to do that much for themselves. The things to consider are whether or not the protagonists have succeeded in meeting this requirement and, if it appears they have failed, whether one had any right to suppose they would do otherwise.

A final source of uneasiness for contemporary readers of *Romeo and Juliet* is the impression, got mainly from the first two acts, that Verona is really a part of the world of comedy. Many things contribute to this impression. An amusing street fight and a masked ball in the first act, a lovers' meeting in the orchard in the second, a doting young man carrying courtly conventions to laughable excess, parents who would be custom-bound to interfere if they only knew of the affair going on under their noses, an affected troublemaker bent on vindicating honor to the letter in duels conducted with precious precision, a bawdy nurse and an even bawdier friend—such things as these in an Elizabethan play ordinarily lead to the triumph of young love and a marriage or two, with forgiveness and feasting all around. In this play, however, the familiar dream of courtly comedy shatters when Mercutio is slain, and from that point on the lightness quickly dissolves. Romeo is banished, the "comfortable" Friar falls back on desperate remedies, old Capulet grows testy and intolerant, Lady Capulet calls for blood, the amusing Nurse suggests bigamy as a practical course, and Juliet, who has scarcely known life, prepares to be familiar with death. Even the weather adapts itself to the shift in tone: it suddenly gets hot in Act III, and in Act IV it rains; the sky is still overcast as the play comes to an end.

The contrast that Shakespeare gets here between the tone of the first two acts and that of the remaining three is probably intentional and, in any case, more apparent than real. Unless a reader is genuinely sophisticated, his response to literature is always at least partly a matter of habit; he laughs and shudders on signal. Thus there will always be those who find the first two acts of *Romeo and Juliet* mainly laughable, just as there will always be some who consider *Othello* the tragedy of a handkerchief, a farce with unfortunate consequences. Shakespeare must not be held responsible for responses of this kind. The first two acts of *Romeo and Juliet* will appear to be consistently comic only if we read them in the limited light of other, very different things—second-rate farces, dramatic and nondramatic, hack work generally, certain comic strips, even—in which the same conventions have been used. The corrective is to pay attention, for Shakespeare allows us to carry any initial impression of comedy we may have got only so far as the climax of the street brawl in Scene i. At that point, while the servants are still battling, Tybalt still fighting with Benvolio, Capulet yelling for a long sword, and his wife telling him to call for a crutch instead, he brings us up sharply with the Prince's words:

> What, ho! You men, you beasts,
> That quench the fire of your pernicious rage
> With purple fountains issuing from your veins!
> (I.i.86–88)

Comedy can thrive indefinitely on beasts that pass for men, but it cannot long tolerate a reminder of original sin such as lurks in "pernicious rage" or a reminder of royal humanity's self-destructiveness like "purple fountains"; and it is with these in our ears that we pass on to the rest of the Prince's dignified rebuke and thence to the speeches of Benvolio and the Montagues which express their human concern for a youthful friend and son, the absent Romeo.

When Romeo himself appears, later in the same scene, juggling words in a fashionable euphuistic manner and complaining of the contradictions of love, we are more cautious with our laughter. Laugh as we may, Romeo clearly lives in a world where folly can have serious and irrevocable consequences; and we are no longer confident that the conventions of comedy will save him from those consequences or spare us the pain of seeing him destroyed.

The remaining scenes in Acts I and II contain much that confirms our uneasiness. For example, Capulet, who has been very funny calling for his long sword, says tenderly of his daughter in Scene ii:

> . . . too soon marred are those so early made.
> Earth hath swallowèd all my hopes but she;
> She is the hopeful lady of my earth.
>
> (I.ii.13–15)

These three lines are enough to establish him as a dramatic figure who will probably invite our sympathy as readily as he has provoked our ridicule. They also prepare us for Juliet, who never has much of the comic about her and least of all when she disturbs us with a prophetic "My grave is like to be my wedding bed" (I.v.137). Mercutio's bawdiness is perhaps the best argument for taking these two acts as comic, but an attentive listener will receive it all with the long Queen Mab speech still in mind, see that Mercutio's bawdiness and fancy are simply complementary aspects of a single creative and remarkably perceptive imagination, and be prepared to recognize that Verona's one hope of restoration without tragedy has vanished when he dies.

In any case, a feeling that the play represents relatively mature work has disposed most scholars to seek a late date for it. The latest that can reasonably be given is 1596, since the first edition appeared early in 1597 and described the play as having been performed by "Lord Hunsdon's servants," a title that Shakespeare's company held only from July 1596 until the following March. The preferred date seems to be 1595, which is also the preferred date for *Richard II* and *A Midsummer Night's Dream*. The reason usually given for putting these plays in the same year is that the same intense lyricism characterizes all three, but it has also been suggested that *A Midsummer Night's Dream,* in its special concern with the difficulties of young love, reveals itself to be a product of the same mood or preoccupation that caused Shakespeare to write *Romeo and Juliet.* Some interesting parallels have been noted. For example, in the first scene of *A Midsummer Night's Dream* Lysander says:

> Brief as the lightning in the collied night,
> That, in a spleen, unfolds both heaven and earth,
> And ere a man hath power to say "Behold!"
> The jaws of darkness do devour it up:
> So quick bright things come to confusion.
>
> (I.i.145–149)

To this Hermia replies, "If then true lovers have been ever crossed,/ It stands as an edict in destiny." This exchange has been related plausibly both to Juliet's "too rash, too unadvised, too sudden;/ Too like the lightning, which doth cease to be/ Ere one can say it lightens" (II.ii.118– 120) and to the "star-crossed lovers" of the Prologue. But beyond the realm of the plausible in this matter we cannot go. Those who regard the play as immature usually prefer an earlier date, insisting that the Nurse's " 'Tis since the earthquake now eleven years" (I.iii.23), by which she remembers the time of Juliet's weaning, refers to a famous earthquake which struck England in 1580 and that Shakespeare meant to date his play 1591 by having the Nurse mention something that everyone in the audience could date precisely. Against this view one might argue that there were two other earthquakes in England during the 1580's and at least one on the Continent; Shakespeare could easily have referred to one of these or just as easily to no earthquake at all. Moreover, while it is certainly reasonable to suppose that in mentioning an earthquake he would have thought of some earthquake he knew, it is hardly reasonable to think he would have bothered to fix as contemporary the date of a play that apparently had nothing to gain by being considered topical. Everything taken into account, the play seems to come after plays like *The Two Gentlemen of Verona* and *Love's Labor's Lost* and before *The Merchant of Venice* and the Henry IV plays. The most likely date, therefore, is still 1595.

Whatever the date, the style of *Romeo and Juliet* places it at a point which marks the poet's achievement of self-awareness and confidence in his mastery over the medium. The play is rich in set pieces and memorable scenes, so much so in fact that insensitive producers have sometimes turned it into a collection of dramatic recitals. Yet Shakespeare's virtuosity, intrinsically interesting as it is whenever we choose to isolate some specimen of it, never fails to function as a part of the general action of the play; and that is as true in this work, where he seems to be rejoicing openly in his creative power, as it is in the later tragedies, where the power is felt rather than seen. Nothing in *Romeo and Juliet* really stands alone, not even a startling passage like the Queen Mab speech, which almost immediately proves to be an indispensable part of Mercutio's complex personality, just as Mercutio with all his complexity ultimately proves indispensable to the meaning of the play. The creativity displayed in this passage is Shakespeare's, to be sure, but his greatest achievement is in making it credibly Mercutio's. Equally remarkable is the much-admired lyrical quality of the next scene, in which Romeo meets Juliet for the first time; but this scene is remarkable for another reason. Here we have two young people who presumably have had no opportunity to develop any special gift for language. Juliet's talk up to this point has commanded no particular attention; and Romeo's, best displayed perhaps in his first exchange with Benvolio (I.i), has been characterized by extravagant paradoxes and an occasional fortuitous couplet. Suddenly, with Juliet in sight, he begins to make something like poetry:

> O, she doth teach the torches to burn bright!
> It seems she hangs upon the cheek of night

As a rich jewel in an Ethiop's ear—
Beauty too rich for use, for earth too dear!
(I.v.46–49)

Capulet and Tybalt briefly obscure the young man from
view, but as these move aside, we see that he has not
only taken Juliet by the hand but has begun spinning
sonnets with her; and even before the Nurse interrupts,
we have sensed the rightness of this unexpected attach-
ment and its potential for permanence. We are thus prepared for the orchard, or balcony, scene of Act II and for
the lovely *aubade* that the two perform at the parting in
Act III—both among the memorable scenes in Shakespeare because without any formal patterning they achieve
a unity all their own and still serve the larger function of
suggesting the integrity that love can confer briefly upon
two young people who, apart from each other, will remain
children to the end.

In characterization Shakespeare had always been able
to make language work for him, but with *Romeo and
Juliet* he mastered it so completely that the play almost
became a gallery of individuals. The language of the extremes in the social scale must have been easiest to catch,
with the banter of servingmen at one end and the formal
periods of Prince Escalus at the other; but in between the
extremes we get the Nurse's peasant speech, most notice-
ably of peasant origin when she tries to imitate her betters,
beautifully contrasted with the self-assured and warmly
healthy country-gentry talk of old Capulet; Mercutio's
mature command of language at all levels and Tybalt's
narrow range of sharp insolence; Friar Lawrence's moralizing, formal and sententious but never tedious, and the tiny
voice of the complaisant Apothecary. Some of these characters change attitude as external circumstances require,
but in general their personalities simply unfold in the language that establishes them. This is also true of Benvolio,
Paris, and Lady Capulet. Romeo and Juliet, however,
undergo development, and he undergoes more than she.
From her first appearance the younger Juliet is more mature than her lover. Romeo is fertile in figures and can

occasionally invent fresh things like "Night's candles are burnt out, and jocund day/ Stands tiptoe on the misty mountaintops" (III.v.9–10); but it is always Juliet who leads the talk in their two great scenes together, and it is also she who knows what language cannot do:

> Conceit, more rich in matter than in words,
> Brags of his substance, not of ornament.
> They are but beggars that can count their worth;
> But my true love is grown to such excess
> I cannot sum up sum of half my wealth.
>
> (II.vi.30–34)

Her best lines are those in which she draws upon language to invent for her the images of death which she must confront before Romeo can be permanently hers (IV.iii.14–58); yet when she wakes to find Romeo lifeless, she can muster no language capable of helping her in such an extremity and quickly joins her lover in death. By contrast, Romeo's best speech is perhaps the one he delivers in the tomb; with it he gives dignity, meaning, and finality to the one act he plans and executes, however unwisely, without the help of friends, Friar, or Juliet. His language here, like the deed, is his own, as the courtly conventions and fashionable euphuism of many of his earlier scenes were not. His paradoxes, his puns, even his lamentations in the Friar's cell, are borrowed things, as his mature friends know; yet Romeo's "misshapen chaos of well-seeming forms" is catalyzed into inchoate poetry whenever Juliet comes upon the scene, and in the end he achieves in her presence a man's power to act if not a man's gift of discretion.

If *Romeo and Juliet* fails to achieve the highest rank of tragedy, the reason for that failure must be sought in the protagonists themselves and not in some extraterrestrial power or agency. The reason Romeo and Juliet do not stand out clearly as protagonists in a great tragedy is simply that Shakespeare created them to be protagonists in a different kind of play, one which has many of the circumstances that we find in the other tragedies but which lacks at the center a figure capable of achieving the terrible but satisfying perception of man's involvement in the mystery of creation. "Failure" is an inappropriate word for such an achievement. The notable thing about Romeo and Juliet is not that they fail to reach a Hamlet's degree of awareness but that as very young people they behave better and mature more rapidly in that direction than we have any right to expect them to. They learn that Verona is flawed, but they do not dream that the whole world is flawed in the same way. They discover that some actions are good and some bad, but never achieve the Friar's catholic view that only will can make an action bad and only grace can redeem it. They confront imperfection courageously; they fail to see in it an image of themselves. Death overtakes them in their innocence and their unknowing; and we remember them not as we remember tragic heroes, in pity and fear, but in admiration for their loveliness, as we remember dead children.

All things considered, the Verona which serves as their testing ground is not a bad place. The Prologue refers darkly to "the continuance of their parents' rage,/ Which but their children's end, naught could remove"; but as H. B. Charlton has observed, the old people in the play seem to have little interest in continuing a quarrel. Apart from the ancient rift, one might describe the city as a reservoir of high spirits and good will, full of attractive people like the witty Mercutio, Benvolio and Paris, the wise and tolerant Friar, and the young ladies who brighten the evenings in Capulet's great hall. Yet the Prologue is right. The rift created by the old people's almost forgotten rage is still there, wide enough for irresponsible young servingmen to see and make a game of and wide enough, too, for irresponsible young noblemen, like Tybalt, to aggravate into a civic crisis. One might say of it, as Mercutio says of his death wound, " 'Tis not so deep as a well, nor so wide as a church door; but 'tis enough, 'twill serve." In the end it has served as a conduit for some of the best blood in the city, including Mercutio's own, and for the tears of all the rest.

Apart from the two protagonists, the people of Verona,

or rather those that Shakespeare has presented to us, may be arranged in two groups. The first of these, by far the larger, includes all the supernumeraries, such minor characters as Peter and the Apothecary, and a few relatively important figures like Tybalt, the Capulets, the Nurse, Paris, and Benvolio. These are the static or "flat" characters, who are "by nature" what they are; and their functions are to present the limited range of values they embody and to make the plot go. Tybalt, for example, is by nature choleric and determined to pick quarrels; Benvolio, by nature the opposite, is equally determined to avoid them. There are no surprises in either, even when Tybalt precipitates the climactic crisis of the play, just as there are no surprises in Paris and should be none in the Nurse. The latter is interesting to us precisely because Shakespeare's detailed unfolding of her reveals a consistent personality, yet she too is static. From the beginning, she is garrulous, corruptible, and insensitive; and as long as nothing requires her to be otherwise, she can also be amusing. At her crisis, when Juliet asks her to be wise, the Nurse can only suggest bigamy, a course quite in keeping with the values she herself is made of. Here the Nurse is no longer funny, but she has not changed. It is Juliet who has done that. The other characters in this group do not change either. They may be said to represent the abiding conditions of human intercourse in any representative community; and a lesser playwright, assembling a similar collection, would probably have included the same kind of servants and dignitaries, a Nurse or someone like her, Tybalts and Benvolios, all performing essentially the same functions as Shakespeare's and exhibiting many of the same qualities. The unique excellence of the static characters in *Romeo and Juliet* comes from Shakespeare's having particularized them so deftly that, like the protagonists in the play, we hopefully take them at first for people of larger dimensions. Their vitality tempts us to expect them to be more than they are and to give more than they have any capacity for giving. Thus when Tybalt fails to respond to Romeo's generous appeal and Lady Capulet proves blind to her daughter's need for sympathy, we feel the disappointment as sharply as if we were discovering for ourselves the limitations of common humanity.

The second group consists of three characters who give a doubly strong impression of life because they include among their qualities some degree of perception or understanding. Prince Escalus, slight as he is, is one of these, and Friar Lawrence another. Normally we should expect a magistrate to belong to the group of static or flat characters, but Shakespeare has given his magistrate a conscience and a growing presentiment of what must happen to everyone in Verona if the wound in the civil body cannot be healed. Others want to keep the peace, too, but mainly because they have a perfunctory sense of duty or perhaps because they dislike fighting. Escalus knows from the beginning that keeping the peace here is a matter of life or death, and in the end he readily takes his share of responsibility for the bloody sacrifice he has failed to avert:

> Capulet, Montague,
> See what a scourge is laid upon your hate,
> That heaven finds means to kill your joys with love.
> And I, for winking at your discords too,
> Have lost a brace of kinsmen. All are punished.
> (V.iii.291–95)

The Friar is included in this "all"; and the Friar, moreover, has preceded the Prince in accepting blame:

> . . . if aught in this
> Miscarried by my fault, let my old life
> Be sacrificed some hour before his time
> Unto the rigor of severest law.
> (V.iii.266–69)

Like the Prince, the Friar has had from the start a clear perception of the danger latent in the old quarrel, and like the Prince he has taken steps appropriate to his position to mend the differences and restore order. Yet whereas the Prince by nature has moved openly and erred in not moving vigorously enough, Friar Lawrence by nature works in secret and his secrecy does him in. Actually his much-criticized plan for ending the quarrel is sound enough in principle. Any faithful son of the Church, accustomed to cementing alliances with the sacrament of matrimony, would naturally have considered the young people's sudden affection for each other an opportunity sent by Heaven. Friar Lawrence's error lies all in the execution of the thing, in letting a Heaven-made marriage remain an affair of secret messages, rope ladders, and unorthodox sleeping potions, a clandestine remedy doomed to miscarriage long before the thwarted message determines the shape of the inevitable catastrophe. What was desperately needed in this case was a combination of virtues, the forthrightness of the Prince and the vigor and ingenuity of the Friar; and these virtues were combined only in Mercutio, who fell victim to the deficiencies of both in that he confronted a needlessly active Tybalt at a disadvantage caused in part by bumbling Romeo's adherence to the Friar's secret plot.

Mercutio, who is the third member of this more perceptive group, stands next to Romeo and Juliet in importance in the play. In fact, some critics who consider him more interesting than the two protagonists have suggested that Shakespeare finished him off in Act III out of necessity. This is almost as absurd as the view that Shakespeare wrote Falstaff out of *Henry V* because the fat man had become unmanageable. Others have found Mercutio's wit embarrassing and tried to relieve Shakespeare of the responsibility for some parts of it, but this is absurd too. An edited Mercutio becomes either sentimental or obscene; he also becomes meaningless, and without him the play as a whole reverts to the condition of melodrama that it had in Shakespeare's source. Consider for a moment the climax of the play, which is almost solely Shakespeare's invention. In Brooke the matter is relatively simple: Tybalt provokes Romeo, and Romeo slays him. Shakespeare has it that Tybalt deliberately sought to murder Romeo and Romeo so badly underestimated his challenger that he declined to defend himself; whereupon Mercutio, in defense of both Romeo's honor and his person, picked up the challenge and would have killed Tybalt but for Romeo's intervention. Tybalt then killed Mercutio, and Romeo killed Tybalt in revenge. But, one should ask, what if Romeo had not intervened? Tybalt would have been slain, surely, and Mercutio would have survived to receive the Prince's rebuke; at most, however, he would have been punished only slightly, for Mercutio was of the Prince's line and not of the feuding families. The feud thus would have died with Tybalt, and in time Capulet and Montague might have been reconciled openly, as Friar Lawrence hoped. In short, Mercutio was on the point of bringing to pass what neither civil authority nor well-intentioned but misplaced ingenuity had been able to accomplish, and Romeo with a single sentimental action ("I thought all for the best," he says) destroyed his only hope of averting tragedy long enough to achieve the maturity he needed in order to avoid it altogether.

Many critics have commented on the breathless pace of this play, and no wonder. Shakespeare has made it the story of a race against time. What Romeo needs most of all is a teacher, and the only one capable of giving him instruction worth having and giving it quickly is Mercutio. All the rest are unavailable, or ineffectual, like Benvolio, or unapt for dealing practically with human relations. Mercutio, however, for all his superficial show of irresponsibility, is made in the image of his creator; he is a poet, who gives equal value to flesh and spirit, sees them as inseparable aspects of total being, and accepts each as the necessary mode of the other. His first line in the play, discharged at a young fool who is playing the ascetic for love, is revealing: "Nay, gentle Romeo, we must have you dance" (I.iv.13). And when gentle Romeo persists in daydreaming, he says, "Be rough with love," declares that love is a mire and that dreamers are often liars. The long fairy speech which follows dignifies idle dreams by marrying them to earth; its intent is to compel Romeo to acknowledge his senses and to bring him to an honest and healthy confession of what he is really looking for, but Romeo is too wrapped up in self-deception to listen. In Act II Mercutio tries harder, speaks more plainly, but prompts from his pupil only the fatuous "He jests at scars that never felt a wound." Later still, in the battle of wits (II.iv), Mercutio imagines briefly that he has succeeded: "Why, is not this better now than groaning for love? Now art thou sociable, now art thou Romeo; now art thou what thou art, by art as well as by nature" (II.iv.92–95). There are no wiser words in the whole play, and none more ironic; for Romeo even here has not found his identity and is never really to find it except for those fleeting moments when Juliet is there to lead him by the hand.

Time runs out for both principals in this play, but it is Juliet who makes the race exciting. Her five-day maturation is a miracle which only a Shakespeare could have made credible; yet at the end she is still a fourteen-year-old girl, and she succumbs to an adolescent's despair. Mercutio might have helped had he been available, but Mercutio is dead. All the others have deserted her—parents, Nurse, the Friar, who takes fright at the crucial moment, and Romeo, who lies dead at her feet. She simply has not lived long enough in her wisdom to stand entirely alone. This is really the source of pathos in *Romeo and Juliet*. One hears much about the portrayal of young love here, about the immortality of the lovers and the eternality of their love; but such talk runs toward vapid sentimentality and does an injustice to Shakespeare. No one has more poignantly described the beauty of young love than he, and no one has portrayed more honestly than he the destructiveness of any love which ignores the mortality of those who make it. Romeo struggled toward full understanding but fell far short of achievement, leaving a trail of victims behind him. Juliet came much closer than we had any right to expect, but she too failed. Both have a legitimate claim to our respect, she more than he; and the youth of both relieves them of our ultimate censure, which falls not on the stars but on all those whose thoughtlessness denied them the time they so desperately needed.

J. A. BRYANT, JR.
The University of North Carolina at Greensboro

The Tragedy of Romeo and Juliet

Chorus
Escalus, Prince of Verona
Paris, a young count, kinsman to the Prince
Montague
Capulet
An old Man, of the Capulet family
Romeo, son to Montague
Mercutio, kinsman to the Prince and friend to Romeo
Benvolio, nephew to Montague and friend to Romeo
Tybalt, nephew to Lady Capulet
Friar Lawrence } Franciscans
Friar John
Balthasar, servant to Romeo
Sampson } servants to Capulet
Gregory
Peter, servant to Juliet's nurse
Abram, servant to Montague
An Apothecary
Three Musicians
An Officer
Lady Montague, wife to Montague
Lady Capulet, wife to Capulet
Juliet, daughter to Capulet
Nurse to Juliet
Citizens of Verona, Gentlemen and Gentlewomen of both
    houses, Maskers, Torchbearers, Pages, Guards, Watch-
    men, Servants, and Attendants
                Scene: Verona; Mantua]

The Tragedy of Romeo and Juliet

THE PROLOGUE

[Enter Chorus.]

Chorus. Two households, both alike in dignity,°¹
    In fair Verona, where we lay our scene,
From ancient grudge break to new mutiny,°
    Where civil blood makes civil hands unclean.
From forth the fatal loins of these two foes   *5*
    A pair of star-crossed° lovers take their life;
Whose misadventured piteous overthrows
    Doth with their death bury their parents' strife.
The fearful passage of their death-marked love,
    And the continuance of their parents' rage,   *10*
Which, but their children's end, naught could
    remove,
    Is now the two hours' traffic of our stage;°
The which if you with patient ears attend,
What here shall miss, our toil shall strive to mend.
                            [Exit.]

¹ The degree sign (°) indicates a footnote, which is keyed to the text by line number. Text references are printed in **boldface** type; the annotation follows in roman type.
Prologue 1 **dignity** rank   3 **mutiny** violence   6 **star-crossed** fated to disaster   12 **two hours' traffic of our stage** i.e., the business of our play

[ACT I

Scene I. *Verona. A public place.*]

*Enter Sampson and Gregory, with swords and
bucklers,° of the house of Capulet.*

Sampson. Gregory, on my word, we'll not carry coals.°

Gregory. No, for then we should be colliers.°

Sampson. I mean, and° we be in choler, we'll draw.°

Gregory. Ay, while you live, draw your neck out of
5   collar.

Sampson. I strike quickly, being moved.

Gregory. But thou art not quickly moved to strike.

Sampson. A dog of the house of Montague moves me.

Gregory. To move is to stir, and to be valiant is to
10   stand. Therefore, if thou art moved, thou run'st
away.

Sampson. A dog of that house shall move me to
stand. I will take the wall° of any man or maid of
Montague's.

I.i.s.d. **bucklers** small shields   1 **carry coals** endure insults   2 **colliers** coal venders (this leads to puns on "choler" = anger, and
"collar" = hangman's noose)   3 **and** if   3 **draw** draw swords
13 **take the wall** take the preferred place on the walk

Gregory. That shows thee a weak slave; for the weak-   15
est goes to the wall.°

Sampson. 'Tis true; and therefore women, being the
weaker vessels, are ever thrust to the wall.° Therefore I will push Montague's men from the wall and
thrust his maids to the wall.   20

Gregory. The quarrel is between our masters and us
their men.

Sampson. 'Tis all one. I will show myself a tyrant.
When I have fought with the men, I will be civil
with the maids—I will cut off their heads.   25

Gregory. The heads of the maids?

Sampson. Ay, the heads of the maids or their maiden-
heads. Take it in what sense thou wilt.

Gregory. They must take it in sense that feel it.

Sampson. Me they shall feel while I am able to stand; 30
and 'tis known I am a pretty piece of flesh.

Gregory. 'Tis well thou art not fish; if thou hadst,
thou hadst been Poor John.° Draw thy tool!° Here
comes two of the house of Montagues.

Enter two other Servingmen [Abram and Balthasar].

Sampson. My naked weapon is out. Quarrel! I will   35
back thee.

Gregory. How? Turn thy back and run?

Sampson. Fear me not.

Gregory. No, marry.° I fear thee!

15-16 **weakest goes to the wall** i.e., is pushed to the rear   18 **thrust to
the wall** assaulted against the wall   33 **Poor John** hake salted and
dried (poor man's fare)   33 **tool** weapon (with bawdy innuendo)
39 **marry** (an interjection, from "By the Virgin Mary")

40 *Sampson.* Let us take the law of our sides;° let them
begin.

Gregory. I will frown as I pass by, and let them take
it as they list.

Sampson. Nay, as they dare. I will bite my thumb° at
45 them, which is disgrace to them if they bear it.

Abram. Do you bite your thumb at us, sir?

Sampson. I do bite my thumb, sir.

Abram. Do you bite your thumb at us, sir?

Sampson. [*Aside to Gregory*] Is the law of our side
50 if I say ay?

Gregory. [*Aside to Sampson*] No.

Sampson. No, sir, I do not bite my thumb at you, sir;
but I bite my thumb, sir.

Gregory. Do you quarrel, sir?

55 *Abram.* Quarrel, sir? No, sir.

Sampson. But if you do, sir, I am for you. I serve as
good a man as you.

Abram. No better.

Sampson. Well, sir.

Enter Benvolio.

60 *Gregory.* Say "better." Here comes one of my master's
kinsmen.

Sampson. Yes, better, sir.

Abram. You lie.

Sampson. Draw, if you be men. Gregory, remember
65 thy swashing° blow.   *They fight.*

---

40 **take the law of our sides** keep ourselves in the right   44 **bite my
thumb** i.e., make a gesture of contempt   65 **swashing** slashing

Benvolio. Part, fools!
  Put up your swords. You know not what you do.

          Enter Tybalt.

Tybalt. What, art thou drawn among these heartless
    hinds?°
  Turn thee, Benvolio; look upon thy death.

Benvolio. I do but keep the peace. Put up thy sword,   70
  Or manage it to part these men with me.

Tybalt. What, drawn, and talk of peace? I hate the
    word
  As I hate hell, all Montagues, and thee.
  Have at thee, coward!   [*They fight.*]

    *Enter [an Officer, and] three or four Citizens
        with clubs or partisans.*

Officer. Clubs, bills, and partisans!° Strike! Beat them   75
  down! Down with the Capulets! Down with the
  Montagues!

    Enter old Capulet in his gown, and his Wife.

Capulet. What noise is this? Give me my long sword,
  ho!

Lady Capulet. A crutch, a crutch! Why call you for
  a sword?

Capulet. My sword, I say! Old Montague is come   80
  And flourishes his blade in spite° of me.

    Enter old Montague and his Wife.

Montague. Thou villain Capulet!—Hold me not; let
  me go.

Lady Montague. Thou shalt not stir one foot to seek
  a foe.

---

68 **heartless hinds** cowardly rustics   75 **bills, and partisans** varieties
of halberd, a combination spear and battle-ax   81 **spite** defiance

Enter Prince Escalus, with his Train.

Prince. Rebellious subjects, enemies to peace,
85   Profaners of this neighbor-stainèd steel—
     Will they not hear? What, ho! You men, you beasts,
     That quench the fire of your pernicious rage
     With purple fountains issuing from your veins!
     On pain of torture, from those bloody hands
90   Throw your mistempered° weapons to the ground
     And hear the sentence of your movèd prince.
     Three civil brawls, bred of an airy word
     By thee, old Capulet, and Montague,
     Have thrice disturbed the quiet of our streets
95   And made Verona's ancient citizens
     Cast by their grave beseeming° ornaments
     To wield old partisans, in hands as old,
     Cank'red with peace, to part your cank'red° hate.
     If ever you disturb our streets again,
100   Your lives shall pay the forfeit of the peace.
     For this time all the rest depart away.
     You, Capulet, shall go along with me;
     And, Montague, come you this afternoon,
     To know our farther pleasure in this case,
105   To old Freetown, our common judgment place.
     Once more, on pain of death, all men depart.
                 Exeunt [all but Montague, his Wife,
                          and Benvolio].

Montague. Who set this ancient quarrel new abroach?°
     Speak, nephew, were you by when it began?

Benvolio. Here were the servants of your adversary
110   And yours, close fighting ere I did approach.
     I drew to part them. In the instant came
     The fiery Tybalt, with his sword prepared;
     Which, as he breathed defiance to my ears,
     He swung about his head and cut the winds,

---

90 **mistempered** (1) ill-made (2) used with ill will   96 **grave beseeming** dignified and appropriate   98 **cank'red . . . cank'red** rusted . . . malignant   107 **new abroach** newly open

Who, nothing hurt withal,° hissed him in scorn.   *115*
While we were interchanging thrusts and blows,
Came more and more, and fought on part and
    part,°
Till the Prince came, who parted either part.

Lady Montague. O, where is Romeo? Saw you him
    today?
Right glad I am he was not at this fray.   *120*

Benvolio. Madam, an hour before the worshiped sun
Peered forth the golden window of the East,
A troubled mind drave me to walk abroad;
Where, underneath the grove of sycamore
That westward rooteth from this city side,   *125*
So early walking did I see your son.
Towards him I made, but he was ware° of me
And stole into the covert of the wood.
I, measuring his affections by my own,
Which then most sought where most might not be
    found,°   *130*
Being one too many by my weary self,
Pursued my humor not pursuing his,°
And gladly shunned who gladly fled from me.

Montague. Many a morning hath he there been seen,
With tears augmenting the fresh morning's dew,   *135*
Adding to clouds more clouds with his deep sighs;
But all so soon as the all-cheering sun
Should in the farthest East begin to draw
The shady curtains from Aurora's° bed,
Away from light steals home my heavy° son   *140*
And private in his chamber pens himself,
Shuts up his windows, locks fair daylight out,
And makes himself an artificial night.

---

115 **withal** thereby   117 **on part and part** some on one side, some
on another   127 **ware** aware   130 **most sought . . . found** i.e.,
wanted most to be alone   132 **Pursued . . . his** i.e., followed my
own inclination by not inquiring into his mood   139 **Aurora** goddess of the dawn   140 **heavy** melancholy, moody

Black and portentous must this humor° prove
145 Unless good counsel may the cause remove.

Benvolio. My noble uncle, do you know the cause?

Montague. I neither know it nor can learn of him.

Benvolio. Have you importuned him by any means?

Montague. Both by myself and many other friends;
150 But he, his own affections' counselor,
Is to himself—I will not say how true—
But to himself so secret and so close,
So far from sounding° and discovery,
As is the bud bit with an envious° worm
155 Ere he can spread his sweet leaves to the air
Or dedicate his beauty to the sun.
Could we but learn from whence his sorrows grow,
We would as willingly give cure as know.

Enter Romeo.

Benvolio. See, where he comes. So please you step
        aside;
160 I'll know his grievance, or be much denied.

Montague. I would thou wert so happy° by thy stay
To hear true shrift.° Come, madam, let's away.
            Exeunt [*Montague and Wife*].

Benvolio. Good morrow,° cousin.

Romeo.   Is the day so young?

Benvolio. But new struck nine.

Romeo.   Ay me! Sad hours seem long.
165 Was that my father that went hence so fast?

Benvolio. It was. What sadness lengthens Romeo's
        hours?

---

144 **humor** mood   153 **So far from sounding** so far from measuring the depth of his mood   154 **envious** malign   161 **happy** lucky
162 **true shrift** i.e., Romeo's confession of the truth   163 **morrow**
morning

Romeo. Not having that which having makes them
   short.

Benvolio. In love?

Romeo. Out—

Benvolio. Of love?   170

Romeo. Out of her favor where I am in love.

Benvolio. Alas that love, so gentle in his view,°
   Should be so tyrannous and rough in proof!

Romeo. Alas that love, whose view is muffled still,°
   Should without eyes see pathways to his will!   175
   Where shall we dine? O me! What fray was here?
   Yet tell me not, for I have heard it all.
   Here's much to do with hate, but more with love.°
   Why then, O brawling love, O loving hate,
   O anything, of nothing first created!°   180
   O heavy lightness, serious vanity,
   Misshapen chaos of well-seeming forms,
   Feather of lead, bright smoke, cold fire, sick health,
   Still-waking sleep, that is not what it is!
   This love feel I, that feel no love in this.   185
   Dost thou not laugh?

Benvolio.   No, coz,° I rather weep.

Romeo. Good heart, at what?

Benvolio.   At thy good heart's oppression.

Romeo. Why, such is love's transgression.
   Griefs of mine own lie heavy in my breast,
   Which thou wilt propagate, to have it prest°   190
   With more of thine. This love that thou hast shown

---

172 **gentle in his view** mild in appearance   174 **muffled still** always
blindfolded   178 **more with love** i.e., the combatants enjoyed their
fighting   180 **O anything, of nothing first created** (Romeo here re-
lates his own succession of witty paradoxes to the dogma that God
created everything out of nothing)   186 **coz** cousin (relative)
190 **Which . . . prest** i.e., which griefs you will increase by burdening
my breast

Doth add more grief to too much of mine own.
Love is a smoke made with the fume of sighs;
Being purged, a fire sparkling in lovers' eyes;
195 Being vexed, a sea nourished with loving tears.
What is it else? A madness most discreet,°
A choking gall, and a preserving sweet.
Farewell, my coz.

Benvolio.   Soft!° I will go along.
And if° you leave me so, you do me wrong.

200 *Romeo.* Tut! I have lost myself; I am not here;
This is not Romeo, he's some other where.

Benvolio. Tell me in sadness,° who is that you love?

Romeo. What, shall I groan and tell thee?

Benvolio.   Groan? Why, no;
But sadly° tell me who.

205 *Romeo.* Bid a sick man in sadness° make his will.
Ah, word ill urged to one that is so ill!
In sadness, cousin, I do love a woman.

Benvolio. I aimed so near when I supposed you loved.

Romeo. A right good markman. And she's fair I love.

210 *Benvolio.* A right fair mark,° fair coz, is soonest hit.

Romeo. Well, in that hit you miss. She'll not be hit
With Cupid's arrow. She hath Dian's wit,°
And, in strong proof° of chastity well armed,
From Love's weak childish bow she lives un-
    charmed.
215 She will not stay° the siege of loving terms,
Nor bide° th' encounter of assailing eyes,

---

196 **discreet** discriminating   198 **Soft** hold on   199 **And if** if
202 **in sadness** in all seriousness   204 **sadly** seriously   205 **in sadness** (1) in seriousness (2) in unhappiness at the prospect of death
210 **fair mark** target easily seen   212 **Dian's wit** the cunning of
Diana, huntress and goddess of chastity   213 **proof** tested power
215 **stay** submit to   216 **bide** abide (put up with)

Nor ope her lap to saint-seducing gold.
O, she is rich in beauty; only poor
That, when she dies, with beauty dies her store.°

Benvolio. Then she hath sworn that she will still° live
    chaste?   220

Romeo. She hath, and in that sparing make huge
    waste;
For beauty, starved with her severity,
Cuts beauty off from all posterity.
She is too fair, too wise, wisely too fair,
To merit bliss° by making me despair.   225
She hath forsworn to love, and in that vow
Do I live dead that live to tell it now.

Benvolio. Be ruled by me; forget to think of her.

Romeo. O, teach me how I should forget to think!

Benvolio. By giving liberty unto thine eyes.   230
    Examine other beauties.

Romeo.   'Tis the way
To call hers, exquisite, in question° more.
These happy masks that kiss fair ladies' brows,
Being black puts us in mind they hide the fair.
He that is strucken blind cannot forget   235
The precious treasure of his eyesight lost.
Show me a mistress that is passing fair:
What doth her beauty serve but as a note°
Where I may read who passed that passing fair?
Farewell. Thou canst not teach me to forget.   240

Benvolio. I'll pay that doctrine, or else die in debt.°
                             Exeunt.

---

219 with beauty dies her store i.e., she will leave no progeny to perpetuate her beauty   **220 still** always   **225 merit bliss** win heavenly
bliss   **232 To call hers . . . in question** to keep bringing her beauty
to mind   **238 note** written reminder   **241 I'll . . . debt** I will teach
you or else die trying

[Scene II. *A street.*]

Enter Capulet, County Paris, and the Clown,
[his Servant].

Capulet. But Montague is bound° as well as I,
In penalty alike; and 'tis not hard, I think,
For men so old as we to keep the peace.

Paris. Of honorable reckoning° are you both,
5 And pity 'tis you lived at odds so long.
But now, my lord, what say you to my suit?

Capulet. But saying o'er what I have said before:
My child is yet a stranger in the world,
She hath not seen the change of fourteen years;
10 Let two more summers wither in their pride
Ere we may think her ripe to be a bride.

Paris. Younger than she are happy mothers made.

Capulet. And too soon marred are those so early
made.
Earth hath swallowèd all my hopes° but she;
15 She is the hopeful lady of my earth.
But woo her, gentle Paris, get her heart;
My will to her consent is but a part.
And she agreed,° within her scope of choice°
Lies my consent and fair according° voice.
20 This night I hold an old accustomed° feast,
Whereto I have invited many a guest,
Such as I love; and you among the store,
One more, most welcome, makes my number more.

I.ii.1 **bound** under bond   4 **reckoning** reputation   14 **hopes** children   18 **And she agreed** if she agrees   18 **within her scope of**
choice among those she favors   19 **according** agreeing   20 **accus-**
tomed established by custom

At my poor house look to behold this night
<u>Earth-treading stars° that make dark heaven light.</u> *25*
Such comfort as do lusty young men feel
When well-appareled April on the heel
Of limping Winter treads, even such delight
Among fresh fennel° buds shall you this night
Inherit° at my house. Hear all, all see, *30*
And like her most whose merit most shall be;
Which, on more view of many, mine, being one,
May stand in number,° though in reck'ning none.°
Come, go with me. [*To Servant, giving him a paper*]
  Go, sirrah,° trudge about
Through fair Verona; find those persons out *35*
Whose names are written there, and to them say
My house and welcome on their pleasure stay.°
                    Exit [*with Paris*].

Servant. Find them out whose names are written here?
It is written that the shoemaker should meddle with
his yard and the tailor with his last, the fisher with *40*
his pencil and the painter with his nets;° but I am
sent to find those persons whose names are here
writ, and can never find° what names the writing
person hath here writ. I must to the learned. In
good time!° *45*

Enter Benvolio and Romeo.

Benvolio. Tut, man, one fire burns out another's
    burning;
  One pain is less'ned by another's anguish;°
Turn giddy, and be holp by backward turning;°

---

25 **Earth-treading stars** i.e., young girls   29 **fennel** flowering herb
30 **Inherit** have   33 **stand in number** constitute one of the crowd
33 **in reck'ning none** not worth special consideration   34 **sirrah** (a
term of familiar address)   37 **stay** wait   39–41 **shoemaker . . . nets**
i.e., one should stick to what one knows how to do (but the servant,
being illiterate, reverses the proverbial expressions)   43 **find** understand   44–45 **In good time** i.e., here come some learned ones
47 **another's anguish** the pain of another   48 **be holp by backward
turning** be helped by turning in the opposite direction

    One desperate grief cures with another's languish.
50 Take thou some new infection to thy eye,
    And the rank poison of the old will die.

Romeo. Your plantain leaf is excellent for that.

Benvolio. For what, I pray thee?

Romeo.   For your broken° shin.

Benvolio. Why, Romeo, art thou mad?

55 *Romeo.* Not mad, but bound more than a madman is;
    Shut up in prison, kept without my food,
    Whipped and tormented and—God-den,° good fel-
        low.
Servant. God gi' go-den. I pray, sir, can you read?

Romeo. Ay, mine own fortune in my misery.

60 *Servant.* Perhaps you have learned it without book.
    But, I pray, can you read anything you see?

Romeo. Ay, if I know the letters and the language.°

Servant. Ye say honestly. Rest you merry.°

Romeo. Stay, fellow; I can read.   *He reads the letter.*
65 "Signior Martino and his wife and daughters;
    County Anselm and his beauteous sisters;
    The lady widow of Vitruvio;
    Signior Placentio and his lovely nieces;
    Mercutio and his brother Valentine;
70 Mine uncle Capulet, his wife and daughters;
    My fair niece Rosaline; Livia;
    Signior Valentio and his cousin Tybalt;
    Lucio and the lively Helena."
    A fair assembly. Whither should they come?

75 *Servant.* Up.

---

53 **broken** scratched   57 **God-den** good evening (good afternoon)
62 **if I know the letters and the language** i.e., if I already know
what the writing says   63 **Rest you merry** may God keep you
merry

Romeo. Whither? To supper?

Servant. To our house.

Romeo. Whose house?

Servant. My master's.

Romeo. Indeed I should have asked you that before.   80

Servant. Now I'll tell you without asking. My master
is the great rich Capulet; and if you be not of the
house of Montagues, I pray come and crush a cup°
of wine. Rest you merry.   [*Exit.*]

Benvolio. At this same ancient° feast of Capulet's   85
Sups the fair Rosaline whom thou so loves;
With all the admirèd beauties of Verona.
Go thither, and with unattainted° eye
Compare her face with some that I shall show,
And I will make thee think thy swan a crow.   90

Romeo. When the devout religion of mine eye
      Maintains such falsehood, then turn tears to fires;
And these, who, often drowned, could never die,
      Transparent° heretics, be burnt for liars!
One fairer than my love? The all-seeing sun   95
Ne'er saw her match since first the world begun.

Benvolio. Tut! you saw her fair, none else being by,
Herself poised° with herself in either eye;
But in that crystal scales° let there be weighed
Your lady's love against some other maid   100
That I will show you shining at this feast,
And she shall scant° show well that now seems best.

Romeo. I'll go along, no such sight to be shown,
      But to rejoice in splendor of mine own.°   [*Exeunt.*]

---

83 **crush a cup** have a drink   85 **ancient** established by custom
88 **unattainted** impartial   94 **Transparent** obvious   98 **poised** bal-
anced   99 **crystal scales** i.e., Romeo's pair of eyes   102 **scant**
scarcely   104 **splendor of mine own** my own lady's splendor

[Scene III. *A room in Capulet's house.*]

Enter Capulet's Wife, and Nurse.

Lady Capulet. Nurse, where's my daughter? Call her
  forth to me.

Nurse. Now, by my maidenhead at twelve year old,
  I bade her come. What,° lamb! What, ladybird!
  God forbid, where's this girl? What, Juliet!

Enter Juliet.

Juliet. How now? Who calls?

Nurse.   Your mother.

5 *Juliet.*   Madam, I am here.
  What is your will?

Lady Capulet. This is the matter—Nurse, give leave
  awhile;
  We must talk in secret. Nurse, come back again.
  I have rememb'red me; thou 's° hear our counsel.
10 Thou knowest my daughter's of a pretty age.

Nurse. Faith, I can tell her age unto an hour.

Lady Capulet. She's not fourteen.

Nurse.   I'll lay fourteen of my teeth—
  And yet, to my teen° be it spoken, I have but
  four—
  She's not fourteen. How long is it now
  To Lammastide?°

15 *Lady Capulet.*   A fortnight and odd days.

I.iii.3 **What** (an impatient call)   9 **thou 's** thou shalt   13 **teen** sorrow   15 **Lammastide** August 1

Nurse. Even or odd, of all days in the year,
　Come Lammas Eve at night shall she be fourteen.
　Susan and she (God rest all Christian souls!)
　Were of an age.° Well, Susan is with God;
　She was too good for me. But, as I said,　　　　　20
　On Lammas Eve at night shall she be fourteen;
　That shall she, marry; I remember it well.
　'Tis since the earthquake° now eleven years;
　And she was weaned (I never shall forget it),
　Of all the days of the year, upon that day;　　　25
　For I had then laid wormwood to my dug,
　Sitting in the sun under the dovehouse wall.
　My lord and you were then at Mantua.
　Nay, I do bear a brain.° But, as I said,
　When it did taste the wormwood on the nipple　30
　Of my dug and felt it bitter, pretty fool,
　To see it tetchy° and fall out with the dug!
　Shake, quoth the dovehouse!° 'Twas no need, I
　　trow,°
　To bid me trudge.
　And since that time it is eleven years,　　　　33
　For then she could stand high-lone;° nay, by th'
　　rood,°
　She could have run and waddled all about;
　For even the day before, she broke her brow;
　And then my husband (God be with his soul!
　'A° was a merry man) took up the child.　　　40
　"Yea," quoth he, "dost thou fall upon thy face?
　Thou wilt fall backward when thou hast more wit;
　Wilt thou not, Jule?" and, by my holidam,°
　The pretty wretch left crying and said, "Ay."
　To see now how a jest shall come about!　　　　45
　I warrant, and I should live a thousand years,

---

19 **of an age** the same age　23 **earthquake** (see Introduction)　29 **I
do bear a brain** i.e., my mind is still good　32 **tetchy** irritable
33 **Shake, quoth the dovehouse** i.e., the dovehouse (which the Nurse
personifies) began to tremble　33 **trow** believe　36 **high-lone** alone
36 **rood** cross　40 **'A** he　43 **holidam** holy thing, relic

I never should forget it. "Wilt thou not, Jule?"
quoth he,
And, pretty fool, it stinted° and said, "Ay."

Lady Capulet. Enough of this. I pray thee hold thy
peace.

50 *Nurse.* Yes, madam. Yet I cannot choose but laugh
To think it should leave crying and say, "Ay."
And yet, I warrant, it had upon it° brow
A bump as big as a young cock'rel's stone;
A perilous knock; and it cried bitterly.
55 "Yea," quoth my husband, "fall'st upon thy face?
Thou wilt fall backward when thou comest to age,
Wilt thou not, Jule?" It stinted and said, "Ay."

Juliet. And stint thou too, I pray thee, nurse, say I.

Nurse. Peace, I have done. God mark thee to His
grace!
60 Thou wast the prettiest babe that e'er I nursed.
And I might live to see thee married once,
I have my wish.

Lady Capulet. Marry,° that "marry" is the very theme
I came to talk of. Tell me, daughter Juliet,
65 How stands your dispositions to be married?

Juliet. It is an honor that I dream not of.

Nurse. An honor? Were not I thine only nurse,
I would say thou hadst sucked wisdom from thy
teat.

Lady Capulet. Well, think of marriage now. Younger
than you,
70 Here in Verona, ladies of esteem,
Are made already mothers. By my count,
I was your mother much upon these years°
That you are now a maid. Thus then in brief:
The valiant Paris seeks you for his love.

48 **stinted** stopped   52 **it** its   63 **Marry** indeed   72 **much upon
these years** the same length of time

Nurse. A man, young lady! Lady, such a man   *75*
　　As all the world— Why, he's a man of wax.°

Lady Capulet. Verona's summer hath not such a
　　flower.

Nurse. Nay, he's a flower, in faith—a very flower.

Lady Capulet. What say you? Can you love the gentle-
　　man?
　　This night you shall behold him at our feast.   *80*
　　Read o'er the volume of young Paris' face,
　　And find delight writ there with beauty's pen;
　　Examine every married lineament,°
　　And see how one another lends content;°
　　And what obscured in this fair volume lies   *85*
　　Find written in the margent° of his eyes.
　　This precious book of love, this unbound° lover,
　　To beautify him only lacks a cover.°
　　The fish lives in the sea, and 'tis much pride
　　For fair without the fair within to hide.°   *90*
　　That book in many's eyes doth share the glory,
　　That in gold clasps locks in the golden story;
　　So shall you share all that he doth possess,
　　By having him making yourself no less.

Nurse. No less? Nay, bigger! Women grow by men.   *95*

Lady Capulet. Speak briefly, can you like of° Paris'
　　love?

Juliet. I'll look to like, if looking liking move;
　　But no more deep will I endart mine eye
　　Than your consent gives strength to make it fly.

　　　　　Enter Servingman.

Servingman. Madam, the guests are come, supper   *100*

---

76 **man of wax** man of perfect figure   83 **married lineament** har-
monious feature   84 **one another lends content** all enhance one
another   86 **margent** marginal commentary   87 **unbound** (1) without cover (2) uncaught   88 **only lacks a cover** i.e., only a wife is
lacking   89–90 **The fish . . . to hide** i.e., the fair sea is made even
fairer by hiding fair fish within it   96 **like of** be favorable to

served up, you called, my young lady asked for,
the nurse cursed° in the pantry, and everything in
extremity. I must hence to wait.° I beseech you
follow straight.°   [*Exit.*]

Lady Capulet. We follow thee. Juliet, the County
105   stays.°

Nurse. Go, girl, seek happy nights to happy days.
                                        Exeunt.

[*Scene IV. A street.*]

*Enter Romeo, Mercutio, Benvolio, with five
or six other Maskers; Torchbearers.*

Romeo. What, shall this speech be spoke for our
    excuse?°
Or shall we on without apology?

Benvolio. The date is out of such prolixity.°
We'll have no Cupid hoodwinked° with a scarf,
5   Bearing a Tartar's painted bow of lath,
Scaring the ladies like a crowkeeper;°
Nor no without-book prologue,° faintly spoke
After the prompter, for our entrance;
But, let them measure° us by what they will,
10   We'll measure them a measure° and be gone.

Romeo. Give me a torch. I am not for this ambling.
Being but heavy, I will bear the light.

102 **the nurse cursed** i.e., because she is not helping   103 **to wait**
to serve   104 **straight** straightway   105 **the County stays** the Count
is waiting   I.iv.1 **shall . . . excuse** i.e., shall we introduce ourselves
with the customary prepared speech   3 **date . . . prolixity** i.e., such
wordiness is out of fashion   4 **hoodwinked** blindfolded   6 **crowkeeper** boy set to scare crows away   7 **without-book prologue**
memorized speech   9 **measure** judge   10 **measure them a measure**
dance one dance with them

Mercutio. Nay, gentle Romeo, we must have you
  dance.

Romeo. Not I, believe me. You have dancing shoes
  With nimble soles; I have a soul of lead   15
  So stakes me to the ground I cannot move.

Mercutio. You are a lover. Borrow Cupid's wings
  And soar with them above a common bound.°

Romeo. I am too sore enpiercèd with his shaft
  To soar with his light feathers; and so bound   20
  I cannot bound a pitch° above dull woe.
  Under love's heavy burden do I sink.

Mercutio. And, to sink in it, should you burden love—
  Too great oppression for a tender thing.

Romeo. Is love a tender thing? It is too rough,   25
  Too rude, too boist'rous, and it pricks like thorn.

Mercutio. If love be rough with you, be rough with
  love;
  Prick love for pricking,° and you beat love down.
  Give me a case to put my visage in.
  A visor for a visor! What care I   30
  What curious eye doth quote deformities?°
  Here are the beetle brows° shall blush° for me.

Benvolio. Come, knock and enter; and no sooner in
  But every man betake him to his legs.°

Romeo. A torch for me! Let wantons light of heart   35
  Tickle the senseless rushes° with their heels;
  For I am proverbed with a grandsire phrase,°
  I'll be a candleholder° and look on;

18 **bound** (1) leap (2) limit   21 **pitch** height (as in a falcon's soar-
ing)   28 **Prick love for pricking** i.e., give love the spur in return
29–31 **Give . . . deformities** i.e., give me a bag for my mask. A mask
for a mask. What do I care who notices my ugliness?   32 **beetle
brows** bushy eyebrows (?)   32 **blush** be red, i.e., be grotesque   34 **betake him to his legs** begin dancing   36 **rushes** (used for floor covering)   37 **grandsire phrase** old saying   38 **candleholder** attendant

The game was ne'er so fair, and I am done.°

Mercutio. Tut! Dun's the mouse, the constable's own
40   word!°
If thou art Dun,° we'll draw thee from the mire
Of this sir-reverence° love, wherein thou stickest
Up to the ears. Come, we burn daylight,° ho!

Romeo. Nay, that's not so.

Mercutio.   I mean, sir, in delay
45   We waste our lights° in vain, like lights by day.
Take our good meaning, for our judgment sits
Five times in that° ere once in our five wits.

Romeo. And we mean well in going to this masque,
But 'tis no wit° to go.

Mercutio.   Why, may one ask?

Romeo. I dreamt a dream tonight.°

50 *Mercutio.*   And so did I.

Romeo. Well, what was yours?

Mercutio.   That dreamers often lie.

Romeo. In bed asleep, while they do dream things true.

Mercutio. O, then I see Queen Mab° hath been with
you.
She is the fairies' midwife, and she comes
55   In shape no bigger than an agate stone

---

39 **The game . . . done** i.e., I'll give up dancing, now that I have enjoyed it as much as I ever shall   40 **Dun's . . . word** (Mercutio puns
on Romeo's last clause, saying in effect "You are not done [i.e.,
"dun": "dark," by extension, "silent"] but the mouse is, and it's time
to be quiet)   41 **Dun** (a common name for a horse, used in an old
game, "Dun is in the mire," in which the players try to haul a heavy
log)   42 **sir-reverence** save your reverence (an apologetic expression, used to introduce indelicate expressions; here used humor-
ously with the word "love")   43 **burn daylight** delay   45 **lights**
(1) torches (2) mental faculties   47 **that** i.e., our good meaning
49 **'tis no wit** it shows no discretion   50 **tonight** last night
53 **Queen Mab** Fairy Queen (Celtic)

On the forefinger of an alderman,
Drawn with a team of little atomies°
Over men's noses as they lie asleep;
Her wagon spokes made of long spinners'° legs,
The cover, of the wings of grasshoppers;   60
Her traces, of the smallest spider web;
Her collars, of the moonshine's wat'ry beams;
Her whip, of cricket's bone; the lash, of film;°
Her wagoner, a small gray-coated gnat,
Not half so big as a round little worm   65
Pricked from the lazy finger of a maid;°
Her chariot is an empty hazelnut,
Made by the joiner squirrel or old grub,°
Time out o' mind the fairies' coachmakers.
And in this state° she gallops night by night   70
Through lovers' brains, and then they dream of
    love;
On courtiers' knees, that dream on curtsies straight;
O'er lawyers' fingers, who straight dream on fees;
O'er ladies' lips, who straight on kisses dream,
Which oft the angry Mab with blisters plagues,   75
Because their breath with sweetmeats tainted are.
Sometime she gallops o'er a courtier's nose,
And then dreams he of smelling out a suit;°
And sometime comes she with a tithe pig's° tail
Tickling a parson's nose as 'a lies asleep,   80
Then he dreams of another benefice.°
Sometime she driveth o'er a soldier's neck,
And then dreams he of cutting foreign throats,
Of breaches, ambuscadoes, Spanish blades,
Of healths° five fathom deep; and then anon   85
Drums in his ear, at which he starts and wakes,
And being thus frighted, swears a prayer or two

---

57 **atomies** tiny creatures   59 **spinners** spiders   63 **film** fine fila-
ment of some kind   65–66 **worm . . . maid** (lazy maids were said
to have worms breeding in their fingers)   68 **joiner squirrel or old
grub** (both woodworkers and adept at hollowing out nuts)   70 **state**
stately array   78 **suit** i.e., a petitioner, who may be induced to pay
for the courtier's influence   79 **tithe pig** tenth pig (considered part
of the parson's tithe)   81 **benefice** income, "living"   85 **healths**
toasts

And sleeps again. This is that very Mab
That plats the manes of horses in the night
90 And bakes the elflocks° in foul sluttish hairs,
Which once untangled much misfortune bodes.
This is the hag,° when maids lie on their backs,
That presses them and learns them first to bear,
Making them women of good carriage.°
This is she—

95 *Romeo.*   Peace, peace, Mercutio, peace!
Thou talk'st of nothing.

Mercutio.   True, I talk of dreams;
Which are the children of an idle brain,
Begot of nothing but vain fantasy;°
Which is as thin of substance as the air,
100 And more inconstant than the wind, who woos
Even now the frozen bosom of the North
And, being angered, puffs away from thence,
Turning his side to the dew-dropping South.

Benvolio. This wind you talk of blows us from ourselves.
105 Supper is done, and we shall come too late.

Romeo. I fear, too early; for my mind misgives
Some consequence° yet hanging in the stars
Shall bitterly begin his fearful date°
With this night's revels and expire the term
110 Of a despisèd life, closed in my breast,
By some vile forfeit of untimely death.°
But he that hath the steerage of my course
Direct my sail! On, lusty gentlemen!

Benvolio. Strike, drum.
                    They march about the stage, and
                    [*retire to one side*].

90 **elflocks** hair tangled by elves   92 **hag** nightmare or incubus
94 **carriage** (1) posture (2) capacity for carrying children   98 **fan-**
tasy fancy   107 **consequence** future event   108 **date** duration (of
the consequence or event)   109–11 **expire . . . death** (the event is
personified here as one who deliberately lends in expectation that
the borrower will have to forfeit at great loss)

[Scene V. *A hall in Capulet's house.*]

Servingmen come forth with napkins.°

First Servingman. Where's Potpan, that he helps not
to take away? He shift a trencher!° He scrape a
trencher!

Second Servingman. When good manners shall lie all
in one or two men's hands, and they unwashed too,   *5*
'tis a foul thing.

First Servingman. Away with the join-stools,° remove
the court cupboard,° look to the plate. Good thou,
save me a piece of marchpane,° and, as thou loves
me, let the porter let in Susan Grindstone and Nell.   *10*
Anthony, and Potpan!

Second Servingman. Ay, boy, ready.

First Servingman. You are looked for and called for,
asked for and sought for, in the great chamber.

Third Servingman. We cannot be here and there too.   *15*
Cheerly, boys! Be brisk awhile, and the longer liver
take all.   *Exeunt.*

Enter [Capulet, his Wife, Juliet, Tybalt, Nurse, and]
all the Guests and Gentlewomen to the Maskers.

Capulet. Welcome, gentlemen! Ladies that have their
toes

I.v. s.d. (although for reference purposes this edition employs the
conventional post-Elizabethan divisions into scenes, the reader is
reminded that they are merely editorial; in the quarto this stage
direction is part of the preceding one)   2 **trencher** wooden plate
7 **join-stools** stools fitted together by a joiner   8 **court cupboard**
sideboard, displaying plate   9 **marchpane** marzipan, a confection
made of sugar and almonds

Unplagued with corns will walk a bout° with you.
20 Ah, my mistresses, which of you all
Will now deny° to dance? She that makes dainty,°
She I'll swear hath corns. Am I come near ye now?
Welcome, gentlemen! I have seen the day
That I have worn a visor and could tell
25 A whispering tale in a fair lady's ear,
Such as would please. 'Tis gone, 'tis gone, 'tis gone.
You are welcome, gentlemen! Come, musicians, play.
                    Music plays, and they dance.
A hall,° a hall! Give room! And foot it, girls.
More light, you knaves, and turn the tables up,
30 And quench the fire; the room is grown too hot.
Ah, sirrah, this unlooked-for sport° comes well.
Nay, sit; nay, sit, good cousin Capulet;
For you and I are past our dancing days.
How long is't now since last yourself and I
Were in a mask?

35 *Second Capulet.*   By'r Lady, thirty years.

Capulet. What, man? 'Tis not so much, 'tis not so
    much;
'Tis since the nuptial of Lucentio,
Come Pentecost as quickly as it will,
Some five-and-twenty years, and then we masked.

Second Capulet. 'Tis more, 'tis more. His son is elder,
40   sir;
His son is thirty.

Capulet.   Will you tell me that?
His son was but a ward° two years ago.

Romeo. [*To a Servingman*] What lady's that which
    doth enrich the hand
Of yonder knight?

45 *Servingman.* I know not, sir.

19 **walk a bout** dance a turn   21 **deny** refuse   21 **makes dainty**
seems to hesitate   28 **A hall** clear the floor   31 **unlooked-for sport**
(they had not expected maskers)   42 **ward** minor

Romeo. O, she doth teach the torches to burn bright!
It seems she hangs upon the cheek of night
As a rich jewel in an Ethiop's ear—
Beauty too rich for use, for earth too dear!
So shows a snowy dove trooping with crows
As yonder lady o'er her fellows shows.
The measure done, I'll watch her place of stand
And, touching hers, make blessèd my rude° hand.
Did my heart love till now? Forswear it, sight!
For I ne'er saw true beauty till this night.

Tybalt. This, by his voice, should be a Montague.
Fetch me my rapier, boy. What! Dares the slave
Come hither, covered with an antic face,°
To fleer° and scorn at our solemnity?
Now, by the stock and honor of my kin,   60
To strike him dead I hold it not a sin.

Capulet. Why, how now, kinsman? Wherefore storm
      you so?

Tybalt. Uncle, this is a Montague, our foe,
A villain, that is hither come in spite°
To scorn at our solemnity this night.   65

Capulet. Young Romeo is it?

Tybalt.   'Tis he, that villain Romeo.

Capulet. Content thee, gentle coz, let him alone.
'A bears him like a portly° gentleman,
And, to say truth, Verona brags of him
To be a virtuous and well-governed youth.   70
I would not for the wealth of all this town
Here in my house do him disparagement.
Therefore be patient; take no note of him.
It is my will, the which if thou respect,
Show a fair presence and put off these frowns,   75
An ill-beseeming semblance for a feast.

Tybalt. It fits when such a villain is a guest.

53 **rude** rough   58 **antic face** fantastic mask   59 **fleer** jeer   64 **in spite** insultingly   68 **portly** of good deportment

I'll not endure him.

Capulet.   He shall be endured.
What, goodman° boy! I say he shall. Go to!°
80 Am I the master here, or you? Go to!
You'll not endure him, God shall mend my soul!°
You'll make a mutiny° among my guests!
You will set cock-a-hoop.° You'll be the man!

Tybalt. Why, uncle, 'tis a shame.

Capulet.   Go to, go to!
85 You are a saucy boy. Is't so, indeed?
This trick may chance to scathe° you. I know what.
You must contrary me! Marry, 'tis time—
Well said, my hearts!—You are a princox°—go!
Be quiet, or— More light, more light!—For shame!
90 I'll make you quiet. What!—Cheerly, my hearts!

Tybalt. Patience perforce° with willful choler° meeting
Makes my flesh tremble in their different greeting.
I will withdraw; but this intrusion shall,
Now seeming sweet, convert to bitt'rest gall.   *Exit.*

95 *Romeo.* If° I profane with my unworthiest hand
This holy shrine,° the gentle sin is this:°
My lips, two blushing pilgrims, ready stand
To smooth that rough touch with a tender kiss.

Juliet. Good pilgrim, you do wrong your hand too
much,
100   Which mannerly devotion shows in this;
For saints have hands that pilgrims' hands do touch,
And palm to palm is holy palmers'° kiss.

---

79 **goodman** (a term applied to someone below the rank of gentleman)   79 **Go to** (impatient exclamation)   81 **God shall mend my
soul** (roughly equivalent to our "Indeed")   82 **mutiny** disturbance
83 **set cock-a-hoop** be cock of the walk   86 **scathe** hurt, harm
88 **princox** impertinent youngster   91 **Patience perforce** enforced
self-control   91 **choler** anger   95 **If** (here begins an English, or
Shakespearean, sonnet)   96 **shrine** i.e., Juliet's hand   96 **the gentle
sin is this** this is the sin of well-bred people   102 **palmer** religious
pilgrim (the term originally signified one who carried a palm branch;
here it is used as a pun meaning one who holds another's hand)

Romeo. Have not saints lips, and holy palmers too?

Juliet. Ay, pilgrim, lips that they must use in prayer.

Romeo. O, then, dear saint, let lips do what hands do! 105
　　They pray; grant thou, lest faith turn to despair.

Juliet. Saints do not move,° though grant for prayers'
　　sake.

Romeo. Then move not while my prayer's effect I take.
　　Thus from my lips, by thine my sin is purged.
　　　　　　　　　　　　　　　　[*Kisses her.*]

Juliet. Then have my lips the sin that they have took. 110

Romeo. Sin from my lips? O trespass sweetly urged!
　　Give me my sin again.　　　　[*Kisses her.*]

Juliet.　　　　　　　You kiss by th' book.°

Nurse. Madam, your mother craves a word with you.

Romeo. What is her mother?

Nurse.　　　　　　Marry, bachelor,
　　Her mother is the lady of the house,　　　　　　115
　　And a good lady, and a wise and virtuous.
　　I nursed her daughter that you talked withal.°
　　I tell you, he that can lay hold of her
　　Shall have the chinks.°

Romeo.　　　　　　Is she a Capulet?
　　O dear account! My life is my foe's debt.°　　　120

Benvolio. Away, be gone; the sport is at the best.

Romeo. Ay, so I fear; the more is my unrest.

Capulet. Nay, gentlemen, prepare not to be gone;
　　We have a trifling foolish banquet towards.°
　　Is it e'en so?° Why then, I thank you all.　　　125

---

107 **do not move** (1) do not initiate action (2) stand still　112 **kiss
by th' book** i.e., you take my words literally to get more kisses
117 **withal** with　119 **the chinks** plenty of money　120 **my life is
my foe's debt** my foe now owns my life　124 **towards** in preparation　125 **Is it e'en so?** (the maskers insist on leaving)

I thank you, honest gentlemen. Good night.
More torches here! Come on then; let's to bed.
Ah, sirrah, by my fay,° it waxes late;
I'll to my rest.   [*Exeunt all but Juliet and Nurse.*]

130 *Juliet.* Come hither, nurse. What is yond gentleman?

Nurse. The son and heir of old Tiberio.

Juliet. What's he that now is going out of door?

Nurse. Marry, that, I think, be young Petruchio.

Juliet. What's he that follows here, that would not
dance?

135 *Nurse.* I know not.

Juliet. Go ask his name.—If he is marrièd,
My grave is like to be my wedding bed.

Nurse. His name is Romeo, and a Montague,
The only son of your great enemy.

140 *Juliet.* My only love, sprung from my only hate!
Too early seen unknown, and known too late!
Prodigious° birth of love it is to me
That I must love a loathèd enemy.

Nurse. What's this? What's this?

Juliet.   A rhyme I learnt even now
145 Of one I danced withal.   *One calls within,* "Juliet."

Nurse.   Anon,° anon!
Come, let's away; the strangers all are gone.

                                        Exeunt.

---

128 **fay** faith   142 **Prodigious** (1) monstrous (2) of evil portent
145 **Anon** at once

[ACT II

Enter] *Chorus.*

Chorus. Now old desire doth in his deathbed lie,
 And young affection gapes° to be his heir;
That fair° for which love groaned for and would
 die,
 With tender Juliet matched, is now not fair.
Now Romeo is beloved and loves again,   *5*
 Alike bewitchèd° by the charm of looks;
But to his foe supposed he must complain,°
 And she steal love's sweet bait from fearful
 hooks.
Being held a foe, he may not have access
 To breathe such vows as lovers use to° swear, *10*
And she as much in love, her means much less
 To meet her new belovèd anywhere;
But passion lends them power, time means, to meet,
Temp'ring extremities with extreme sweet.° [*Exit.*]

II. Prologue 2 **young affection gapes** the new love is eager 3 **That
fair** i.e., Rosaline 6 **Alike bewitchèd** i.e., both are bewitched
7 **complain** address his lover's suit 10 **use to** customarily 14 **Temp'ring . . . sweet** softening difficulties with extraordinary delights

[Scene I.   *Near Capulet's orchard.*]

Enter Romeo alone.

Romeo. Can I go forward when my heart is here?
Turn back, dull earth, and find thy center out.°

Enter Benvolio with Mercutio. [Romeo retires.]

Benvolio. Romeo! My cousin Romeo! Romeo!

Mercutio.   He is wise
And, on my life, hath stol'n him home to bed.

5 *Benvolio.* He ran this way and leapt this orchard wall.
Call, good Mercutio.

Mercutio.   Nay, I'll conjure too.
Romeo! Humors! Madman! Passion! Lover!
Appear thou in the likeness of a sigh;
Speak but one rhyme, and I am satisfied!
Cry but "Ay me!" pronounce but "love" and
10   "dove";
Speak to my gossip° Venus one fair word,
One nickname for her purblind° son and heir,
Young Abraham Cupid,° he that shot so true
When King Cophetua loved the beggar maid!°
15 He heareth not, he stirreth not, he moveth not;
The ape is dead,° and I must conjure him.
I conjure thee by Rosaline's bright eyes,
By her high forehead and her scarlet lip,

II.i.1–2 **Can . . . out** (Romeo refuses to pass Capulet's house, commanding his body, or *earth*, to stop and join its proper soul, or *center*—i.e., Juliet) 11 **gossip** crony 12 **purblind** quite blind 13 **Abraham Cupid** (the phrase may mean "ancient youth" or, since "abram man" was slang for "trickster," "rascally Cupid") 14 **King Cophetua . . . maid** (reference to an old familiar ballad) 16 **The ape is dead** i.e., Romeo plays dead, like a performing ape

By her fine foot, straight leg, and quivering thigh,
And the demesnes° that there adjacent lie,   20
That in thy likeness thou appear to us!

Benvolio. And if° he hear thee, thou wilt anger him.

Mercutio. This cannot anger him. 'Twould anger him
To raise a spirit in his mistress' circle°
Of some strange nature, letting it there stand   25
Till she had laid it and conjured it down.
That were some spite;° my invocation
Is fair and honest:° in his mistress' name,
I conjure only but to raise up him.

Benvolio. Come, he hath hid himself among these trees 30
To be consorted° with the humorous° night.
Blind is his love and best befits the dark.

Mercutio. If love be blind, love cannot hit the mark.
Now will he sit under a medlar tree
And wish his mistress were that kind of fruit   35
As maids call medlars° when they laugh alone.
O, Romeo, that she were, O that she were
An open *et cetera,* thou a pop'rin pear!
Romeo, good night. I'll to my truckle bed;°
This field bed is too cold for me to sleep.   40
Come, shall we go?

Benvolio.   Go then, for 'tis in vain
To seek him here that means not to be found.
                                        Exit [*with others*].

20 **demesnes** domains   22 **And if** if   24 **circle** (conjurers worked
within a magic circle, but there is also a bawdy innuendo, as in
stand, laid, down, raise)   27 **spite** vexation   28 **fair and honest**
respectable   31 **consorted** associated   31 **humorous** (1) damp (2)
moody   36 **medlars** applelike fruit, eaten when decayed (like
pop'rin, in line 38, the word was often used to refer to sexual or-
gans)   39 **I'll to my truckle bed** I'll go to my trundle bed, or baby
bed (i.e., I'm innocent in affairs of this kind)

[Scene II. *Capulet's orchard.*]

Romeo. [*Coming forward*] He jests at scars that never
    felt a wound.

[*Enter Juliet at a window.*]

But soft! What light through yonder window breaks?
It is the East, and Juliet is the sun!
Arise, fair sun, and kill the envious moon,
5 Who is already sick and pale with grief
That thou her maid° art far more fair than she.
Be not her maid, since she is envious.
Her vestal livery° is but sick and green,°
And none but fools do wear it. Cast it off.
10 It is my lady! O, it is my love!
O, that she knew she were!
She speaks, yet she says nothing. What of that?
Her eye discourses; I will answer it.
I am too bold; 'tis not to me she speaks.
15 Two of the fairest stars in all the heaven,
Having some business, do entreat her eyes
To twinkle in their spheres° till they return.
What if her eyes were there, they in her head?
The brightness of her cheek would shame those stars
20 As daylight doth a lamp; her eyes in heaven
Would through the airy region stream so bright
That birds would sing and think it were not night.
See how she leans her cheek upon her hand!
O, that I were a glove upon that hand,
That I might touch that cheek!

Juliet.   Ay me!

II.ii.6 **her maid** (the moon is here thought of as Diana, goddess and
patroness of virgins) 8 **vestal livery** i.e., virginity 8 **sick and
green** sickly, bearing the characteristics of greensickness, the virgin's
malady 17 **spheres** orbits

Romeo.   She speaks.   *25*
  O, speak again, bright angel, for thou art
  As glorious to this night, being o'er my head,
  As is a wingèd messenger of heaven
  Unto the white-upturnèd wond'ring eyes
  Of mortals that fall back to gaze on him   *30*
  When he bestrides the lazy puffing clouds
  And sails upon the bosom of the air.

Juliet. O Romeo, Romeo! Wherefore art thou Romeo?
  Deny thy father and refuse thy name;
  Or, if thou wilt not, be but sworn my love,   *35*
  And I'll no longer be a Capulet.

Romeo. [*Aside*] Shall I hear more, or shall I speak
  at this?

Juliet. 'Tis but thy name that is my enemy.
  Thou art thyself, though not° a Montague.
  What's Montague? It is nor hand, nor foot,   *40*
  Nor arm, nor face. O, be some other name
  Belonging to a man.
  What's in a name? That which we call a rose
  By any other word would smell as sweet.
  So Romeo would, were he not Romeo called,   *45*
  Retain that dear perfection which he owes°
  Without that title. Romeo, doff thy name;
  And for thy name, which is no part of thee,
  Take all myself.

Romeo.   I take thee at thy word.
  Call me but love, and I'll be new baptized;   *50*
  Henceforth I never will be Romeo.

Juliet. What man art thou, that, thus bescreened in
  night,
  So stumblest on my counsel?

Romeo.   By a name
  I know not how to tell thee who I am.   *55*
  My name, dear saint, is hateful to myself

---

39 **though not** even if you were not   46 **owes** owns

Because it is an enemy to thee.
Had I it written, I would tear the word.

Juliet. My ears have yet not drunk a hundred words
Of thy tongue's uttering, yet I know the sound.
60   Art thou not Romeo, and a Montague?

Romeo. Neither, fair maid, if either thee dislike.°

Juliet. How camest thou hither, tell me, and wherefore?
The orchard walls are high and hard to climb,
And the place death, considering who thou art,
65   If any of my kinsmen find thee here.

Romeo. With love's light wings did I o'erperch° these
walls;
For stony limits cannot hold love out,
And what love can do, that dares love attempt.
Therefore thy kinsmen are no stop to me.

70   *Juliet.* If they do see thee, they will murder thee.

Romeo. Alack, there lies more peril in thine eye
Than twenty of their swords! Look thou but sweet,
And I am proof° against their enmity.

Juliet. I would not for the world they saw thee here.

75   *Romeo.* I have night's cloak to hide me from their eyes;
And but° thou love me, let them find me here.
My life were better ended by their hate
Than death proroguèd,° wanting of thy love.

Juliet. By whose direction found'st thou out this place?

80   *Romeo.* By love, that first did prompt me to inquire.
He lent me counsel, and I lent him eyes.
I am no pilot; yet, wert thou as far
As that vast shore washed with the farthest sea,
I should adventure° for such merchandise.

85   *Juliet.* Thou knowest the mask of night is on my face;

61 **dislike** displeases   66 **o'erperch** fly over   73 **proof** protected
76 **but** if only   78 **proroguèd** deferred   84 **adventure** risk the
journey

Else would a maiden blush bepaint my cheek
For that which thou hast heard me speak tonight.
Fain would I dwell on form—fain, fain deny
What I have spoke; but farewell compliment!°
Dost thou love me? I know thou wilt say "Ay";   90
And I will take thy word. Yet, if thou swear'st,
Thou mayst prove false. At lovers' perjuries,
They say Jove laughs. O gentle Romeo,
If thou dost love, pronounce it faithfully.
Or if thou thinkest I am too quickly won,   95
I'll frown and be perverse and say thee nay,
So thou wilt woo; but else, not for the world.
In truth, fair Montague, I am too fond,°
And therefore thou mayst think my havior° light;
But trust me, gentleman, I'll prove more true   100
Than those that have more cunning to be strange.°
I should have been more strange, I must confess,
But that thou overheard'st, ere I was ware,
My truelove passion. Therefore pardon me,
And not impute this yielding to light love,   105
Which the dark night hath so discovered.°

Romeo. Lady, by yonder blessèd moon I vow,
  That tips with silver all these fruit-tree tops—

Juliet. O, swear not by the moon, th' inconstant moon,
  That monthly changes in her circle orb,   110
  Lest that thy love prove likewise variable.

Romeo. What shall I swear by?

Juliet.   Do not swear at all;
  Or if thou wilt, swear by thy gracious self,
  Which is the god of my idolatry,
  And I'll believe thee.

Romeo.   If my heart's dear love—   115

Juliet. Well, do not swear. Although I joy in thee,
  I have no joy of this contract tonight.

89 **compliment** formal courtesy 98 **fond** (1) affectionate (2) fool-
ishly tender 99 **havior** behavior 101 **strange** aloof 106 **discov-
erèd** revealed

It is too rash, too unadvised, too sudden;
Too like the lightning, which doth cease to be
120 Ere one can say it lightens. Sweet, good night!
This bud of love, by summer's ripening breath,
May prove a beauteous flow'r when next we meet.
Good night, good night! As sweet repose and rest
Come to thy heart as that within my breast!

125 *Romeo.* O, wilt thou leave me so unsatisfied?

Juliet. What satisfaction canst thou have tonight?

Romeo. Th' exchange of thy love's faithful vow for
mine.

Juliet. I gave thee mine before thou didst request it;
And yet I would it were to give again.

Romeo. Wouldst thou withdraw it? For what purpose,
130 love?

Juliet. But to be frank° and give it thee again.
And yet I wish but for the thing I have.
My bounty° is as boundless as the sea,
My love as deep; the more I give to thee,
135 The more I have, for both are infinite.
I hear some noise within. Dear love, adieu!
                         [*Nurse calls within.*]
Anon, good nurse! Sweet Montague, be true.
Stay but a little, I will come again.   [*Exit.*]

Romeo. O blessèd, blessèd night! I am afeard,
140 Being in night, all this is but a dream,
Too flattering-sweet to be substantial.

                [Enter Juliet again.]

Juliet. Three words, dear Romeo, and good night
indeed.
If that thy bent° of love be honorable,
Thy purpose marriage, send me word tomorrow,
145 By one that I'll procure to come to thee,
Where and what time thou wilt perform the rite;

131 **frank** generous   133 **bounty** capacity for giving   143 **bent** aim

And all my fortunes at thy foot I'll lay
And follow thee my lord throughout the world.

[*Nurse. Within*] Madam!

Juliet. I come anon.—But if thou meanest not well,   *150*
I do beseech thee—

[*Nurse. Within*] Madam!

Juliet.   By and by° I come.—
To cease thy strife° and leave me to my grief.
Tomorrow will I send.

Romeo.   So thrive my soul—

Juliet. A thousand times good night!   [*Exit.*]

Romeo. A thousand times the worse, to want thy light!   *155*
Love goes toward love as schoolboys from their
      books;
But love from love, toward school with heavy looks.

            Enter Juliet again.

Juliet. Hist! Romeo, hist! O for a falc'ner's voice
To lure this tassel gentle° back again!
Bondage is hoarse° and may not speak aloud,   *160*
Else would I tear the cave where Echo lies
And make her airy tongue more hoarse than mine
With repetition of "My Romeo!"

Romeo. It is my soul that calls upon my name.
How silver-sweet sound lovers' tongues by night,   *165*
Like softest music to attending° ears!

Juliet. Romeo!

Romeo.   My sweet?

Juliet.   What o'clock tomorrow
Shall I send to thee?

151 **By and by** at once   152 **strife** efforts   159 **tassel gentle** tercel
gentle, male falcon   160 **Bondage is hoarse** i.e., being surrounded
by "protectors," I cannot cry loudly   166 **attending** attentive

Romeo.   By the hour of nine.

Juliet. I will not fail. 'Tis twenty year till then.
170   I have forgot why I did call thee back.

Romeo. Let me stand here till thou remember it.

Juliet. I shall forget, to have thee still stand there,
     Rememb'ring how I love thy company.

Romeo. And I'll still stay, to have thee still forget,
175   Forgetting any other home but this.

Juliet. 'Tis almost morning. I would have thee gone—
     And yet no farther than a wanton's° bird,
     That lets it hop a little from his hand,
     Like a poor prisoner in his twisted gyves,°
180   And with a silken thread plucks it back again,
     So loving-jealous of his liberty.

Romeo. I would I were thy bird.

Juliet.   Sweet, so would I.
     Yet I should kill thee with much cherishing.
     Good night, good night! Parting is such sweet
      sorrow
185   That I shall say good night till it be morrow.°
                          [Exit.]

Romeo. Sleep dwell upon thine eyes, peace in thy
     breast!
     Would I were sleep and peace, so sweet to rest!°
     Hence will I to my ghostly friar's° close cell,
     His help to crave and my dear hap° to tell.   *Exit.*

---

177 **wanton's** capricious child's   179 **gyves** fetters   185 **morrow**
morning   187 **rest** (the four lines that follow in the quarto are
here deleted because they are virtually identical with the first four
lines of the next scene. See Textual Note. Apparently Shakespeare
wrote them and then decided to use them at the start of the next
scene, but forgot to delete their first occurrence)   188 **ghostly friar**
spiritual father (i.e., confessor)   189 **dear hap** good fortune

[Scene III.   *Friar Lawrence's cell.*]

Enter Friar [Lawrence] alone, with a basket.

Friar. The gray-eyed morn smiles on the frowning
     night,
  Check'ring the eastern clouds with streaks of light;
  And fleckèd° darkness like a drunkard reels
  From forth day's path and Titan's burning wheels.°
  Now, ere the sun advance his burning eye   5
  The day to cheer and night's dank dew to dry,
  I must upfill this osier cage° of ours
  With baleful° weeds and precious-juicèd flowers.
  The earth that's nature's mother is her tomb.
  What is her burying grave, that is her womb;   10
  And from her womb children of divers kind
  We sucking on her natural bosom find,
  Many for many virtues excellent,
  None but for some, and yet all different.
  O, mickle° is the powerful grace that lies   15
  In plants, herbs, stones, and their true qualities;
  For naught so vile that on the earth doth live
  But to the earth some special good doth give;
  Nor aught so good but, strained° from that fair use,
  Revolts from true birth,° stumbling on abuse.   20
  Virtue itself turns vice, being misapplied,
  And vice sometime by action dignified.°

Enter Romeo.°

II.iii.3 **fleckèd** spotted   4 **Titan's burning wheels** wheels of the
sun's chariot   7 **osier cage** willow basket   8 **baleful** (1) evil (2)
poisonous   15 **mickle** much   19 **strained** diverted   20 **Revolts
from true birth** falls away from its real purpose   22 **dignified** made
worthy   22 s.d. **Enter Romeo** (the entry of Romeo at this point,
unseen by the Friar, emphasizes the appropriateness of the remaining eight lines of the Friar's speech, not only to the flower but to
Romeo)

Within the infant rind° of this weak flower
Poison hath residence and medicine° power;
For this, being smelt, with that part cheers each
25   part;°
Being tasted, stays all senses with the heart.
Two such opposèd kings encamp them still°
In man as well as herbs—grace and rude will;
And where the worser is predominant,
30   Full soon the canker° death eats up that plant.

Romeo. Good morrow, father.

Friar.   *Benedicite!°*
What early tongue so sweet saluteth me?
Young son, it argues a distemperèd head°
So soon to bid good morrow to thy bed.
35   Care keeps his watch in every old man's eye,
And where care lodges, sleep will never lie;
But where unbruisèd youth with unstuffed° brain
Doth couch his limbs, there golden sleep doth reign.
Therefore thy earliness doth me assure
40   Thou art uproused with some distemp'rature;
Or if not so, then here I hit it right—
Our Romeo hath not been in bed tonight.

Romeo. That last is true. The sweeter rest was mine.

Friar. God pardon sin! Wast thou with Rosaline?

45 *Romeo.* With Rosaline, my ghostly father? No.
I have forgot that name and that name's woe.

Friar. That's my good son! But where hast thou been
then?

Romeo. I'll tell thee ere thou ask it me again.
I have been feasting with mine enemy,
50   Where on a sudden one hath wounded me
That's by me wounded. Both our remedies

23 **infant rind** tender bark, skin   24 **medicine** medicinal   25 **For
. . . part** i.e., being smelled, this flower stimulates every part of the
body   27 **still** always   30 **canker** cankerworm, larva that feeds
on leaves   31 **Benedicite** bless you   33 **distemperèd head** troubled
mind   37 **unstuffed** untroubled

Within thy help and holy physic° lies.
I bear no hatred, blessèd man, for, lo,
My intercession° likewise steads° my foe.

Friar. Be plain, good son, and homely in thy drift.°   55
Riddling confession finds but riddling shrift.°

Romeo. Then plainly know my heart's dear love is set
On the fair daughter of rich Capulet;
As mine on hers, so hers is set on mine,
And all combined,° save what thou must combine   60
By holy marriage. When and where and how
We met, we wooed, and made exchange of vow,
I'll tell thee as we pass; but this I pray,
That thou consent to marry us today.

Friar. Holy Saint Francis! What a change is here!   65
Is Rosaline, that thou didst love so dear,
So soon forsaken? Young men's love then lies
Not truly in their hearts, but in their eyes.
Jesu Maria! What a deal of brine
Hath washed thy sallow cheeks for Rosaline!   70
How much salt water thrown away in waste
To season° love, that of it doth not taste!
The sun not yet thy sighs from heaven clears,
Thy old groans ring yet in mine ancient ears.
Lo, here upon thy cheek the stain doth sit   75
Of an old tear that is not washed off yet.
If e'er thou wast thyself, and these woes thine,
Thou and these woes were all for Rosaline.
And art thou changed? Pronounce this sentence
    then:
Women may fall° when there's no strength° in men.   80

Romeo. Thou chidst me oft for loving Rosaline.

Friar. For doting, not for loving, pupil mine.

---

52 **physic** medicine   54 **intercession** entreaty   54 **steads** helps
55 **homely in thy drift** plain in your talk   56 **shrift** absolution
60 **combined** (1) brought into unity (2) settled   72 **season** (1) preserve (2) flavor   80 **may fall** i.e., may be expected to be fickle
80 **strength** constancy

Romeo. And badst me bury love.

Friar. Not in a grave
To lay one in, another out to have.

85　*Romeo.* I pray thee chide me not. Her I love now
Doth grace° for grace and love for love allow.
The other did not so.

Friar. O, she knew well
Thy love did read by rote, that could not spell.°
But come, young waverer, come go with me.
90　In one respect° I'll thy assistant be;
For this alliance may so happy prove
To turn your households' rancor to pure love.

Romeo. O, let us hence! I stand on° sudden haste.

Friar. Wisely and slow. They stumble that run fast.
Exeunt.

[Scene IV. *A street.*]

Enter Benvolio and Mercutio.

Mercutio. Where the devil should this Romeo be?
Came he not home tonight?

Benvolio. Not to his father's. I spoke with his man.

Mercutio. Why, that same pale hardhearted wench,
that Rosaline,
5　Torments him so that he will sure run mad.

Benvolio. Tybalt, the kinsman to old Capulet,
Hath sent a letter to his father's house.

Mercutio. A challenge, on my life.

86 **grace** favor　88 **did read . . . spell** i.e., said words without understanding them　90 **In one respect** with respect to one particular
93 **stand on** insist on

Benvolio. Romeo will answer it.

Mercutio. Any man that can write may answer a letter.   *10*

Benvolio. Nay, he will answer the letter's master, how
he dares, being dared.

Mercutio. Alas, poor Romeo, he is already dead:
stabbed with a white wench's black eye; run through
the ear with a love song; the very pin° of his heart   *15*
cleft with the blind bow-boy's butt-shaft;° and is he
a man to encounter Tybalt?

Benvolio. Why, what is Tybalt?

Mercutio. More than Prince of Cats.° O, he's the
courageous captain of compliments.° He fights as   *20*
you sing pricksong°—keeps time, distance, and pro-
portion; he rests his minim rests,° one, two, and
the third in your bosom! The very butcher of a silk
button,° a duelist, a duelist! A gentleman of the
very first house,° of the first and second cause.°   *25*
Ah, the immortal *passado!*° The *punto reverso!*°
The hay!°

Benvolio. The what?

Mercutio. The pox of such antic, lisping, affecting
fantasticoes°—these new tuners of accent! "By   *30*
Jesu, a very good blade! A very tall° man! A very
good whore!" Why, is not this a lamentable thing,
grandsir, that we should be thus afflicted with these

II.iv.15 **pin** center (of a target)   16 **blind bow-boy's butt-shaft** Cupid's blunt arrow   19 **Prince of Cats** (Tybalt's name, or some vari-
ant of it, was given to the cat in medieval stories of Reynard the
Fox)   20 **compliments** formal courtesies   21 **sing pricksong** (1)
sing from a text (2) sing with attention to accuracy   22 **he rests
his minim rests** i.e., he scrupulously observes every formality (literally, he observes even the shortest rests in the notation)   24 **button** (on his opponent's shirt)   25 **first house** first rank   25 **first and
second cause** (dueling terms, meaning formal grounds for taking
offense and giving a challenge)   26 **passado** lunge   26 **punto reverso** backhanded stroke   27 **hay** home thrust (Italian *hai*)
30 **fantasticoes** fops   31 **tall** brave

35 strange flies, these fashionmongers, these pardon-
me's,° who stand so much on the new form° that
they cannot sit at ease on the old bench? O, their
bones,° their bones!

Enter Romeo.

Benvolio. Here comes Romeo! Here comes Romeo!

Mercutio. Without his roe,° like a dried herring. O
40 flesh, flesh, how art thou fishified! Now is he for
the numbers° that Petrarch flowed in. Laura,° to
his lady, was a kitchen wench (marry, she had a
better love to berhyme her), Dido° a dowdy,°
Cleopatra a gypsy,° Helen and Hero° hildings° and
45 harlots, Thisbe° a gray eye° or so, but not to the
purpose. Signior Romeo, *bon jour!* There's a French
salutation to your French slop.° You gave us the
counterfeit fairly last night.

Romeo. Good morrow to you both. What counterfeit
50 did I give you?

Mercutio. The slip,° sir, the slip. Can you not conceive?

Romeo. Pardon, good Mercutio. My business was
great, and in such a case as mine a man may strain
55 courtesy.

Mercutio. That's as much as to say, such a case° as
yours constrains a man to bow in the hams.

34–35 **pardon-me's** i.e., persons who affect foreign phrases (cf.
Italian *perdona mi*) 35 **form** (1) fashion (2) bench 37 **bones**
(pun on French *bon*) 39 **Without his roe** i.e., (1) emaciated like
a fish that has spawned or (2) stripped of "Ro," leaving only "me-o"
(a sigh) 41 **numbers** verses 41 **Laura** (Petrarch's beloved)
43 **Dido** (Queen of Carthage, enamored of Aeneas) 43 **dowdy** a
drab woman 44 **gypsy** a deceitful woman (gypsies were commonly
believed to be Egyptians) 44 **Helen and Hero** (beloved respec-
tively of Paris and Leander) 44 **hildings** good-for-nothings
45 **Thisbe** (beloved of Pyramus in a story analogous to that of
Romeo and Juliet) 45 **gray eye** i.e., gleam in the eye 47 **slop** loose
breeches 51 **slip** (1) escape (2) counterfeit coin 56 **case** (1) situation (2) physical condition

Romeo. Meaning, to curtsy.

Mercutio. Thou hast most kindly hit° it.

Romeo. A most courteous exposition.　　　　　　　60

Mercutio. Nay, I am the very pink° of courtesy.

Romeo. Pink for flower.

Mercutio. Right.

Romeo. Why, then is my pump° well-flowered.°

Mercutio. Sure wit, follow me this jest now till thou　65
hast worn out thy pump, that, when the single sole
of it is worn, the jest may remain, after the wearing,
solely singular.°

Romeo. O single-soled jest, solely singular for the
singleness!　　　　　　　　　　　　　　　　　　70

Mercutio. Come between us, good Benvolio! My wits
faints.

Romeo. Swits° and spurs, swits and spurs; or I'll cry
a match.°

Mercutio. Nay, if our wits run the wild-goose chase,°　75
I am done; for thou hast more of the wild goose in
one of thy wits than, I am sure, I have in my whole
five. Was I with you there for the goose?°

Romeo. Thou wast never with me for anything when
thou wast not there for the goose.°　　　　　　　80

Mercutio. I will bite thee by the ear for that jest.

59 **most kindly hit** most politely interpreted　61 **pink** perfection
(but Romeo proceeds to exploit two other meanings: [1] flower
[2] punches in an ornamental design)　64 **pump** shoe　64 **well-flowered** ornamented with pinking (with pun on "floored")
68 **solely singular** (1) single-soled (i.e., weak) (2) uniquely remarkable (literally, "uniquely unique")　73 **Swits** switches　73–74 **cry a match** claim a victory　75 **wild-goose chase** cross-country game
of "follow the leader" on horseback　78 **goose** end of the chase
(i.e., end of the punning match)　80 **goose** prostitute

Romeo. Nay, good goose, bite not!°

Mercutio. Thy wit is a very bitter sweeting;° it is a most sharp sauce.

85 *Romeo.* And is it not, then, well served in to a sweet goose?°

Mercutio. O, here's a wit of cheveril,° that stretches from an inch narrow to an ell broad!°

Romeo. I stretch it out for that word "broad," which
90 added to the goose, proves thee far and wide a broad° goose.

Mercutio. Why, is not this better now than groaning for love? Now art thou sociable, now art thou Romeo; now art thou what thou art, by art as well
95 as by nature. For this driveling love is like a great natural° that runs lolling° up and down to hide his bauble° in a hole.

Benvolio. Stop there, stop there!

Mercutio. Thou desirest me to stop in my tale against
100 the hair.°

Benvolio. Thou wouldst else have made thy tale large.°

Mercutio. O, thou art deceived! I would have made it short; for I was come to the whole depth of my
105 tale, and meant indeed to occupy the argument° no longer.

Romeo. Here's goodly gear!°

---

82 **good goose, bite not** (proverbial for "Spare me!")   83 **bitter sweeting** tart kind of apple   85–86 **sweet goose** tender goose (here probably referring to Mercutio; but the expression "Sour sauce for sweet meat" was proverbial)   87 **cheveril** kid leather, easily stretched   88 **ell broad** forty-five inches wide   91 **broad** indecent (?)   96 **natural** idiot   96 **lolling** with tongue hanging out   97 **bauble** trinket (with ribald innuendo)   99–100 **against the hair** against my inclination   102 **large** indecent   105 **occupy the argument** discuss the matter   107 **gear** stuff

Enter Nurse and her Man [Peter].

A sail, a sail!

Mercutio. Two, two! A shirt and a smock.°

Nurse. Peter!   110

Peter. Anon.

Nurse. My fan, Peter.

Mercutio. Good Peter, to hide her face; for her fan's the fairer face.

Nurse. God ye good morrow, gentlemen.   115

Mercutio. God ye good-den,° fair gentlewoman.

Nurse. Is it good-den?

Mercutio. 'Tis no less, I tell ye; for the bawdy hand of the dial is now upon the prick° of noon.

Nurse. Out upon you! What a man are you!   120

Romeo. One, gentlewoman, that God hath made, himself to mar.

Nurse. By my troth, it is well said. "For himself to mar," quoth 'a?° Gentlemen, can any of you tell me where I may find the young Romeo?   125

Romeo. I can tell you; but young Romeo will be older when you have found him than he was when you sought him. I am the youngest of that name, for fault of a worse.°

Nurse. You say well.   130

Mercutio. Yea, is the worst well? Very well took,° i' faith! Wisely, wisely.

Nurse. If you be he, sir, I desire some confidence° with you.

109 **A shirt and a smock** i.e., a man and a woman   116 **good-den** good evening (i.e., afternoon)   119 **prick** point on the dial of a clock (with bawdy innuendo)   124 **quoth 'a** indeed (literally, "said he")   128–29 **for fault of a worse** (mock-modestly parodying "for want of a better")   131 **took** understood   133 **confidence** conference (possibly a malapropism)

135 *Benvolio.* She will endite° him to some supper.

Mercutio. A bawd, a bawd, a bawd! So ho!°

Romeo. What hast thou found?

Mercutio. No hare,° sir; unless a hare, sir, in a lenten
    pie,° that is something stale and hoar° ere it be
140 spent.

          [*He walks by them and sings.*]

          An old hare hoar,
          And an old hare hoar,
      Is very good meat in Lent;
          But a hare that is hoar
145   Is too much for a score
      When it hoars ere it be spent.

Romeo, will you come to your father's? We'll to
dinner thither.

Romeo. I will follow you.

150 *Mercutio.* Farewell, ancient lady. Farewell, [*singing*]
    "Lady, lady, lady."°   *Exeunt* [*Mercutio, Benvolio*].

Nurse. I pray you, sir, what saucy merchant was this
    that was so full of his ropery?°

Romeo. A gentleman, nurse, that loves to hear himself
155 talk and will speak more in a minute than he will
    stand to in a month.

Nurse. And 'a speak anything against me, I'll take him
    down, and 'a were lustier than he is, and twenty
    such Jacks; and if I cannot, I'll find those that shall.
160 Scurvy knave! I am none of his flirt-gills;° I am

---

136 **endite** invite (Benvolio's intentional malapropism?)　136 **So
ho!** (cry on sighting a quarry)　138 **hare** prostitute　138–39 **lenten
pie** rabbit pie (eaten sparingly and hence stale)　139 **hoar** gray-
haired, moldy (wordplay on "hare" and "whore")　151 **Lady, lady,
lady** (ballad refrain from "Chaste Susanna")　153 **ropery** rascally
talk　160 **flirt-gills** flirting wenches

none of his skainsmates.° And thou must stand
by too, and suffer every knave to use me at his
pleasure!

Peter. I saw no man use you at his pleasure. If I had,
my weapon should quickly have been out, I warrant   *165*
you. I dare draw as soon as another man, if I see
occasion in a good quarrel, and the law on my side.

Nurse. Now, afore God, I am so vexed that every part
about me quivers. Scurvy knave! Pray you, sir, a
word; and, as I told you, my young lady bid me   *170*
inquire you out. What she bid me say, I will keep
to myself; but first let me tell ye, if ye should lead
her in a fool's paradise,° as they say, it were a very
gross kind of behavior, as they say; for the gentlewoman is young; and therefore, if you should deal   *175*
double with her, truly it were an ill thing to be
off'red to any gentlewoman, and very weak° dealing.

Romeo. Nurse, commend me to thy lady and mistress.
I protest unto thee—

Nurse. Good heart, and i' faith I will tell her as much.   *180*
Lord, Lord, she will be a joyful woman.

Romeo. What wilt thou tell her, nurse? Thou dost not
mark me.

Nurse. I will tell her, sir, that you do protest, which,
as I take it, is a gentlemanlike offer.   *185*

Romeo. Bid her devise
Some means to come to shrift this afternoon;
And there she shall at Friar Lawrence' cell
Be shrived and married. Here is for thy pains.

Nurse. No, truly, sir; not a penny.   *190*

Romeo. Go to! I say you shall.

Nurse. This afternoon, sir? Well, she shall be there.

---

161 **skainsmates** harlots (?) daggers' mates (i.e., outlaws' mates)
173 **fool's paradise** seduction   177 **weak** unmanly, unscrupulous

Romeo. And stay, good nurse, behind the abbey wall.
Within this hour my man shall be with thee
195 And bring thee cords made like a tackled stair,°
Which to the high topgallant° of my joy
Must be my convoy° in the secret night.
Farewell. Be trusty, and I'll quit° thy pains.
Farewell. Commend me to thy mistress.

200 *Nurse.* Now God in heaven bless thee! Hark you, sir.

Romeo. What say'st thou, my dear nurse?

Nurse. Is your man secret? Did you ne'er hear say,
Two may keep counsel, putting one away?

Romeo. Warrant thee my man's as true as steel.

205 *Nurse.* Well, sir, my mistress is the sweetest lady. Lord,
Lord! When 'twas a little prating thing— O, there is
a nobleman in town, one Paris, that would fain lay
knife aboard;° but she, good soul, had as lieve° see
a toad, a very toad, as see him. I anger her some-
210 times, and tell her that Paris is the properer man;
but I'll warrant you, when I say so, she looks as
pale as any clout° in the versal world.° Doth not
rosemary and Romeo begin both with a letter?

Romeo. Ay, nurse; what of that? Both with an R.

215 *Nurse.* Ah, mocker! That's the dog's name.° R is for
the— No; I know it begins with some other letter;
and she hath the prettiest sententious° of it, of you
and rosemary, that it would do you good to hear it.

Romeo. Commend me to thy lady.

220 *Nurse.* Ay, a thousand times. [*Exit Romeo.*] Peter!

Peter. Anon.

Nurse. Before, and apace.   *Exit [after Peter].*

---

195 **tackled stair** rope ladder   196 **topgallant** summit (mast above
the topmast)   197 **convoy** conveyance   198 **quit** reward   207–08
lay knife aboard take a slice   208 **had as lieve** would rather
212 **clout** cloth   212 **versal world** universe   215 **dog's name** (the
R sound suggests a dog's growl)   217 **sententious** sentences, pithy
sayings

[Scene V. *Capulet's orchard.*]

Enter Juliet.

Juliet. The clock struck nine when I did send the
    nurse;
  In half an hour she promised to return.
  Perchance she cannot meet him. That's not so.
  O, she is lame! Love's heralds should be thoughts,
  Which ten times faster glides than the sun's beams   *5*
  Driving back shadows over low'ring hills.
  Therefore do nimble-pinioned doves° draw Love,
  And therefore hath the wind-swift Cupid wings.
  Now is the sun upon the highmost hill
  Of this day's journey, and from nine till twelve   *10*
  Is three long hours; yet she is not come.
  Had she affections and warm youthful blood,
  She would be as swift in motion as a ball;
  My words would bandy her° to my sweet love,
  And his to me.   *15*
  But old folks, many feign as they were dead°—
  Unwieldy, slow, heavy and pale as lead.

Enter Nurse [and Peter].

  O God, she comes! O honey nurse, what news?
  Hast thou met with him? Send thy man away.

Nurse. Peter, stay at the gate.   [*Exit Peter.*] *20*

Juliet. Now, good sweet nurse—O Lord, why lookest
    thou sad?
  Though news be sad, yet tell them merrily;

II.v.7 **nimble-pinioned doves** swift-winged doves (sacred to Venus)
14 **bandy her** speed her   16 **old . . . dead** i.e., many old people
move about as if they were almost dead

If good, thou shamest the music of sweet news
By playing it to me with so sour a face.

25 *Nurse.* I am aweary, give me leave awhile.
Fie, how my bones ache! What a jaunce° have I!

Juliet. I would thou hadst my bones, and I thy news.
Nay, come, I pray thee speak. Good, good nurse,
speak.

Nurse. Jesu, what haste! Can you not stay° awhile?
30 Do you not see that I am out of breath?

Juliet. How art thou out of breath when thou hast
breath
To say to me that thou art out of breath?
The excuse that thou dost make in this delay
Is longer than the tale thou dost excuse.
35 Is thy news good or bad? Answer to that.
Say either, and I'll stay the circumstance.°
Let me be satisfied, is't good or bad?

Nurse. Well, you have made a simple° choice; you
know not how to choose a man. Romeo? No, not
40 he. Though his face be better than any man's, yet
his leg excels all men's; and for a hand and a foot,
and a body, though they be not to be talked on,
yet they are past compare. He is not the flower of
courtesy, but, I'll warrant him, as gentle as a lamb.
45 Go thy ways, wench; serve God. What, have you
dined at home?

Juliet. No, no. But all this did I know before.
What says he of our marriage? What of that?

Nurse. Lord, how my head aches! What a head have I!
50 It beats as it would fall in twenty pieces.
My back a° t' other side—ah, my back, my back!
Beshrew° your heart for sending me about
To catch my death with jauncing up and down!

---

26 **jaundice** jaunt, fatiguing walk   29 **stay** wait   36 **stay the circumstance** wait for the details   38 **simple** foolish   51 a on   52 **Beshrew** curse (in the sense of "shame on")

Juliet. I' faith, I am sorry that thou art not well.
  Sweet, sweet, sweet nurse, tell me, what says my
    love?   55

Nurse. Your love says, like an honest gentleman, and
  a courteous, and a kind, and a handsome, and, I
  warrant, a virtuous— Where is your mother?

Juliet. Where is my mother? Why, she is within.
  Where should she be? How oddly thou repliest!   60
  "Your love says, like an honest gentleman,
  'Where is your mother?'"

Nurse.   O God's Lady dear!
  Are you so hot?° Marry come up, I trow.°
  Is this the poultice for my aching bones?
  Henceforward do your messages yourself.   85

Juliet. Here's such a coil!° Come, what says Romeo?

Nurse. Have you got leave to go to shrift today?

Juliet. I have.

Nurse. Then hie you hence to Friar Lawrence' cell;
  There stays a husband to make you a wife.   70
  Now comes the wanton blood up in your cheeks:
  They'll be in scarlet straight° at any news.
  Hie you to church; I must another way,
  To fetch a ladder, by the which your love
  Must climb a bird's nest soon when it is dark.   75
  I am the drudge, and toil in your delight;
  But you shall bear the burden soon at night.
  Go; I'll to dinner; hie you to the cell.

Juliet. Hie to high fortune! Honest nurse, farewell.
                                        Exeunt.

---

63 **hot** angry   63 **Marry . . . trow** indeed, come now, by the Virgin
66 **coil** disturbance   72 **straight** straightway

[Scene VI. *Friar Lawrence's cell.*]

Enter Friar [*Lawrence*] *and Romeo.*

Friar. So smile the heavens upon this holy act
    That afterhours with sorrow chide us not!

Romeo. Amen, amen! But come what sorrow can,
    It cannot countervail° the exchange of joy
5   That one short minute gives me in her sight.
    Do thou but close our hands with holy words,
    Then love-devouring death do what he dare—
    It is enough I may but call her mine.

Friar. These violent delights have violent ends
10   And in their triumph die, like fire and powder,
    Which, as they kiss, consume. The sweetest honey
    Is loathsome in his own deliciousness
    And in the taste confounds° the appetite.
    Therefore love moderately: long love doth so;
15   Too swift arrives as tardy as too slow.

Enter Juliet.

    Here comes the lady. O, so light a foot
    Will ne'er wear out the everlasting flint.°
    A lover may bestride the gossamers°
    That idles in the wanton° summer air,
20   And yet not fall; so light is vanity.°

Juliet. Good even to my ghostly confessor.

Friar. Romeo shall thank thee, daughter, for us both.

II.vi.4 **countervail** equal   13 **confounds** destroys   17 **Will . . .
flint** i.e., Juliet's feet are lighter than waterdrops, which are pro-
verbially said to wear away stones   18 **gossamers** spiders' webs
19 **wanton** capricious   20 **vanity** a transitory thing (an earthly lover
and his love)

Juliet. As much to him,° else is his thanks too much.

Romeo. Ah, Juliet, if the measure of thy joy
  Be heaped like mine, and that thy skill be more   25
  To blazon it,° then sweeten with thy breath
  This neighbor air, and let rich music's tongue
  Unfold the imagined happiness that both
  Receive in either by this dear encounter.

Juliet. Conceit, more rich in matter than in words,   30
  Brags of his substance, not of ornament.°
  They are but beggars that can count their worth;
  But my true love is grown to such excess
  I cannot sum up sum of half my wealth.

Friar. Come, come with me, and we will make short
      work;   35
  For, by your leaves, you shall not stay alone
  Till Holy Church incorporate two in one. [*Exeunt.*]

---

23 As much to him i.e., the same greeting to Romeo   **25–26 thy
skill . . . blazon it** you are better able to set it forth   **30–31 Conceit
. . . ornament** i.e., true understanding is its own proud manifestation
and does not need words

[ACT III

Scene I. *A public place.*]

Enter Mercutio, Benvolio, and Men.

Benvolio. I pray thee, good Mercutio, let's retire.
    The day is hot, the Capels are abroad,
    And, if we meet, we shall not 'scape a brawl,
    For now, these hot days, is the mad blood stirring.

5 *Mercutio.* Thou art like one of these fellows that,
    when he enters the confines of a tavern, claps me
    his sword upon the table and says, "God send me
    no need of thee!" and by the operation of the
    second cup draws him on the drawer,° when indeed
10   there is no need.

Benvolio. Am I like such a fellow?

Mercutio. Come, come, thou art as hot a Jack in thy
    mood as any in Italy; and as soon moved to be
    moody,° and as soon moody to be moved.°

15 *Benvolio.* And what to?

Mercutio. Nay, and there were two such, we should
    have none shortly, for one would kill the other.
    Thou! Why, thou wilt quarrel with a man that hath

III.i.9 **draws him on the drawer** draws his sword on the waiter
14 **moody** angry   14 **moody to be moved** quick-tempered

a hair more or a hair less in his beard than thou
hast. Thou wilt quarrel with a man for cracking   20
nuts, having no other reason but because thou hast
hazel eyes. What eye but such an eye would spy
out such a quarrel? Thy head is as full of quarrels
as an egg is full of meat; and yet thy head hath
been beaten as addle as an egg for quarreling. Thou   25
hast quarreled with a man for coughing in the street,
because he hath wakened thy dog that hath lain
asleep in the sun. Didst thou not fall out with a
tailor for wearing his new doublet° before Easter?
With another for tying his new shoes with old   30
riband?° And yet thou wilt tutor me from quarreling!

Benvolio. And I were so apt to quarrel as thou art, any
man should buy the fee simple° of my life for an
hour and a quarter.°

Mercutio. The fee simple? O simple!°   35

    Enter Tybalt, Petruchio,° and others.

Benvolio. By my head, here comes the Capulets.

Mercutio. By my heel, I care not.

Tybalt. Follow me close, for I will speak to them.
Gentlemen, good-den.° A word with one of you.

Mercutio. And but one word with one of us? Couple   40
it with something; make it a word and a blow.

Tybalt. You shall find me apt enough to that, sir, and
you will give me occasion.

Mercutio. Could you not take some occasion without
giving?   45

Tybalt. Mercutio, thou consortest with Romeo.

---

29 **doublet** jacket   31 **riband** ribbon   33 **fee simple** absolute possession   33–34 **for an hour and a quarter** i.e., the life expectancy
of one with Mercutio's penchant for quarreling   35 **O simple** O
stupid   35 **Petruchio** (in I.v he was one of Capulet's guests, but he
has no lines)   39 **good-den** good evening (i.e., afternoon)

Mercutio. Consort?° What, dost thou make us minstrels? And thou make minstrels of us, look to hear
nothing but discords. Here's my fiddlestick;° here's
50 that shall make you dance. Zounds,° consort!

Benvolio. We talk here in the public haunt of men.
Either withdraw unto some private place,
Or reason coldly of your grievances,
Or else depart. Here all eyes gaze on us.

Mercutio. Men's eyes were made to look, and let them
55   gaze.
I will not budge for no man's pleasure, I.

Enter Romeo.

Tybalt. Well, peace be with you, sir. Here comes my
man.°

Mercutio. But I'll be hanged, sir, if he wear your
livery.°
Marry, go before to field,° he'll be your follower!
60 Your worship in that sense may call him man.

Tybalt. Romeo, the love I bear thee can afford
No better term than this: thou art a villain.°

Romeo. Tybalt, the reason that I have to love thee
Doth much excuse the appertaining° rage
65 To such a greeting. Villain am I none.
Therefore farewell. I see thou knowest me not.

Tybalt. Boy, this shall not excuse the injuries
That thou hast done me; therefore turn and draw.

Romeo. I do protest I never injured thee,
70 But love thee better than thou canst devise°
Till thou shalt know the reason of my love;
And so, good Capulet, which name I tender°
As dearly as mine own, be satisfied.

---

47 Consort (1) to keep company with (2) company of musicians
49 fiddlestick i.e., sword   **50 Zounds** by God's wounds   **57 man**
(Mercutio takes this to mean "manservant")   **58 livery** servant's
uniform   **59 field** dueling field   **62 villain** low fellow   **64 apper-
taining** appropriate   **70 devise** imagine   **72 tender** value

Mercutio. O calm, dishonorable, vile submission!
  Alla stoccata° carries it away. [*Draws.*] 75
  Tybalt, you ratcatcher, will you walk?°

Tybalt. What wouldst thou have with me?

Mercutio. Good King of Cats, nothing but one of your
  nine lives. That I mean to make bold withal,° and,
  as you shall use me hereafter, dry-beat° the rest of
  the eight. Will you pluck your sword out of his 80
  pilcher° by the ears? Make haste, lest mine be about
  your ears ere it be out.

Tybalt. I am for you. [*Draws.*]

Romeo. Gentle Mercutio, put thy rapier up. 85

Mercutio. Come, sir, your *passado!*° [*They fight.*]

Romeo. Draw, Benvolio; beat down their weapons.
  Gentlemen, for shame! Forbear this outrage!
  Tybalt, Mercutio, the Prince expressly hath
  Forbid this bandying° in Verona streets. 90
  Hold, Tybalt! Good Mercutio!
          [*Tybalt under Romeo's arm thrusts
            Mercutio in, and flies.*]

Mercutio.   I am hurt.
  A plague a° both houses! I am sped.°
  Is he gone and hath nothing?

Benvolio.   What, art thou hurt?

Mercutio. Ay, ay, a scratch, a scratch. Marry, 'tis
  enough.
  Where is my page? Go, villain, fetch a surgeon. 95
          [*Exit Page.*]

Romeo. Courage, man. The hurt cannot be much.

Mercutio. No, 'tis not so deep as a well, nor so wide

---

75 **Alla stoccata** (a term in fencing, "At the thrust," which Mercutio uses contemptuously as a nickname for Tybalt) 76 **walk**
step aside 79 **make bold withal** make bold with, take 80 **dry-
beat** thrash 82 **pilcher** scabbard 86 **passado** lunge 90 **bandy-
ing** brawling 92 **a** on 92 **sped** wounded

as a church door; but 'tis enough, 'twill serve. Ask
for me tomorrow, and you shall find me a grave°
100   man. I am peppered,° I warrant, for this world. A
plague a both your houses! Zounds, a dog, a rat, a
mouse, a cat, to scratch a man to death! A braggart,
a rogue, a villain, that fights by the book of arithmetic!° Why the devil came you between us? I was
105   hurt under your arm.

Romeo. I thought all for the best.

Mercutio. Help me into some house, Benvolio,
Or I shall faint. A plague a both your houses!
They have made worms' meat of me. I have it,°
110   And soundly too. Your houses!
                    Exit [Mercutio and Benvolio].

Romeo. This gentleman, the Prince's near ally,°
My very° friend, hath got this mortal hurt
In my behalf—my reputation stained
With Tybalt's slander—Tybalt, that an hour
115   Hath been my cousin. O sweet Juliet,
Thy beauty hath made me effeminate
And in my temper soft'ned valor's steel!°

                    Enter Benvolio.

Benvolio. O Romeo, Romeo, brave Mercutio is dead!
That gallant spirit hath aspired° the clouds,
120   Which too untimely here did scorn the earth.

Romeo. This day's black fate on moe° days doth
X   depend;°
This but begins the woe others must end.

                    [Enter Tybalt.]

Benvolio. Here comes the furious Tybalt back again.

Romeo. Alive in triumph, and Mercutio slain?

99 **grave** (1) extremely serious (2) ready for the grave   100 **am
peppered** have been given a deathblow   103–04 **by the book of
arithmetic** by formal rules   109 **I have it** i.e., I have received my
deathblow   111 **ally** relative   112 **very** true   117 **in . . . steel**
softened the valorous part of my character   119 **aspired** climbed
to   121 **moe** more   121 **depend** hang over

Away to heaven respective lenity,°   *125*
And fire-eyed fury be my conduct° now!
Now, Tybalt, take the "villain" back again
That late thou gavest me; for Mercutio's soul
Is but a little way above our heads,
Staying for thine to keep him company.   *130*
Either thou or I, or both, must go with him.

Tybalt. Thou, wretched boy, that didst consort him here,
 Shalt with him hence.

Romeo.   This shall determine that.
                    They fight. Tybalt falls.

Benvolio. Romeo, away, be gone!
 The citizens are up, and Tybalt slain.   *135*
 Stand not amazed. The Prince will doom thee death
 If thou art taken. Hence, be gone, away!

Romeo. O, I am fortune's fool!°

Benvolio.   Why dost thou stay?
                    Exit Romeo.

Enter Citizens.

Citizen. Which way ran he that killed Mercutio?
 Tybalt, that murderer, which way ran he?   *140*

Benvolio. There lies that Tybalt.

Citizen.   Up, sir, go with me.
 I charge thee in the Prince's name obey.

*Enter Prince, old Montague, Capulet, their Wives,
 and all.*

Prince. Where are the vile beginners of this fray?

Benvolio. O noble Prince, I can discover° all
 The unlucky manage° of this fatal brawl.   *145*

---

125 **respective lenity** discriminating mercifulness 126 **conduct**
guide 138 **fool** plaything, dupe 144 **discover** reveal 145 **manage** course

There lies the man, slain by young Romeo,
That slew thy kinsman, brave Mercutio.

Lady Capulet. Tybalt, my cousin! O my brother's child!
  O Prince! O cousin! Husband! O, the blood is
    spilled
150 Of my dear kinsman! Prince, as thou art true,
  For blood of ours shed blood of Montague.
  O cousin, cousin!

Prince. Benvolio, who began this bloody fray?

Benvolio. Tybalt, here slain, whom Romeo's hand did
    slay.
155 Romeo, that spoke him fair, bid him bethink
  How nice° the quarrel was, and urged° withal
  Your high displeasure. All this—utterèd
  With gentle breath, calm look, knees humbly
    bowed—
  Could not take truce with the unruly spleen°
160 Of Tybalt deaf to peace, but that he tilts°
  With piercing steel at bold Mercutio's breast;
  Who, all as hot, turns deadly point to point,
  And, with a martial scorn, with one hand beats
  Cold death aside and with the other sends
165 It back to Tybalt, whose dexterity
  Retorts it. Romeo he cries aloud,
  "Hold, friends! Friends, part!" and swifter than his
    tongue,
  His agile arm beats down their fatal points,
  And 'twixt them rushes; underneath whose arm
170 An envious° thrust from Tybalt hit the life
  Of stout Mercutio, and then Tybalt fled;
  But by and by comes back to Romeo,
  Who had but newly entertained° revenge,
  And to't they go like lightning; for, ere I
175 Could draw to part them, was stout Tybalt slain;
  And, as he fell, did Romeo turn and fly.
  This is the truth, or let Benvolio die.

156 **nice** trivial 156 **urged** mentioned 159 **spleen** ill nature
160 **tilts** thrusts 170 **envious** full of enmity 173 **entertained** contemplated

Lady Capulet. He is a kinsman to the Montague;
    Affection makes him false, he speaks not true.
    Some twenty of them fought in this black strife,   *180*
    And all those twenty could but kill one life.
    I beg for justice, which thou, Prince, must give.
    Romeo slew Tybalt; Romeo must not live.

Prince. Romeo slew him; he slew Mercutio.
    Who now the price of his dear blood doth owe?   *185*

Capulet. Not Romeo, Prince; he was Mercutio's friend;
    His fault concludes but what the law should end,
    The life of Tybalt.

Prince.   And for that offense
    Immediately we do exile him hence.
    I have an interest in your hate's proceeding,   *190*
    My blood° for your rude brawls doth lie a-bleeding;
    But I'll amerce° you with so strong a fine
    That you shall all repent the loss of mine.
    I will be deaf to pleading and excuses;
    Nor tears nor prayers shall purchase out abuses.   *195*
    Therefore use none. Let Romeo hence in haste,
    Else, when he is found, that hour is his last.
    Bear hence this body and attend our will.°
    Mercy but murders, pardoning those that kill.
                          Exit [*with others*].

[Scene II. *Capulet's orchard.*]

Enter Juliet alone.

Juliet. Gallop apace, you fiery-footed steeds,°
    Towards Phoebus' lodging!° Such a wagoner

---

191 My blood (Mercutio was the Prince's relative)   **192 amerce**
punish by fine   **198 attend our will** respect my decision   **III.ii.1**
fiery-footed steeds horses of the sun god, Phoebus   **2 Towards**
Phoebus' lodging i.e., beneath the horizon

As Phaëton° would whip you to the west
And bring in cloudy night immediately.
5 Spread thy close curtain, love-performing night,
That runaways'° eyes may wink,° and Romeo
Leap to these arms untalked of and unseen.
Lovers can see to do their amorous rites,
And by their own beauties; or, if love be blind,
10 It best agrees with night. Come, civil night,
Thou sober-suited matron all in black,
And learn me how to lose a winning match,
Played for a pair of stainless maidenhoods.
Hood° my unmanned° blood, bating° in my cheeks,
15 With thy black mantle till strange° love grow bold,
Think true love acted simple modesty.
Come, night; come, Romeo; come, thou day in
night;
For thou wilt lie upon the wings of night
Whiter than new snow upon a raven's back.
Come, gentle night; come, loving, black-browed
20 night;
Give me my Romeo; and, when I shall die,
Take him and cut him out in little stars,
And he will make the face of heaven so fine
That all the world will be in love with night
25 And pay no worship to the garish sun.
O, I have bought the mansion of a love,
But not possessed it; and though I am sold,
Not yet enjoyed. So tedious is this day
As is the night before some festival
30 To an impatient child that hath new robes
And may not wear them. O, here comes my nurse,

Enter Nurse, with cords.

And she brings news; and every tongue that speaks
But Romeo's name speaks heavenly eloquence.

---

3 Phaëton Phoebus' son, who mismanaged the horses and let them
run away   **6 runaways'** of the horses (?)   **6 wink** shut   **14 Hood**
i.e., cover with a hood, as in falconry   **14 unmanned** (1) untamed
(2) unmated   **14 bating** fluttering   **15 strange** unfamiliar

Now, nurse, what news? What hast thou there, the
    cords
That Romeo bid thee fetch?

Nurse.   Ay, ay, the cords.   35

Juliet. Ay me! What news? Why dost thou wring thy
    hands?

Nurse. Ah, weraday!° He's dead, he's dead, he's dead!
    We are undone, lady, we are undone!
    Alack the day! He's gone, he's killed, he's dead!

Juliet. Can heaven be so envious?

Nurse.   Romeo can,   40
    Though heaven cannot. O Romeo, Romeo!
    Who ever would have thought it? Romeo!

Juliet. What devil art thou that dost torment me thus?
    This torture should be roared in dismal hell.
    Hath Romeo slain himself? Say thou but "Ay,"   45
    And that bare vowel "I" shall poison more
    Than the death-darting eye of cockatrice.°
    I am not I, if there be such an "Ay,"°
    Or those eyes' shot° that makes thee answer "Ay."
    If he be slain, say "Ay"; or if not, "No."   50
    Brief sounds determine of my weal or woe.

Nurse. I saw the wound, I saw it with mine eyes,
    (God save the mark!°) here on his manly breast.
    A piteous corse,° a bloody piteous corse;
    Pale, pale as ashes, all bedaubed in blood,   55
    All in gore-blood. I sounded° at the sight.

Juliet. O, break, my heart! Poor bankrout,° break at
    once!
    To prison, eyes; ne'er look on liberty!

---

37 **weraday** wellaway, alas   47 **cockatrice** basilisk (a serpent fabled
to have a killing glance)   48 **Ay** (1) I (2) eye   49 **eyes' shot** i.e.,
the Nurse's glance   53 **God save the mark** God avert the bad
omen   54 **corse** corpse   56 **sounded** swooned   57 **bankrout** bank-
rupt

Vile earth,° to earth resign;° end motion here,
60 And thou and Romeo press one heavy bier!

Nurse. O Tybalt, Tybalt, the best friend I had!
O courteous Tybalt! Honest gentleman!
That ever I should live to see thee dead!

Juliet. What storm is this that blows so contrary?
65 Is Romeo slaught'red, and is Tybalt dead?
My dearest cousin, and my dearer lord?
Then, dreadful trumpet, sound the general doom!°
For who is living, if those two are gone?

Nurse. Tybalt is gone, and Romeo banishèd;
70 Romeo that killed him, he is banishèd.

Juliet. O God! Did Romeo's hand shed Tybalt's blood?

Nurse. It did, it did! Alas the day, it did!

Juliet. O serpent heart, hid with a flow'ring face!
Did ever dragon keep so fair a cave?
75 Beautiful tyrant! Fiend angelical!
Dove-feathered raven! Wolvish-ravening lamb!
Despisèd substance of divinest show!
Just opposite to what thou justly seem'st—
A damnèd saint, an honorable villain!
80 O nature, what hadst thou to do in hell
When thou didst bower the spirit of a fiend
In mortal paradise of such sweet flesh?
Was ever book containing such vile matter
So fairly bound? O, that deceit should dwell
In such a gorgeous palace!

85 *Nurse.*   There's no trust,
No faith, no honesty in men; all perjured,
All forsworn, all naught, all dissemblers.
Ah, where's my man? Give me some *aqua vitae.*°
These griefs, these woes, these sorrows make me old.

---

59 **vile earth** referring to her own body   59 **resign** return   67 **dreadful . . . doom** i.e., sound the trumpet of Doomsday   88 **aqua vitae** spirits

Shame come to Romeo!

Juliet   Blistered be thy tongue   **90**
For such a wish! He was not born to shame.
Upon his brow shame is ashamed to sit;
For 'tis a throne where honor may be crowned
Sole monarch of the universal earth.
O, what a beast was I to chide at him!   **95**

Nurse. Will you speak well of him that killed your
    cousin?

Juliet. Shall I speak ill of him that is my husband?
    Ah, poor my lord, what tongue shall smooth thy
      name
    When I, thy three-hours wife, have mangled it?
    But wherefore, villain, didst thou kill my cousin?   **100**
    That villain cousin would have killed my husband.
    Back, foolish tears, back to your native spring!
    Your tributary° drops belong to woe,
    Which you, mistaking, offer up to joy.
    My husband lives, that Tybalt would have slain;   **105**
    And Tybalt's dead, that would have slain my hus-
      band.
    All this is comfort; wherefore weep I then?
    Some word there was, worser than Tybalt's death,
    That murd'red me. I would forget it fain;
    But O, it presses to my memory   **110**
    Like damnèd guilty deeds to sinners' minds!
    "Tybalt is dead, and Romeo—banishèd."
    That "banishèd," that one word "banishèd,"
    Hath slain ten thousand Tybalts. Tybalt's death
    Was woe enough, if it had ended there;   **115**
    Or, if sour woe delights in fellowship
    And needly will be ranked with° other griefs,
    Why followed not, when she said "Tybalt's dead,"

---

103 **tributary** contributed   117 **needly . . . with** must be accompanied by

Thy father, or thy mother, nay, or both,
120 Which modern° lamentation might have moved?
But with a rearward° following Tybalt's death,
"Romeo is banishèd"—to speak that word
Is father, mother, Tybalt, Romeo, Juliet,
All slain, all dead. "Romeo is banishèd"—
125 There is no end, no limit, measure, bound,
In that word's death; no words can that woe sound.
Where is my father and my mother, nurse?

Nurse. Weeping and wailing over Tybalt's corse.
Will you go to them? I will bring you thither.

Juliet. Wash they his wounds with tears? Mine shall be
130 ——spent,
When theirs are dry, for Romeo's banishment.
Take up those cords. Poor ropes, you are beguiled,
Both you and I, for Romeo is exiled.
He made you for a highway to my bed;
135 But I, a maid, die maiden-widowèd.
Come, cords; come, nurse. I'll to my wedding bed;
And death, not Romeo, take my maidenhead!

Nurse. Hie to your chamber. I'll find Romeo
To comfort you. I wot° well where he is.
140 Hark ye, your Romeo will be here at night.
I'll to him; he is hid at Lawrence' cell.

Juliet. O, find him! Give this ring to my true knight
And bid him come to take his last farewell.
                              Exit [with Nurse].

[Scene III. *Friar Lawrence's cell.*]

Enter Friar [Lawrence].

Friar. Romeo, come forth; come forth, thou fearful°
    man.
Affliction is enamored of thy parts,°
And thou art wedded to calamity.

120 **modern** ordinary   121 **rearward** rear guard   139 **wot** know
III.iii.1 **fearful** frightened   2 **Affliction . . . parts** affliction is in
love with your attractive qualities

[*Enter Romeo.*]

Romeo. Father, what news? What is the Prince's doom?°
     What sorrow craves acquaintance at my hand
     That I yet know not?   *5*

Friar.   Too familiar
     Is my dear son with such sour company.
     I bring thee tidings of the Prince's doom.

Romeo. What less than doomsday° is the Prince's
     doom?

Friar. A gentler judgment vanished° from his lips—   *10*
     Not body's death, but body's banishment.

Romeo. Ha, banishment? Be merciful, say "death";
     For exile hath more terror in his look,
     Much more than death. Do not say "banishment."

Friar. Here from Verona art thou banishèd.   *15*
     Be patient, for the world is broad and wide.

Romeo. There is no world without Verona walls,
     But purgatory, torture, hell itself.
     Hence banishèd is banished from the world,
     And world's exile is death. Then "banishèd"
     Is death mistermed. Calling death "banishèd,"   *20*
     Thou cut'st my head off with a golden ax
     And smilest upon the stroke that murders me.

Friar. O deadly sin! O rude unthankfulness!
     Thy fault our law calls death; but the kind Prince,   *25*
     Taking thy part, hath rushed° aside the law,
     And turned that black word "death" to "banish-
       ment."
     This is dear mercy, and thou seest it not.

<u>*Romeo.*</u> 'Tis torture, and not mercy. Heaven is here,
     Where Juliet lives; and every cat and dog   *30*
     And little mouse, every unworthy thing,
     Live here in heaven and may look on her;
     But Romeo may not. More validity,°

4 **doom** final decision 9 **doomsday** i.e., my death 10 **vanished**
escaped 26 **rushed** pushed 33 **validity** value

More honorable state, more courtship° lives
33   In carrion flies than Romeo. They may seize
On the white wonder of dear Juliet's hand
And steal immortal blessing from her lips,
Who, even in pure and vestal° modesty,
Still blush, as thinking their own kisses sin;°
40   But Romeo may not, he is banishèd.
Flies may do this but I from this must fly;
They are freemen, but I am banishèd.
And sayest thou yet that exile is not death?
Hadst thou no poison mixed, no sharp-ground
      knife,
45   No sudden mean of death, though ne'er so mean,°
But "banishèd" to kill me—"banishèd"?
O friar, the damnèd use that word in hell;
Howling attends it! How hast thou the heart,
Being a divine, a ghostly confessor,
50   A sin-absolver, and my friend professed,
To mangle me with that word "banishèd"?

Friar. Thou fond° mad man, hear me a little speak.

Romeo. O, thou wilt speak again of banishment.

Friar. I'll give thee armor to keep off that word;
55   Adversity's sweet milk, philosophy,
To comfort thee, though thou art banishèd.

Romeo. Yet° "banishèd"? Hang up philosophy!
Unless philosophy can make a Juliet,
Displant a town, reverse a prince's doom,
60   It helps not, it prevails not. Talk no more.

Friar. O, then I see that madmen have no ears.

Romeo. How should they, when that wise men have
      no eyes?

Friar. Let me dispute° with thee of thy estate.°

___

34 courtship opportunity for courting   **38 vestal** virgin   **39 their
own kisses sin** i.e., sin when they touch each other   **45 mean . . .
mean** method . . . lowly   **52 fond** foolish   **57 Yet** still   **63 dispute**
discuss   **63 estate** situation

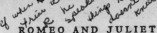

Romeo. Thou canst not speak of that thou dost not
    feel.
    Wert thou as young as I, Juliet thy love,   *65*
    An hour but married, Tybalt murderèd,
    Doting like me, and like me banishèd,
    Then mightst thou speak, then mightst thou tear thy
        hair,
    And fall upon the ground, as I do now,
    Taking the measure° of an unmade grave.   *70*
                        Enter Nurse and knock.

Friar. Arise, one knocks. Good Romeo, hide thyself.

Romeo. Not I; unless the breath of heartsick groans
    Mistlike infold me from the search of eyes. [*Knock.*]

Friar. Hark, how they knock! Who's there? Romeo,
    arise;
    Thou wilt be taken.—Stay awhile!—Stand up;   *75*
                                        [*Knock.*]
    Run to my study.—By and by!°—God's will,
    What simpleness° is this.—I come, I come! *Knock.*
    Who knocks so hard? Whence come you? What's
        your will?

                        Enter Nurse.

Nurse. Let me come in, and you shall know my er-
    rand.
    I come from Lady Juliet.

Friar.   Welcome then.   *80*

Nurse. O holy friar, O, tell me, holy friar,
    Where is my lady's lord, where's Romeo?

Friar. There on the ground, with his own tears made
    drunk.

Nurse. O, he is even in my mistress' case,°

70 **Taking the measure** i.e., measuring by my outstretched body
76 **By and by** in a moment (said to the person knocking)   77 **sim-
pleness** silly behavior (Romeo refuses to rise)   84 **case** (with bawdy
innuendo complementing "stand," "rise," etc. But the Nurse is
unaware of this possible interpretation)

83 Just in her case! O woeful sympathy!
    Piteous predicament! Even so lies she,
    Blubb'ring and weeping, weeping and blubb'ring.
    Stand up, stand up! Stand, and you be a man.
    For Juliet's sake, for her sake, rise and stand!
90 Why should you fall into so deep an O?°

Romeo. [*Rises.*] Nurse—

Nurse. Ah sir, ah sir! Death's the end of all.

Romeo. Spakest thou of Juliet? How is it with her?
    Doth not she think me an old murderer,
95 Now I have stained the childhood of our joy
    With blood removed but little from her own?
    Where is she? And how doth she! And what says
    My concealed lady to our canceled° love?

Nurse. O, she says nothing, sir, but weeps and weeps;
100 And now falls on her bed, and then starts up,
    And Tybalt calls; and then on Romeo cries,
    And then down falls again.

Romeo.   As if that name,
    Shot from the deadly level° of a gun,
    Did murder her; as that name's cursèd hand
105 Murdered her kinsman. O, tell me, friar, tell me,
    In what vile part of this anatomy
    Doth my name lodge? Tell me, that I may sack°
    The hateful mansion.
                    [*He offers to stab himself, and Nurse
                        snatches the dagger away.*]

Friar.   Hold thy desperate hand.
    Art thou a man? Thy form cries out thou art;
110 Thy tears are womanish, thy wild acts denote
    The unreasonable° fury of a beast.
    Unseemly° woman in a seeming man!
    And ill-beseeming beast in seeming both!°

---

90 **so deep an O** such a fit of moaning   98 **canceled** invalidated
103 **level** aim   107 **sack** plunder   111 **unreasonable** irrational
112 **Unseemly** indecorous   113 **ill-beseeming . . . both** i.e., inappropriate even to a beast in being both man and woman

Thou hast amazed me. By my holy order,
I thought thy disposition better tempered.   *113*
Hast thou slain Tybalt? Wilt thou slay thyself?
And slay thy lady that in thy life lives,
By doing damnèd hate upon thyself?
Why railest thou on thy birth, the heaven, and
    earth?
Since birth and heaven and earth,° all three do meet   *120*
In thee at once; which thou at once wouldst lose.°
Fie, fie, thou shamest thy shape, thy love, thy wit,°
Which,° like a usurer, abound'st in all,
And usest none in that true use indeed
Which should bedeck° thy shape, thy love, thy wit.   *125*
Thy noble shape is but a form of wax,
Digressing from the valor of a man;°
Thy dear love sworn but hollow perjury,
Killing that love which thou hast vowed to cherish;
Thy wit, that ornament to shape and love,   *130*
Misshapen in the conduct° of them both,
Like powder in a skilless soldier's flask,°
Is set afire by thine own ignorance,
And thou dismemb'red with thine own defense.°
What, rouse thee, man! Thy Juliet is alive,   *135*
For whose dear sake thou wast but lately dead.°
There art thou happy.° Tybalt would kill thee,
But thou slewest Tybalt. There art thou happy.
The law, that threat'ned death, becomes thy friend
And turns it to exile. There art thou happy.   *140*
A pack of blessings light upon thy back;
Happiness courts thee in her best array;
But, like a misbehaved and sullen wench,
Thou puts up thy fortune and thy love.
Take heed, take heed, for such die miserable.   *145*

---

120 **birth and heaven and earth** family origin, soul, and body
121 **lose** abandon   122 **wit** intellect   123 **Which** who   125 **bedeck**
do honor to   127 **valor of a man** i.e., his manly qualities   131 **conduct** management   132 **flask** powder flask   134 **dismemb'red . . .
defense** (i.e., your intellect, properly the defender of shape and
love, is set off independently and destroys all)   136 **dead** i.e., de-
claring yourself dead   137 **happy** fortunate

Go get thee to thy love, as was decreed,
Ascend her chamber, hence and comfort her.
But look thou stay not till the watch be set,
For then thou canst not pass to Mantua,
150 Where thou shalt live till we can find a time
To blaze° your marriage, reconcile your friends,
Beg pardon of the Prince, and call thee back
With twenty hundred thousand times more joy
Than thou went'st forth in lamentation.
155 Go before, nurse. Commend me to thy lady,
And bid her hasten all the house to bed,
Which heavy sorrow makes them apt unto.
Romeo is coming.

Nurse. O Lord, I could have stayed here all the night
160 To hear good counsel. O, what learning is!
My lord, I'll tell my lady you will come.

Romeo. Do so, and bid my sweet prepare to chide.
　　　　　　[Nurse offers to go in and turns again.]

Nurse. Here, sir, a ring she bid me give you, sir.
Hie you, make haste, for it grows very late. *[Exit.]*

165 *Romeo.* How well my comfort is revived by this!

Friar. Go hence; good night; and here stands all your
　　state:°
Either be gone before the watch be set,
Or by the break of day disguised from hence.
Sojourn in Mantua. I'll find out your man,
170 And he shall signify from time to time
Every good hap to you that chances here.
Give me thy hand. 'Tis late. Farewell; good night.

Romeo. But that a joy past joy calls out on me,
It were a grief so brief to part with thee.
173 Farewell.　　　　　　　　　　　　　　*Exeunt.*

151 **blaze** announce publicly　166 **here . . . state** this is your situation

[Scene IV. *A room in Capulet's house.*]

Enter old Capulet, his Wife, and Paris.

Capulet. Things have fall'n out, sir, so unluckily
  That we have had no time to move° our daughter.
  Look you, she loved her kinsman Tybalt dearly,
  And so did I. Well, <u>we were born to die.</u>
  'Tis very late; she'll not come down tonight.   *5*
  I promise° you, but for your company,
  I would have been abed an hour ago.

Paris. These times of woe afford no times to woo.
  Madam, good night. Commend me to your daughter.

Lady. I will, and know her mind early tomorrow;   *10*
  Tonight she's mewed up to her heaviness.°

Capulet. Sir Paris, I will make a desperate tender°
  Of my child's love. I think she will be ruled
  In all respects by me; nay more, I doubt it not.
  Wife, go you to her ere you go to bed;   *15*
  Acquaint her here of my son Paris' love
  And bid her (mark you me?) on Wednesday next—
  But soft! What day is this?

Paris.   Monday, my lord.

Capulet. Monday! Ha, ha! Well, Wednesday is too
    soon.
  A° Thursday let it be—a Thursday, tell her,   *20*
  She shall be married to this noble earl.
  Will you be ready? Do you like this haste?
  We'll keep no great ado—a friend or two;
  For hark you, Tybalt being slain so late,

III.iv.2 **move** discuss the matter with   6 **promise** assure   11 **mewed**
. . . heaviness shut up with her grief   12 **make . . . tender** risk an
offer   20 **A** on

25   It may be thought we held him carelessly,
      Being our kinsman, if we revel much.
      Therefore we'll have some half a dozen friends,
      And there an end. But what say you to Thursday?

Paris. My lord, I would that Thursday were tomorrow.

30   *Capulet.* Well, get you gone. A Thursday be it then.
      Go you to Juliet ere you go to bed;
      Prepare her, wife, against° this wedding day.
      Farewell, my lord.—Light to my chamber, ho!
      Afore me,° it is so very late
35   That we may call it early by and by.°
      Good night.   *Exeunt.*

[Scene V. *Capulet's orchard.*]

Enter Romeo and Juliet aloft.

Juliet. Wilt thou be gone? It is not yet near day.
      It was the nightingale, and not the lark,
      That pierced the fearful° hollow of thine ear.
      Nightly she sings on yond pomegranate tree.
3   Believe me, love, it was the nightingale.

Romeo. It was the lark, the herald of the morn;
      No nightingale. Look, love, what envious streaks
      Do lace the severing clouds in yonder East.
      Night's candles are burnt out, and jocund day
10   Stands tiptoe on the misty mountaintops.
      I must be gone and live, or stay and die.

Juliet. Yond light is not daylight; I know it, I.
      It is some meteor that the sun exhales°
      To be to thee this night a torchbearer
13   And light thee on thy way to Mantua.

32 **against** in preparation for   34 **Afore me** indeed (a light oath)
35 **by and by** soon   III.v.3 **fearful** fearing   13 **exhales** gives out

Therefore stay yet; thou need'st not to be gone.

Romeo. Let me be ta'en, let me be put to death.
   I am content, so thou wilt have it so.
   I'll say yon gray is not the morning's eye,
   'Tis but the pale reflex of Cynthia's brow;°   20
   Nor that is not the lark whose notes do beat
   The vaulty heaven so high above our heads.
   I have more care to stay than will to go.
   Come, death, and welcome! Juliet wills it so.
   How is't, my soul? Let's talk; it is not day.   25

Juliet. It is, it is! Hie hence, be gone, away!
   It is the lark that sings so out of tune,
   Straining harsh discords and unpleasing sharps.
   Some say the lark makes sweet division;°
   This doth not so, for she divideth us.   30
   Some say the lark and loathèd toad change eyes;
   O, now I would they had changed voices too,
   Since arm from arm that voice doth us affray,°
   Hunting thee hence with hunt's-up° to the day.
   O, now be gone! More light and light it grows.   35

Romeo. More light and light—more dark and dark
   our woes.

PARADOX
Conventional.

                    Enter Nurse.

Nurse. Madam!

Juliet. Nurse?

Nurse. Your lady mother is coming to your chamber.
   The day is broke; be wary, look about.   [*Exit.*]   40

Juliet. Then, window, let day in, and let life out.

Romeo. Farewell, farewell! One kiss, and I'll descend.
                    [*He goeth down.*]

Juliet. Art thou gone so, love-lord, ay husband-friend?°

---

20 **reflex of Cynthia's brow** reflection of the edge of the moon
29 **division** melody (i.e., a division of notes) 33 **affray** frighten
34 **hunt's-up** morning song (for hunters) 43 **husband-friend** husband-lover

I must hear from thee every day in the hour,
45   For in a minute there are many days.
O, by this count I shall be much in years°
Ere I again behold my Romeo!

Romeo. Farewell!
I will omit no opportunity
50   That may convey my greetings, love, to thee.

Juliet. O, think'st thou we shall ever meet again?

Romeo. I doubt it not; and all these woes shall serve
For sweet discourses in our times to come.

Juliet. O God, I have an ill-divining° soul!
55   Methinks I see thee, now thou art so low,
As one dead in the bottom of a tomb.
Either my eyesight fails, or thou lookest pale.

Romeo. And trust me, love, in my eye so do you.
Dry° sorrow drinks our blood. Adieu, adieu! *Exit.*

60   *Juliet.* O Fortune, Fortune! All men call thee fickle.
If thou art fickle, what dost thou° with him
That is renowned for faith? Be fickle, Fortune,
For then I hope thou wilt not keep him long
But send him back.

Enter Mother.

65   *Lady Capulet.* Ho, daughter! Are you up?

Juliet. Who is't that calls? It is my lady mother.
Is she not down so late,° or up so early?
What unaccustomed cause procures her hither?

Lady Capulet. Why, how now, Juliet?

Juliet.   Madam, I am not well.

Lady Capulet. Evermore weeping for your cousin's
70   death?

---

46 **much in years** much older   54 **ill-divining** foreseeing evil
59 **Dry** thirsty (as grief was thought to be)   61 **what dost thou**
what business have you   67 **not down so late** so late getting to bed

What, wilt thou wash him from his grave with tears?
And if thou couldst, thou couldst not make him live.
Therefore have done. Some grief shows much of
    love;
But much of grief shows still some want of wit.

Juliet. Yet let me weep for such a feeling loss.°   *75*

Lady Capulet. So shall you feel the loss, but not the
    friend
Which you weep for.

Juliet.   Feeling so the loss,
I cannot choose but ever weep the friend.

Lady Capulet. Well, girl, thou weep'st not so much for
    his death
As that the villain lives which slaughtered him.   *80*

Juliet. What villain, madam?

Lady Capulet.   That same villain Romeo.

Juliet. [*Aside*] Villain and he be many miles asunder.—
God pardon him! I do, with all my heart;
And yet no man like he doth grieve my heart.

Lady Capulet. That is because the traitor murderer
    lives.   *85*

Juliet. Ay, madam, from the reach of these my hands.
Would none but I might venge my cousin's death!

Lady Capulet. We will have vengeance for it, fear
    thou not.
Then weep no more. I'll send to one in Mantua,
Where that same banished runagate° doth live,
     90
Shall give him such an unaccustomed dram
That he shall soon keep Tybalt company;
And then I hope thou wilt be satisfied.

Juliet. Indeed I never shall be satisfied
With Romeo till I behold him—dead°—   *95*

75 **feeling loss** loss to be felt   90 **runagate** renegade   95 **dead**
(Lady Capulet takes this to refer to "him"; Juliet takes it to refer
to "heart")

Is my poor heart so for a kinsman vexed.
Madam, if you could find out but a man
To bear a poison, I would temper° it;
That Romeo should, upon receipt thereof,
100   Soon sleep in quiet. O, how my heart abhors
To hear him named and cannot come to him,
To wreak° the love I bore my cousin
Upon his body that hath slaughtered him!

Lady Capulet. Find thou the means, and I'll find such
a man.
105   But now I'll tell thee joyful tidings, girl.

Juliet. And joy comes well in such a needy time.
What are they, beseech your ladyship?

Lady Capulet. Well, well, thou hast a careful° father,
child;
One who, to put thee from thy heaviness,
110   Hath sorted out° a sudden day of joy
That thou expects not nor I looked not for.

Juliet. Madam, in happy time!° What day is that?

Lady Capulet. Marry, my child, early next Thursday
morn
The gallant, young, and noble gentleman,
115   The County Paris, at Saint Peter's Church,
Shall happily make thee there a joyful bride.

Juliet. Now by Saint Peter's Church, and Peter too,
He shall not make me there a joyful bride!
I wonder at this haste, that I must wed
120   Ere he that should be husband comes to woo.
I pray you tell my lord and father, madam,
I will not marry yet; and when I do, I swear
It shall be Romeo, whom you know I hate,
Rather than Paris. These are news indeed!

---

98 **temper** (1) mix (2) weaken   102 **wreak** (1) avenge (2) give
expression to   108 **careful** solicitous   110 **sorted out** selected
112 **in happy time** most opportunely

Lady Capulet. Here comes your father. Tell him so
    yourself,   *125*
And see how he will take it at your hands.

Enter Capulet and Nurse.

Capulet. When the sun sets the earth doth drizzle dew,
  But for the sunset of my brother's son
  It rains downright.
  How now? A conduit,° girl? What, still in tears?   *130*
  Evermore show'ring? In one little body
  Thou counterfeits a bark, a sea, a wind:
  For still thy eyes, which I may call the sea,
  Do ebb and flow with tears; the bark thy body is,
  Sailing in this salt flood; the winds, thy sighs,   *135*
  Who, raging with thy tears and they with them,
  Without a sudden° calm will overset
  Thy tempest-tossèd body. How now, wife?
  Have you delivered to her our decree?

Lady Capulet. Ay, sir; but she will none, she gives
  you thanks.°   *140*
I would the fool were married to her grave!

Capulet. Soft! Take me with you,° take me with you,
  wife.
How? Will she none? Doth she not give us thanks?
Is she not proud? Doth she not count her blest,
Unworthy as she is, that we have wrought°   *145*
So worthy a gentleman to be her bride?

Juliet. Not proud° you have, but thankful that you
  have.
Proud can I never be of what I hate,
But thankful even for hate that is meant love.

Capulet. How, how, how, how, chopped-logic?° What
  is this?   *150*

---

130 **conduit** water pipe   137 **sudden** unanticipated, immediate
140 **she gives you thanks** she'll have none of it, thank you   142 **Soft
. . . you** Wait! Help me to understand you   145 **wrought** arranged
147 **proud** highly pleased   150 **chopped-logic** chop logic, sophistry

"Proud"—and "I thank you"—and "I thank you
  not"—
And yet "not proud"? Mistress minion° you,
Thank me no thankings, nor proud me no prouds,
But fettle° your fine joints 'gainst Thursday next
155 To go with Paris to Saint Peter's Church,
Or I will drag thee on a hurdle° thither.
Out, you greensickness° carrion! Out, you baggage!°
You tallow-face!

Lady Capulet.   Fie, fie! What, are you mad?

Juliet. Good father, I beseech you on my knees,
160 Hear me with patience but to speak a word.

Capulet. Hang thee, young baggage! Disobedient
  wretch!
I tell thee what—get thee to church a Thursday
Or never after look me in the face.
Speak not, reply not, do not answer me!
165 My fingers itch. Wife, we scarce thought us blest
That God had lent us but this only child;
But now I see this one is one too much,
And that we have a curse in having her.
Out on her, hilding!°

Nurse.   God in heaven bless her!
170 You are to blame, my lord, to rate° her so.

Capulet. And why, my Lady Wisdom? Hold your
  tongue,
Good Prudence. Smatter with your gossips,° go!

Nurse. I speak no treason.

Capulet.   O, God-i-god-en!°

Nurse. May not one speak?

---

152 **minion** minx   154 **fettle** make ready   156 **hurdle** sledge on
which traitors were taken to execution   157 **greensickness** anemic,
after the fashion of young girls   157 **baggage** strumpet   169 **hilding** worthless person   170 **rate** scold   172 **Smatter with your gossips** save your chatter for your cronies   173 **God-i-god-en** God
give you good even (here equivalent to "Get on with you!")

Capulet.   Peace, you mumbling fool!
   Utter your gravity o'er a gossip's bowl,   *175*
   For here we need it not.

Lady Capulet.   You are too hot.

Capulet. God's bread!° It makes me mad.
   Day, night; hour, tide, time; work, play;
   Alone, in company; still my care hath been
   To have her matched; and having now provided   *180*
   A gentleman of noble parentage,
   Of fair demesnes,° youthful, and nobly trained,
   Stuffed, as they say, with honorable parts,
   Proportioned as one's thought would wish a man—
   And then to have a wretched puling° fool,   *185*
   A whining mammet,° in her fortune's tender,°
   To answer "I'll not wed, I cannot love;
   I am too young, I pray you pardon me"!
   But, and you will not wed, I'll pardon you!°
   Graze where you will, you shall not house with me. *190*
   Look to't, think on't; I do not use to jest.°
   Thursday is near; lay hand on heart, advise:°
   And you be mine, I'll give you to my friend;
   And you be not, hang, beg, starve, die in the streets,
   For, by my soul, I'll ne'er acknowledge thee,   *195*
   Nor what is mine shall never do thee good.
   Trust to't. Bethink you. I'll not be forsworn.   *Exit.*

Juliet. Is there no pity sitting in the clouds
   That sees into the bottom of my grief?
   O sweet my mother, cast me not away!   *200*
   Delay this marriage for a month, a week;
   Or if you do not, make the bridal bed
   In that dim monument where Tybalt lies.

Lady Capulet. Talk not to me, for I'll not speak a
      word.

---

177 **God's bread** by the sacred host   182 **demesnes** domains
185 **puling** whining   186 **mammet** puppet   186 **in her fortune's tender** (1) on good fortune's offer (2) subject to fortuitous circumstance (?)   189 **I'll pardon you** i.e., in a way you don't expect
191 **do not use to jest** am not in the habit of joking   192 **advise** consider

205   Do as thou wilt, for I have done with thee.   *Exit.*

Juliet. O God!—O nurse, how shall this be prevented?
      My husband is on earth, my faith in heaven.°
      How shall that faith return again to earth
      Unless that husband send it me from heaven
210   By leaving earth?° Comfort me, counsel me.
      Alack, alack, that heaven should practice stratagems
      Upon so soft a subject as myself!
      What say'st thou? Hast thou not a word of joy?
      Some comfort, nurse.

Nurse.   Faith, here it is.
215   Romeo is banished; and all the world to nothing°
      That he dares ne'er come back to challenge you;
      Or if he do, it needs must be by stealth.
      Then, since the case so stands as now it doth,
      I think it best you married with the County.
220   O, he's a lovely gentleman!
      Romeo's a dishclout° to him. An eagle, madam,
      Hath not so green, so quick, so fair an eye
      As Paris hath. Beshrew° my very heart,
      I think you are happy in this second match,
225   For it excels your first; or if it did not,
      Your first is dead—or 'twere as good he were
      As living here and you no use of him.

Juliet. Speak'st thou from thy heart?

Nurse. And from my soul too; else beshrew them both.

230   *Juliet.* Amen!

Nurse. What?

Juliet. Well, thou hast comforted me marvelous much.
      Go in; and tell my lady I am gone,
      Having displeased my father, to Lawrence' cell,
235   To make confession and to be absolved.

---

207 **my faith in heaven** my vow is recorded in heaven   210 **By leaving earth** i.e., by dying   215 **all the world to nothing** (the Nurse advises a safe bet)   221 **dishclout** dishcloth   223 **Beshrew** curse (used in light oaths)

Nurse. Marry, I will; and this is wisely done.   [*Exit.*]

Juliet. Ancient damnation!° O most wicked fiend!
Is it more sin to wish me thus forsworn,°
Or to dispraise my lord with that same tongue
Which she hath praised him with above compare   260
So many thousand times? Go, counselor!
Thou and my bosom henceforth shall be twain.°
I'll to the friar to know his remedy.
If all else fail, <u>myself</u> have power to die.   *Exit.*

She is also alienated - Nurse is no longer her friend (Nurse has never had experience) Separate worlds - utterly alone - in charge of her own life. Friar's remedy; pretend to die

---

237 Ancient damnation (1) damned old woman (2) ancient devil
(note the term "wicked fiend" immediately following)   **238 forsworn**
guilty of breaking a vow   **242 Thou . . . twain** i.e., you shall henceforth be separated from my trust

[ACT IV

Scene I. *Friar Lawrence's cell.*]

Enter Friar [Lawrence] and County Paris.

Friar. On Thursday, sir? The time is very short.

Paris. My father Capulet will have it so,
And I am nothing slow to slack his haste.°

Friar. You say you do not know the lady's mind.
5 Uneven° is the course; I like it not.

Paris. Immoderately she weeps for Tybalt's death,
And therefore have I little talked of love;
For Venus smiles not in a house of tears.
Now, sir, her father counts it dangerous
10 That she do give her sorrow so much sway,
And in his wisdom hastes our marriage
To stop the inundation of her tears,
Which, too much minded° by herself alone,°
May be put from her by society.
15 Now do you know the reason of this haste.

Friar. [*Aside*] I would I knew not why it should be
slowed.—
Look, sir, here comes the lady toward my cell.

Enter Juliet.

Paris. Happily met, my lady and my wife!

Juliet. That may be, sir, when I may be a wife.

Paris. That "may be" must be, love, on Thursday next.   20

Juliet. What must be shall be.

Friar.   That's a certain text.

Paris. Come you to make confession to this father?

Juliet. To answer that, I should confess to you.

Paris. Do not deny to him that you love me.

Juliet. I will confess to you that I love him.   25

Paris. So will ye, I am sure, that you love me.

Juliet. If I do so, it will be of more price,
   Being spoke behind your back, than to your face.

Paris. Poor soul, thy face is much abused with tears.

Juliet. The tears have got small victory by that,   30
   For it was bad enough before their spite.°

Paris. Thou wrong'st it more than tears with that
   report.

Juliet. That is no slander, sir, which is a truth;
   And what I spake, I spake it to my face.

Paris. Thy face is mine, and thou hast sland'red it.   35

Juliet. It may be so, for it is not mine own.
   Are you at leisure, holy father, now,
   Or shall I come to you at evening mass?°

Friar. My leisure serves me, pensive daughter, now.
   My lord, we must entreat the time alone.°   40

---

31 **before their spite** before they marred it   38 **evening mass** (evening mass was still said occasionally in Shakespeare's time)   40 **entreat the time alone** ask to have this time to ourselves

Paris. God shield° I should disturb devotion!
    Juliet, on Thursday early will I rouse ye.
    Till then, adieu, and keep this holy kiss.   *Exit.*

Juliet. O, shut the door, and when thou hast done so,
    Come weep with me—past hope, past care, past
45   help!

Friar. O Juliet, I already know thy grief;
    It strains me past the compass of my wits.
    I hear thou must, and nothing may prorogue° it,
    On Thursday next be married to this County.

50 *Juliet.* Tell me not, friar, that thou hearest of this,
    Unless thou tell me how I may prevent it.
    If in thy wisdom thou canst give no help,
    Do thou but call my resolution wise
    And with this knife I'll help it presently.°
55   God joined my heart and Romeo's, thou our hands;
    And ere this hand, by thee to Romeo's sealed,
    Shall be the label° to another deed,°
    Or my true heart with treacherous revolt
    Turn to another, this shall slay them both.
60   Therefore, out of thy long-experienced time,
    Give me some present counsel; or, behold,
    'Twixt my extremes and me this bloody knife
    Shall play the umpire, arbitrating that
    Which the commission° of thy years and art
65   Could to no issue of true honor bring.
    Be not so long to speak. I long to die
    If what thou speak'st speak not of remedy.

Friar. Hold, daughter. I do spy a kind of hope,
    Which craves as desperate an execution
70   As that is desperate which we would prevent.
    If, rather than to marry County Paris,
    Thou hast the strength of will to slay thyself,
    Then is it likely thou wilt undertake

---

41 God shield God forbid   **48 prorogue** delay   **54 presently** at
once   **57 label** bearer of the seal   **57 deed** (1) act (2) legal document   **64 commission** authority

A thing like death to chide away this shame,
That cop'st° with death himself to scape from it;   75
And, if thou darest, I'll give thee remedy.

Juliet. O, bid me leap, rather than marry Paris,
From off the battlements of any tower,
Or walk in thievish° ways, or bid me lurk
Where serpents are; chain me with roaring bears,   80
Or hide me nightly in a charnel house,°
O'ercovered quite with dead men's rattling bones,
With reeky° shanks and yellow chapless° skulls;
Or bid me go into a new-made grave
And hide me with a dead man in his shroud—   85
Things that, to hear them told, have made me
   tremble—
And I will do it without fear or doubt,
To live an unstained wife to my sweet love.

Friar. Hold, then. Go home, be merry, give consent
To marry Paris. Wednesday is tomorrow.   90
Tomorrow night look that thou lie alone;
Let not the nurse lie with thee in thy chamber.
Take thou this vial, being then in bed,
And this distilling° liquor drink thou off;
When presently through all thy veins shall run   95
A cold and drowsy humor;° for no pulse
Shall keep his native° progress, but surcease;°
No warmth, no breath, shall testify thou livest;
The roses in thy lips and cheeks shall fade
To wanny° ashes, thy eyes' windows° fall   100
Like death when he shuts up the day of life;
Each part, deprived of supple government,°
Shall, stiff and stark and cold, appear like death;
And in this borrowed likeness of shrunk death
Thou shalt continue two-and-forty hours,   105
And then awake as from a pleasant sleep.

---

75 **cop'st** negotiates   79 **thievish** infested with thieves   81 **charnel house** vault for old bones   83 **reeky** damp   83 **chapless** jawless
94 **distilling** infusing   96 **humor** fluid   97 **native** natural   97 **surcease** stop   100 **wanny** pale   100 **windows** lids   102 **supple government** i.e., faculty for maintaining motion

Now, when the bridegroom in the morning comes
To rouse thee from thy bed, there art thou dead.
Then, as the manner of our country is,
110 In thy best robes uncovered on the bier
Thou shalt be borne to that same ancient vault
Where all the kindred of the Capulets lie.
In the meantime, against° thou shalt awake,
Shall Romeo by my letters know our drift;°
115 And hither shall he come; and he and I
Will watch thy waking, and that very night
Shall Romeo bear thee hence to Mantua.
And this shall free thee from this present shame,
If no inconstant toy° nor womanish fear
120 Abate thy valor in the acting it.

Juliet. Give me, give me! O, tell not me of fear!

Friar. Hold! Get you gone, be strong and prosperous
In this resolve. I'll send a friar with speed
To Mantua, with my letters to thy lord.

Juliet. Love give me strength, and strength shall help
125   afford.
Farewell, dear father.   *Exit [with Friar].*

[Scene II. *Hall in Capulet's house.*]

*Enter Father Capulet, Mother, Nurse, and
Servingmen, two or three.*

Capulet. So many guests invite as here are writ.
                [Exit a Servingman.]
Sirrah, go hire me twenty cunning° cooks.

Servingman. You shall have none ill, sir; for I'll try°
if they can lick their fingers.

113 **against** before   114 **drift** purpose   119 **inconstant toy** whim
IV.ii.2 **cunning** skillful   3 **try** test

Capulet. How canst thou try them so?   3

Servingman. Marry, sir, 'tis an ill cook that cannot
  lick his own fingers.° Therefore he that cannot lick
  his fingers goes not with me.

Capulet. Go, begone.   [*Exit Servingman.*]
  We shall be much unfurnished° for this time.   10
  What, is my daughter gone to Friar Lawrence?

Nurse. Ay, forsooth.

Capulet. Well, he may chance to do some good on her.
  A peevish self-willed harlotry it is.°

                   Enter Juliet.

Nurse. See where she comes from shrift with merry
  look.   15

Capulet. How now, my headstrong? Where have you
  been gadding?

Juliet. Where I have learnt me to repent the sin
  Of disobedient opposition
  To you and your behests, and am enjoined
  By holy Lawrence to fall prostrate here   20
  To beg your pardon. Pardon, I beseech you!
  Henceforward I am ever ruled by you.

Capulet. Send for the County. Go tell him of this.
  I'll have this knot knit up tomorrow morning.

Juliet. I met the youthful lord at Lawrence' cell   25
  And gave him what becomèd° love I might,
  Not stepping o'er the bounds of modesty.

Capulet. Why, I am glad on't. This is well. Stand up.
  This is as't should be. Let me see the County.
  Ay, marry, go, I say, and fetch him hither.   30
  Now, afore God, this reverend holy friar,
  All our whole city is much bound to him.

6–7 **cannot lick his own fingers** i.e., cannot taste his own cooking
10 **unfurnished** unprovisioned   14 **A peevish self-willed harlotry it
is** she's a silly good-for-nothing   26 **becomèd** proper

Juliet. Nurse, will you go with me into my closet°
 To help me sort such needful ornaments
35 As you think fit to furnish me tomorrow?

Lady Capulet. No, not till Thursday. There is time
 enough.

Capulet. Go, nurse, go with her. We'll to church
 tomorrow.   *Exeunt* [*Juliet and Nurse*].

Lady Capulet. We shall be short in our provision.
 'Tis now near night.

Capulet.   Tush, I will stir about,
40 And all things shall be well, I warrant thee, wife.
 Go thou to Juliet, help to deck up her.
 I'll not to bed tonight; let me alone.
 I'll play the housewife for this once. What, ho!
 They are all forth; well, I will walk myself
45 To County Paris, to prepare up him
 Against° tomorrow. My heart is wondrous light,
 Since this same wayward girl is so reclaimed.
        Exit [*with Mother*].

[Scene III. *Juliet's chamber.*]

Enter Juliet and Nurse.

Juliet. Ay, those attires are best; but, gentle nurse,
 I pray thee leave me to myself tonight;
 For I have need of many orisons°
 To move the heavens to smile upon my state,°
5 Which, well thou knowest, is cross° and full of sin.

Enter Mother.

Lady Capulet. What, are you busy, ho? Need you my
 help?

33 closet private chamber **46 Against** in anticipation of **IV.iii.3
orisons** prayers **4 state** condition **5 cross** perverse

Juliet. No, madam; we have culled such necessaries
  As are behoveful° for our state° tomorrow.
  So please you, let me now be left alone,
  And let the nurse this night sit up with you;   *10*
  For I am sure you have your hands full all
  In this so sudden business.

Lady Capulet.   Good night.
  Get thee to bed, and rest; for thou hast need.
                 Exeunt [*Mother and Nurse*].

Juliet. Farewell! God knows when we shall meet again.
  I have a faint° cold fear thrills through my veins   *15*
  That almost freezes up the heat of life.
  I'll call them back again to comfort me.
  Nurse!—What should she do here?
  My dismal scene I needs must act alone.
  Come, vial.   *20*
  What if this mixture do not work at all?
  Shall I be married then tomorrow morning?
  No, no! This shall forbid it. Lie thou there.
                [*Lays down a dagger.*]
  What if it be a poison which the friar
  Subtly hath minist'red° to have me dead,   *25*
  Lest in this marriage he should be dishonored
  Because he married me before to Romeo?
  I fear it is; and yet methinks it should not,
  For he hath still° been tried° a holy man.
  How if, when I am laid into the tomb,   *30*
  I wake before the time that Romeo
  Come to redeem me? There's a fearful point!
  Shall I not then be stifled in the vault,
  To whose foul mouth no healthsome air breathes in,
  And there die strangled ere my Romeo comes?   *35*
  Or, if I live, is it not very like
  The horrible conceit° of death and night,
  Together with the terror of the place—
  As in a vault, an ancient receptacle

8 behoveful expedient   **8 state** pomp   **15 faint** causing faintness
25 minist'red provided   **29 still** always   **29 tried** proved   **37 conceit** thought

40   Where for this many hundred years the bones
    Of all my buried ancestors are packed;
    Where bloody Tybalt, yet but green in earth,°
    Lies fest'ring in his shroud; where, as they say,
    At some hours in the night spirits resort—
45   Alack, alack, is it not like that I,
    So early waking—what with loathsome smells,
    And shrieks like mandrakes° torn out of the earth,
    That living mortals, hearing them, run mad—
    O, if I wake, shall I not be distraught,°
50   Environèd with all these hideous fears,
    And madly play with my forefathers' joints,
    And pluck the mangled Tybalt from his shroud,
    And, in this rage, with some great kinsman's bone
    As with a club dash out my desp'rate brains?
55   O, look! Methinks I see my cousin's ghost
    Seeking out Romeo, that did spit his body
    Upon a rapier's point. Stay, Tybalt, stay!
    Romeo, Romeo, Romeo, I drink to thee.
          [*She falls upon her bed within the curtains.*]

[Scene IV. *Hall in Capulet's house.*]

Enter Lady of the House and Nurse.

Lady Capulet. Hold, take these keys and fetch more
    spices, nurse.

Nurse. They call for dates and quinces in the pastry.°

        Enter old Capulet.

Capulet. Come, stir, stir, stir! The second cock hath
    crowed,
    The curfew bell hath rung, 'tis three o'clock.

42 **green in earth** newly entombed   47 **mandrakes** plant with forked
root, resembling the human body (supposed to shriek when up-
rooted and drive the hearer mad)   49 **distraught** driven mad
IV.iv.2 **pastry** pastry cook's room

Look to the baked meats,° good Angelica;°   5
Spare not for cost.

Nurse.   Go, you cotquean,° go,
Get you to bed! Faith, you'll be sick tomorrow
For this night's watching.°

Capulet. No, not a whit. What, I have watched ere now
All night for lesser cause, and ne'er been sick.   10

Lady Capulet. Ay, you have been a mouse hunt° in
your time;
But I will watch you from such watching now.
                              Exit Lady and Nurse.

Capulet. A jealous hood,° a jealous hood!

          *Enter three or four [Fellows] with spits and
                    logs and baskets.*

                              Now, fellow,
What is there?

First Fellow. Things for the cook, sir; but I know not
what.   15

Capulet. Make haste, make haste. [*Exit first Fellow.*]
Sirrah, fetch drier logs.
Call Peter; he will show thee where they are.

Second Fellow. I have a head, sir, that will find out
logs°
And never trouble Peter for the matter.

Capulet. Mass,° and well said; a merry whoreson,° ha!   20
Thou shalt be loggerhead.° [*Exit second Fellow,
with the others.*] Good faith, 'tis day.
The County will be here with music straight,
For so he said he would.   *Play music.*

5 **baked meats** meat pies   5 **Angelica** (the Nurse's name)   6 **cotquean** man who does woman's work   8 **watching** staying awake
11 **mouse hunt** night prowler, woman chaser   13 **A jealous hood**
i.e., you wear the cap of a jealous person   18 **will find out logs** has
an affinity for logs (i.e., is wooden also)   20 **Mass** by the Mass
20 **whoreson** rascal   21 **loggerhead** blockhead

I hear him near.
Nurse! Wife! What, ho! What, nurse, I say!

Enter Nurse.

25   Go waken Juliet; go and trim her up.
I'll go and chat with Paris. Hie, make haste,
Make haste! The bridegroom he is come already:
Make haste, I say.   [*Exit.*]

[Scene V. *Juliet's chamber.*]

Nurse.° Mistress! What, mistress! Juliet! Fast,° I war-
rant her, she.
Why, lamb! Why, lady! Fie, you slugabed.°
Why, love, I say! Madam; Sweetheart! Why, bride!
What, not a word? You take your pennyworths°
now;
5   Sleep for a week; for the next night, I warrant,
The County Paris hath set up his rest°
That you shall rest but little. God forgive me!
Marry, and amen. How sound is she asleep!
I needs must wake her. Madam, madam, madam!
10   Ay, let the County take you in your bed;
He'll fright you up, i' faith. Will it not be?
                  [*Draws aside the curtains.*]
What, dressed, and in your clothes, and down°
again?
I must needs wake you. Lady! Lady! Lady!
Alas, alas! Help, help! My lady's dead!

IV.v.1 **Nurse** (at the conclusion of the last scene the nurse presumably did not go offstage but remained on the forestage, and
after Capulet's departure she now walks to the rear to open the
curtains, revealing Juliet)   1 **Fast** fast asleep   2 **slugabed** sleepy-
head   4 **pennyworths** small portions (i.e., short naps)   6 **set up
his rest** firmly resolved (with bawdy suggestion of having a lance in
readiness)   12 **down** gone back to bed

O weraday° that ever I was born!
Some *aqua vitae,*° ho! My lord! My lady!

[Enter Mother.]

Lady Capulet. What noise is here?

Nurse.   O lamentable day!

Lady Capulet. What is the matter?

Nurse.   Look, look! O heavy day!

Lady Capulet. O me, O me! My child, my only life!
Revive, look up, or I will die with thee!   *20*
Help, help! Call help.

Enter Father.

Capulet. For shame, bring Juliet forth; her lord is
     come.

Nurse. She's dead, deceased; she's dead, alack the day!

Lady Capulet. Alack the day, she's dead, she's dead,
     she's dead!

Capulet. Ha! Let me see her. Out alas! She's cold,   *25*
Her blood is settled, and her joints are stiff;
Life and these lips have long been separated.
Death lies on her like an untimely frost
Upon the sweetest flower of all the field.

Nurse. O lamentable day!

Lady Capulet.   O woeful time!   *30*

Capulet. Death, that hath ta'en her hence to make me
     wail,
Ties up my tongue and will not let me speak.

*Enter Friar [Lawrence] and the County [Paris,
     with Musicians].*

Friar. Come, is the bride ready to go to church?

<u>*Capulet*</u>. Ready to go, but never to return.

---

15 weraday welladay, alas   **16 aqua vitae** spirits

35   O son, the night before thy wedding day
    Hath Death lain with thy wife. There she lies,
    Flower as she was, deflowerèd by him.
    Death is my son-in-law, Death is my heir;
    My daughter he hath wedded. I will die
40   And leave him all. Life, living, all is Death's.

Paris. Have I thought, love, to see this morning's face,
    And doth it give me such a sight as this?

Lady Capulet. Accursed, unhappy, wretched, hateful
    day!
    Most miserable hour that e'er time saw
45   In lasting labor of his pilgrimage!
    But one, poor one, one poor and loving child,
    But one thing to rejoice and solace in,
    And cruel Death hath catched it from my sight.

Nurse. O woe! O woeful, woeful, woeful day!
50   Most lamentable day, most woeful day
    That ever ever I did yet behold!
    O day, O day, O day! O hateful day!
    Never was seen so black a day as this.
    O woeful day! O woeful day!

55 *Paris.* Beguiled, divorcèd, wrongèd, spited, slain!
    Most detestable Death, by thee beguiled,
    By cruel, cruel thee quite overthrown.
    O love! O life!—not life, but love in death!

Capulet. Despised, distressèd, hated, martyred, killed!
60   Uncomfortable° time, why cam'st thou now
    To murder, murder our solemnity?
    O child, O child! My soul, and not my child!
    Dead art thou—alack, my child is dead,
    And with my child my joys are burièd!

65 *Friar.* Peace, ho, for shame! Confusion's cure lives not
    In these confusions. Heaven and yourself
    Had part in this fair maid—now heaven hath all,
    And all the better is it for the maid.

60 **Uncomfortable** discomforting

Your part in her you could not keep from death,
But heaven keeps his part in eternal life.   70
The most you sought was her promotion,
For 'twas your heaven she should be advanced;
And weep ye now, seeing she is advanced
Above the clouds, as high as heaven itself?
O, in this love, you love your child so ill   75
That you run mad, seeing that she is well.°
She's not well married that lives married long,
But she's best married that dies married young.
Dry up your tears and stick your rosemary°
On this fair corse, and, as the custom is,   80
And in her best array bear her to church;
For though fond nature° bids us all lament,
Yet nature's tears are reason's merriment.

Capulet. All things that we ordainèd festival
Turn from their office to black funeral—   85
Our instruments to melancholy bells,
Our wedding cheer to a sad burial feast;
Our solemn hymns to sullen dirges change;
Our bridal flowers serve for a buried corse;
And all things change them to the contrary.   90

Friar. Sir, go you in; and, madam, go with him;
And go, Sir Paris. Everyone prepare
To follow this fair corse unto her grave.
The heavens do low'r° upon you for some ill;
Move them no more by crossing their high will.   95

> *Exeunt [casting rosemary on her*
> *and shutting the curtains].*
> *Manet° [the Nurse with Musicians].*

First Musician. Faith, we may put up our pipes and
be gone.

Nurse. Honest good fellows, ah, put up, put up!
For well you know this is a pitiful case.°   [*Exit.*]

76 **well** i.e., in blessed condition, in heaven   79 **rosemary** an ever-
green, signifying remembrance   82 **fond nature** foolish human nature   94 **low'r** frown   95 s.d. **Manet** remains (Latin)   99 **case** (1)
situation (2) instrument case

100 First Musician. Ay, by my troth, the case may be
amended.

Enter [Peter].

Peter. Musicians, O, musicians, "Heart's ease,"
"Heart's ease"! O, and you will have me live, play
105 "Heart's ease."

First Musician. Why "Heart's ease"?

Peter. O, musicians, because my heart itself plays
"My heart is full." O, play me some merry dump°
to comfort me.

First Musician. Not a dump we! 'Tis no time to play
110 now.

Peter. You will not then?

First Musician. No.

Peter. I will then give it you soundly.

First Musician. What will you give us?

115 Peter. No money, on my faith, but the gleek.° I will
give you° the minstrel.

First Musician. Then will I give you the serving-
creature.

Peter. Then will I lay the serving-creature's dagger
*120 on your pate. I will carry° no crotchets.° I'll *re*
you, I'll *fa*° you. Do you note° me?

First Musician. And you *re* us and *fa* us, you note
us.°

Second Musician. Pray you put up your dagger, and
*125 put out° your wit. Then have at you with my wit!

---

107 **dump** sad tune   115 **gleek** gibe   116 **give you** call you
120 **carry** endure   120 **crotchets** (1) whims (2) quarter notes
120–21 **re . . . fa** (musical notes, but used perhaps with puns on
"ray," or "bewray" ["befoul"], and "fay" ["polish"]; see H.
Kökeritz, *Shakespeare's Pronunciation*, pp. 105–06)   121 **note** understand   122–23 **note us** set us to music   125 **put out** set out,
display

Peter. I will dry-beat you with an iron wit, and put
up my iron dagger. Answer me like men.

> "When griping·grief the heart doth wound,
>   And doleful dumps the mind oppress,
> Then music with her silver sound"°—   *150*

Why "silver sound"? Why "music with her silver
sound"? What say you, Simon Catling?°

First Musician. Marry, sir, because silver hath a sweet
sound.

Peter. Pretty! What say you, Hugh Rebeck?°   *135*

Second Musician. I say "silver sound" because musicians sound for silver.

Peter. Pretty too! What say you, James Soundpost?°

Third Musician. Faith, I know not what to say.

Peter. O, I cry you mercy,° you are the singer. I will   *140*
say for you. It is "music with her silver sound" because musicians have no gold for sounding.

> "Then music with her silver sound
>   With speedy help doth lend redress."   *Exit.*

First Musician. What a pestilent knave is this same!   *145*

Second Musician. Hang him, Jack! Come, we'll in here,
tarry for the mourners, and stay dinner.
>   *Exit [with others].*

128–30 **When . . . sound** (the song is from Richard Edwards' "In
Commendation of Music," in *The Paradise of Dainty Devices,* 1576)
132 **Catling** catgut, a lute string   135 **Rebeck** a three-stringed fid-
dle   138 **Soundpost** peg that gives internal support to a violin
140 **cry you mercy** beg your pardon

[ACT V

Scene I. *Mantua. A street.*]

Enter Romeo.

Romeo. If I may trust the flattering° truth of sleep,
My dreams presage some joyful news at hand.
My bosom's lord° sits lightly in his throne,
And all this day an unaccustomed spirit
5 Lifts me above the ground with cheerful thoughts.
I dreamt my lady came and found me dead
(Strange dream that gives a dead man leave to think!)
And breathed such life with kisses in my lips
That I revived and was an emperor.
10 Ah me! How sweet is love itself possessed,
When but love's shadows° are so rich in joy!

Enter Romeo's Man [Balthasar, booted].

News from Verona! How now, Balthasar?
Dost thou not bring me letters from the friar?
How doth my lady? Is my father well?
15 How fares my Juliet? That I ask again,
For nothing can be ill if she be well.

Man. Then she is well, and nothing can be ill.
Her body sleeps in Capel's monument,°
And her immortal part with angels lives.

V.i.1 **flattering** illusory   3 **bosom's lord** i.e., heart   11 **shadows** dreams   18 **monument** tomb

I saw her laid low in her kindred's vault   20
And presently took post° to tell it you.
O, pardon me for bringing these ill news,
Since you did leave it for my office,° sir.

Romeo. Is it e'en so? Then I defy you, stars!
Thou knowest my lodging. Get me ink and paper   25
And hire post horses. I will hence tonight.

Man. I do beseech you, sir, have patience.
Your looks are pale and wild and do import°
Some misadventure.

Romeo.   Tush, thou art deceived.
Leave me and do the thing I bid thee do.   30
Hast thou no letters to me from the friar?

Man. No, my good lord.

Romeo.   No matter. Get thee gone.
And hire those horses. I'll be with thee straight.
                              Exit [*Balthasar*].
Well, Juliet, I will lie with thee tonight.
Let's see for means. O mischief, thou art swift   35
To enter in the thoughts of desperate men!
I do remember an apothecary,
And hereabouts 'a dwells, which late I noted
In tatt'red weeds,° with overwhelming° brows,
Culling of simples.° Meager were his looks,   40
Sharp misery had worn him to the bones;
And in his needy shop a tortoise hung,
An alligator stuffed, and other skins
Of ill-shaped fishes; and about his shelves
A beggarly account° of empty boxes,   45
Green earthen pots, bladders, and musty seeds,
Remnants of packthread, and old cakes of roses°
Were thinly scatterèd, to make up a show.
Noting this penury, to myself I said,

---

21 **post** post horses 23 **office** duty 28 **import** suggest 39 **weeds** clothes 39 **overwhelming** overhanging 40 **Culling of simples** collecting medicinal herbs 45 **account** number 47 **cakes of roses** pressed rose petals (for perfume)

50 "And if a man did need a poison now
    Whose sale is present death in Mantua,
    Here lives a caitiff° wretch would sell it him."
    O, this same thought did but forerun my need,
    And this same needy man must sell it me.
55 As I remember, this should be the house.
    Being holiday, the beggar's shop is shut.
    What, ho! Apothecary!

    [*Enter Apothecary.*]

Apothecary.   Who calls so loud?

Romeo. Come hither, man. I see that thou art poor.
    Hold, there is forty ducats. Let me have
60 A dram of poison, such soon-speeding gear°
    As will disperse itself through all the veins
    That the life-weary taker may fall dead,
    And that the trunk° may be discharged of breath
    As violently as hasty powder fired
65 Doth hurry from the fatal cannon's womb.

Apothecary. Such mortal drugs I have; but Mantua's
        law
    Is death to any he that utters° them.

Romeo. Art thou so bare and full of wretchedness
    And fearest to die? Famine is in thy cheeks,
70 Need and oppression starveth° in thy eyes,
    Contempt and beggary hangs upon thy back:
    The world is not thy friend, nor the world's law;
    The world affords no law to make thee rich;
    Then be not poor, but break it and take this.

75 *Apothecary.* My poverty but not my will consents.

Romeo. I pay thy poverty and not thy will.

Apothecary. Put this in any liquid thing you will
    And drink it off, and if you had the strength
    Of twenty men, it would dispatch you straight.

___

52 **caitiff** miserable   60 **soon-speeding gear** fast-working **stuff**
63 **trunk** body   67 **utters** dispenses   70 **starveth** stand starving

Romeo. There is thy gold—worse poison to men's
    souls,   *80*
  Doing more murder in this loathsome world,
  Than these poor compounds that thou mayst not
    sell.
  I sell thee poison; thou hast sold me none.
  Farewell. Buy food and get thyself in flesh.
  Come, cordial° and not poison, go with me   *85*
  To Juliet's grave; for there must I use thee.

                                        Exeunt.

[Scene II. *Friar Lawrence's cell.*]

Enter Friar John to Friar Lawrence.

John. Holy Franciscan friar, brother, ho!

                Enter [Friar] Lawrence.

Lawrence. This same should be the voice of Friar John.
  Welcome from Mantua. What says Romeo?
  Or, if his mind be writ, give me his letter.

John. Going to find a barefoot brother out,   *5*
  One of our order, to associate° me
  Here in this city visiting the sick,
  And finding him, the searchers° of the town,
  Suspecting that we both were in a house
  Where the infectious pestilence did reign,   *10*
  Sealed up the doors, and would not let us forth,
  So that my speed to Mantua there was stayed.

Lawrence. Who bare my letter, then, to Romeo?

John. I could not send it—here it is again—
  Nor get a messenger to bring it thee,   *13*
  So fearful were they of infection.

---

85 **cordial**   restorative   V.ii.6 **associate**   accompany   8 **searchers**
health officers

Lawrence. Unhappy fortune! By my brotherhood,°
        The letter was not nice,° but full of charge,°
        Of dear import; and the neglecting it
20   May do much danger. Friar John, go hence,
        Get me an iron crow° and bring it straight
        Unto my cell.

John.   Brother, I'll go and bring it thee.   *Exit.*

Lawrence. Now must I to the monument alone.
        Within this three hours will fair Juliet wake.
25   She will beshrew° me much that Romeo
        Hath had no notice of these accidents;°
        But I will write again to Mantua,
        And keep her at my cell till Romeo come—
        Poor living corse, closed in a dead man's tomb!   *Exit.*

[Scene III. *A churchyard; in it a monument
        belonging to the Capulets.*]

*Enter Paris and his Page [with flowers and
        sweet water].*

Paris. Give me thy torch, boy. Hence, and stand aloof.
        Yet put it out, for I would not be seen.
        Under yond yew trees lay thee all along,°
        Holding thy ear close to the hollow ground.
5   So shall no foot upon the churchyard tread
        (Being loose, unfirm, with digging up of graves)
        But thou shalt hear it. Whistle then to me,
        As signal that thou hearest something approach.
        Give me those flowers. Do as I bid thee, go.

10   *Page.* [*Aside*] I am almost afraid to stand alone

17 **brotherhood** religious order   18 **nice** trivial   18 **charge** importance   21 **crow** crowbar   25 **beshrew** blame   26 **accidents** hap-
penings   V.iii.3 **lay thee all along** lie at full length

Here in the churchyard; yet I will adventure.°
                                                [*Retires.*]

Paris. Sweet flower, with flowers thy bridal bed I strew
    (O woe! thy canopy is dust and stones)
    Which with sweet° water nightly I will dew;
        Or, wanting that, with tears distilled by moans.   15
    The obsequies that I for thee will keep
    Nightly shall be to strew thy grave and weep.
                                        Whistle Boy.
    The boy gives warning something doth approach.
    What cursèd foot wanders this way tonight
    To cross° my obsequies and true love's rite?   20
    What, with a torch? Muffle° me, night, awhile.
                                                [*Retires.*]

*Enter Romeo, [and Balthasar with a torch, a mattock,
        and a crow of iron].*

Romeo. Give me that mattock and the wrenching iron.
    Hold, take this letter. Early in the morning
    See thou deliver it to my lord and father.
    Give me the light. Upon thy life I charge thee,   25
    Whate'er thou hearest or seest, stand all aloof
    And do not interrupt me in my course.
    Why I descend into this bed of death
    Is partly to behold my lady's face,
    But chiefly to take thence from her dead finger   30
    A precious ring—a ring that I must use
    In dear employment.° Therefore hence, be gone.
    But if thou, jealous,° dost return to pry
    In what I farther shall intend to do,
    By heaven, I will tear thee joint by joint   35
    And strew this hungry churchyard with thy limbs.
    The time and my intents are savage-wild,
    More fierce and more inexorable far
    Than empty tigers or the roaring sea.

11 **adventure** risk it 14 **sweet** perfumed 20 **cross** interrupt
21 **Muffle** hide 32 **dear employment** important business 33 **jealous** curious

40 *Balthasar.* I will be gone, sir, and not trouble ye.

Romeo. So shalt thou show me friendship. Take thou
     that.
 Live, and be prosperous; and farewell, good fellow.

Balthasar. [*Aside*] For all this same, I'll hide me here-
     about.
 His looks I fear, and his intents I doubt.° [*Retires.*]

45 *Romeo.* Thou detestable maw,° thou womb of death,
 Gorged with the dearest morsel of the earth,
 Thus I enforce thy rotten jaws to open,
 And in despite° I'll cram thee with more food.
                              [*Romeo opens the tomb.*]

Paris. This is that banished haughty Montague
50 That murd'red my love's cousin—with which grief
 It is supposed the fair creature died—
 And here is come to do some villainous shame
 To the dead bodies. I will apprehend him.
 Stop thy unhallowèd toil, vile Montague!
55 Can vengeance be pursued further than death?
 Condemnèd villain, I do apprehend thee.
 Obey, and go with me; for thou must die.

Romeo. I must indeed; and therefore came I hither.
 Good gentle youth, tempt not a desp'rate man.
60 Fly hence and leave me. Think upon these gone;
 Let them affright thee. I beseech thee, youth,
 Put not another sin upon my head
 By urging me to fury. O, be gone!
 By heaven, I love thee better than myself,
65 For I come hither armed against myself.
 Stay not, be gone. Live, and hereafter say
 A madman's mercy bid thee run away.

Paris. I do defy thy conjurations.°
 And apprehend thee for a felon here.

70 *Romeo.* Wilt thou provoke me? Then have at thee, boy!
                              [*They fight.*]

44 **doubt** suspect   45 **maw** stomach   48 **in despite** to spite you
68 **conjurations** solemn charges

Page. O Lord, they fight! I will go call the watch.
[*Exit. Paris falls.*]

Paris. O, I am slain! If thou be merciful,
   Open the tomb, lay me with Juliet.   [*Dies.*]

Romeo. In faith, I will. Let me peruse this face.
   Mercutio's kinsman, noble County Paris!   75
   What said my man when my betossèd soul
   Did not attend° him as we rode? I think
   He told me Paris should have married Juliet.
   Said he not so, or did I dream it so?
   Or am I mad, hearing him talk of Juliet,
   To think it was so? O, give me thy hand,
   One writ with me in sour misfortune's book!
   I'll bury thee in a triumphant grave.
   A grave? O, no, a lanthorn,° slaught'red youth,
   For here lies Juliet, and her beauty makes
   This vault a feasting presence° full of light.
   Death, lie thou there, by a dead man interred.
[*Lays him in the tomb.*]
   How oft when men are at the point of death
   Have they been mèrry! Which their keepers° call
   A lightning before death. O, how may I   90
   Call this a lightning? O my love, my wife!
   Death, that hath sucked the honey of thy breath,
   Hath had no power yet upon thy beauty.
   Thou art not conquered. Beauty's ensign° yet
   Is crimson in thy lips and in thy cheeks,   95
   And death's pale flag is not advancèd there.
   Tybalt, liest thou there in thy bloody sheet?
   O, what more favor can I do to thee
   Than with that hand that cut thy youth in twain
   To sunder his that was thine enemy?   100
   Forgive me, cousin! Ah, dear Juliet,
   Why art thou yet so fair? Shall I believe
   That unsubstantial Death is amorous,

---

77 **attend** give attention to   84 **lanthorn** lantern (a windowed erection on the top of a dome or room to admit light)   86 **feasting presence** festive presence chamber   89 **keepers** jailers   94 **ensign** banner

And that the lean abhorrèd monster keeps
105   Thee here in dark to be his paramour?
For fear of that I still will stay with thee
And never from this pallet of dim night
Depart again. Here, here will I remain
With worms that are thy chambermaids. O, here
110   Will I set up my everlasting rest
And shake the yoke of inauspicious stars
From this world-wearied flesh. Eyes, look your last!
Arms, take your last embrace! And, lips, O you
The doors of breath, seal with a righteous kiss
115   A dateless° bargain to engrossing° death!
Come, bitter conduct;° come, unsavory guide!
Thou desperate pilot,° now at once run on
The dashing rocks thy seasick weary bark!
Here's to my love! [*Drinks.*] O true apothecary!
120   Thy drugs are quick. Thus with a kiss I die. [*Falls.*]
   Enter Friar [Lawrence], with lanthorn, crow,
            and spade.

Friar. Saint Francis be my speed!° How oft tonight
   Have my old feet stumbled° at graves! Who's there?

Balthasar. Here's one, a friend, and one that knows
      you well.

Friar. Bliss be upon you! Tell me, good my friend,
125   What torch is yond that vainly lends his light
   To grubs and eyeless skulls? As I discern,
   It burneth in the Capels' monument.

Balthasar. It doth so, holy sir; and there's my master,
   One that you love.

Friar.   Who is it?

Balthasar.   Romeo.

Friar. How long hath he been there?

---

115 **dateless** eternal   115 **engrossing** all-buying, all-encompassing
116 **conduct** guide   117 **desperate pilot** i.e., himself   121 **speed**
help   122 **stumbled** (a bad omen)

Balthasar.   Full half an hour. 130

Friar. Go with me to the vault.

Balthasar.   I dare not, sir.
  My master knows not but I am gone hence,
  And fearfully did menace me with death
  If I did stay to look on his intents.

Friar. Stay then; I'll go alone. Fear comes upon me. 135
  O, much I fear some ill unthrifty° thing.

Balthasar. As I did sleep under this yew tree here,
  I dreamt my master and another fought,
  And that my master slew him.

Friar.   Romeo!
  Alack, alack, what blood is this which stains   140
  The stony entrance of this sepulcher?
  What mean these masterless and gory swords
  To lie discolored by this place of peace?
                       [Enters the tomb.]
  Romeo! O, pale! Who else? What, Paris too?
  And steeped in blood? Ah, what an unkind° hour   145
  Is guilty of this lamentable chance!
  The lady stirs.   *[Juliet rises.]*

Juliet. O comfortable° friar! Where is my lord?
  I do remember well where I should be,
  And there I am. Where is my Romeo?   150

Friar. I hear some noise. Lady, come from that nest
  Of death, contagion, and unnatural sleep.
  A greater power than we can contradict
  Hath thwarted our intents. Come, come away.
  Thy husband in thy bosom there lies dead;   155
  And Paris too. Come, I'll dispose of thee
  Among a sisterhood of holy nuns.
  Stay not to question, for the watch is coming.
  Come, go, good Juliet. I dare no longer stay.

136 **unthrifty** unlucky   145 **unkind** unnatural   148 **comfortable** comforting

160 *Juliet.* Go, get thee hence, for I will not away.

                                    Exit [Friar].

What's here? A cup, closed in my truelove's hand?
Poison, I see, hath been his timeless° end.
O churl!° Drunk all, and left no friendly drop
To help me after? I will kiss thy lips.
165 Haply some poison yet doth hang on them
To make me die with a restorative.   *[Kisses him.]*
Thy lips are warm!

Chief Watchman. [*Within*] Lead, boy. Which way?

Juliet. Yea, noise? Then I'll be brief. O happy°
    dagger!   *[Snatches Romeo's dagger.]*
170 This is thy sheath; there rust, and let me die.

                         [She stabs herself and falls.]

     Enter [Paris'] Boy and Watch.

Boy. This is the place. There, where the torch doth
    burn.

Chief Watchman. The ground is bloody. Search about
    the churchyard.
Go, some of you; whoe'er you find attach.

                       [Exeunt some of the Watch.]

Pitiful sight! Here lies the County slain;
175 And Juliet bleeding, warm, and newly dead,
Who here hath lain this two days burièd.
Go, tell the Prince; run to the Capulets;
Raise up the Montagues; some others search.

                     [Exeunt others of the Watch.]

We see the ground whereon these woes do lie,
180 But the true ground° of all these piteous woes
We cannot without circumstance° descry.

    Enter [some of the Watch, with] Romeo's Man
               [Balthasar].

Second Watchman. Here's Romeo's man. We found
    him in the churchyard.

---

162 **timeless** untimely   163 **churl** rude fellow   169 **happy** opportune   180 **ground** cause   181 **circumstance** details

Chief Watchman. Hold him in safety till the Prince
   come hither.

    Enter Friar [Lawrence] and another Watchman.

Third Watchman. Here is a friar that trembles, sighs,
   and weeps.
We took this mattock and this spade from him   185
As he was coming from this churchyard's side.

Chief Watchman. A great suspicion! Stay the friar too.

    Enter the Prince [and Attendants].

Prince. What misadventure is so early up,
   That calls our person from our morning rest?

    Enter Capulet and his Wife [with others].

Capulet. What should it be, that is so shrieked abroad? 190

Lady Capulet. O, the people in the street cry "Romeo,"
   Some "Juliet," and some "Paris"; and all run
   With open outcry toward our monument.

Prince. What fear is this which startles in your ears?

Chief Watchman. Sovereign, here lies the County Paris
   slain;   195
And Romeo dead; and Juliet, dead before,
Warm and new killed.

Prince. Search, seek, and know how this foul murder
   comes.

Chief Watchman. Here is a friar, and slaughtered
   Romeo's man,
With instruments upon them fit to open   200
These dead men's tombs.

Capulet. O heavens! O wife, look how our daughter
   bleeds!
This dagger hath mista'en, for, lo, his house°
Is empty on the back of Montague,
And it missheathèd in my daughter's bosom!   205

203 his house its sheath

Lady Capulet. O me, this sight of death is as a bell
That warns my old age to a sepulcher.

Enter Montague [and others].

Prince. Come, Montague; for thou art early up
To see thy son and heir more early down.

210 *Montague.* Alas, my liege, my wife is dead tonight!
Grief of my son's exile hath stopped her breath.
What further woe conspires against mine age?

Prince. Look, and thou shalt see.

Montague. O thou untaught! What manners is in this,
215 To press before thy father to a grave?

Prince. Seal up the mouth of outrage° for a while,
Till we can clear these ambiguities
And know their spring, their head, their true
        descent;
And then will I be general of your woes°
220 And lead you even to death. Meantime forbear,
And let mischance be slave to patience.
Bring forth the parties of suspicion.

Friar. I am the greatest, able to do least,
Yet most suspected, as the time and place
225 Doth make against me, of this direful murder;
And here I stand, both to impeach and purge°
Myself condemnèd and myself excused.

Prince. Then say at once what thou dost know in this.

Friar. I will be brief, for my short date of breath°
230 Is not so long as is a tedious tale.
Romeo, there dead, was husband to that Juliet;
And she, there dead, that's Romeo's faithful wife.
I married them; and their stol'n marriage day
Was Tybalt's doomsday, whose untimely death
235 Banished the new-made bridegroom from this city;

216 **the mouth of outrage** these violent cries   219 **general of your woes** leader in your sorrowing   226 **impeach and purge** make charges and exonerate   229 **date of breath** term of life

For whom, and not for Tybalt, Juliet pined.
You, to remove that siege of grief from her,
Betrothed and would have married her perforce
To County Paris. Then comes she to me
And with wild looks bid me devise some mean   240
To rid her from this second marriage,
Or in my cell there would she kill herself.
Then gave I her (so tutored by my art)
A sleeping potion; which so took effect
As I intended, for it wrought on her   245
The form of death. Meantime I writ to Romeo
That he should hither come as° this dire night
To help to take her from her borrowed grave,
Being the time the potion's force should cease.
But he which bore my letter, Friar John,   250
Was stayed by accident, and yesternight
Returned my letter back. Then all alone
At the prefixèd hour of her waking
Came I to take her from her kindred's vault;
Meaning to keep her closely° at my cell   255
Till I conveniently could send to Romeo.
But when I came, some minute ere the time
Of her awakening, here untimely lay
The noble Paris and true Romeo dead.
She wakes; and I entreated her come forth   260
And bear this work of heaven with patience;
But then a noise did scare me from the tomb,
And she, too desperate, would not go with me,
But, as it seems, did violence on herself.
All this I know, and to the marriage   265
Her nurse is privy;° and if aught in this
Miscarried by my fault, let my old life
Be sacrificed some hour before his time
Unto the rigor of severest law.

Prince. We still° have known thee for a holy man.   270
    Where's Romeo's man? What can he say to this?

Balthasar. I brought my master news of Juliet's death;

247 **as** on   255 **closely** hidden   266 **privy** accessory   270 **still** always

And then in post he came from Mantua
To this same place, to this same monument.
This letter he early bid me give his father,
275 And threat'ned me with death, going in the vault,
If I departed not and left him there.

Prince. Give me the letter. I will look on it.
Where is the County's page that raised the watch?
280 Sirrah, what made your master° in this place?

Boy. He came with flowers to strew his lady's grave;
And bid me stand aloof, and so I did.
Anon comes one with light to ope the tomb;
And by and by° my master drew on him;
285 And then I ran away to call the watch.

Prince. This letter doth make good the friar's words,
Their course of love, the tidings of her death;
And here he writes that he did buy a poison
Of a poor pothecary and therewithal°
290 Came to this vault to die and lie with Juliet.
Where be these enemies? Capulet, Montague,
See what a scourge is laid upon your hate,
That heaven finds means to kill your joys with love.
And I, for winking at° your discords too,
295 Have lost a brace° of kinsmen. All are punished.

Capulet. O brother Montague, give me thy hand.
This is my daughter's jointure,° for no more
Can I demand.

Montague.   But I can give thee more;
For I will raise her statue in pure gold,
300 That whiles Verona by that name is known,
There shall no figure at such rate° be set
As that of true and faithful Juliet.

Capulet. As rich shall Romeo's by his lady's lie—
Poor sacrifices of our enmity!

---

280 **made your master** was your master doing   284 **by and by** soon
289 **therewithal** therewith   294 **winking at** closing eyes to   295
brace pair (i.e., Mercutio and Paris)   297 **jointure** marriage settle-
ment   301 **rate** value

Prince. A glooming° peace this morning with it brings.   *305*
    The sun for sorrow will not show his head.
  Go hence, to have more talk of these sad things;
    Some shall be pardoned, and some punishèd;
  For never was a story of more woe
  Than this of Juliet and her Romeo.   *310*

                        [*Exeunt omnes.*]

FINIS

305 **glooming** cloudy

Textual Note

The First Quarto (Q1) of *Romeo and Juliet* was printed in 1597 without previous entry in the Stationers' Register. It bore the following title page: "An/ EXCEL-LENT/ conceited Tragedie/ OF/ Romeo and Iuliet./ As it hath been often (with great applause)/ plaid pub-liquely, by the right Ho-/ nourable the L. of *Hunsdon*/ his Seruants./ LONDON,/ Printed by Iohn Danter./ 1597." Until the present century, editors frequently as-sumed that this text, curtailed and manifestly corrupt, rep-resented an early draft of the play. Most now agree that Q1, like the other "bad" Shakespeare quartos, is a me-morial reconstruction; that is, a version which some of the actors (accusing fingers have been pointed at those who played Romeo and Peter) put together from memory and gave to the printer. The Second Quarto (Q2) was printed in 1599 with the following title page: "THE/ MOST/ EX-/ cellent and lamentable/ Tragedie, of Romeo/ and *Iuliet*./ *Newly corrected, augmented, and/ amended:* As it hath bene sundry times publiquely acted, by the/ right Honourable the Lord Chamberlaine/ his Seruants./ London/ Printed by Thomas Creede, for Cuth-bert Burby, and are to/ be sold at his shop neare the Exchange./ 1599." Apparently Q2 derives directly from the same acting version that is imperfectly reflected in the memorially reconstructed Q1, but it is based on a written script of the play rather than on actors' memories. Q2, however, is the product of careless or hasty printing and does not inspire complete confidence. Lines that the author doubtless had canceled are sometimes printed along with the lines intended to replace them, and occasionally notes about staging appear which are probably the prompter's, or possibly Shakespeare's. Vexing matters like these, together with the fact that some speeches in Q2 are clearly based on Q1 (possibly the manuscript that provided the copy for most of Q2 was illegible in places), have caused editors to make at least limited use of Q1. The other texts of *Romeo and Juliet* have no claim to authority. The Second Quarto provided the basis for a Third Quarto (1609), which in turn served as copy for an undated Fourth Quarto and for the text in the Folio of 1623. A Fifth Quarto, based on the Fourth, appeared in 1637.

None of these texts—including the Second Quarto, upon which the present edition is based—makes any real division of the play into acts and scenes. (The last third of Q1 does have a rough indication of scene division in the form of strips of ornamental border across the page, and the Folio has at the beginning *Actus Primus. Scena Prima,* but nothing further.) The division used here, like that in most modern texts, derives from the Globe edition, as do the *Dramatis Personae* and the various indications of place. Spelling and punctuation have been modernized, a number of stage directions have been added (in square brackets), and speech prefixes have been regularized. This last change will be regretted by those who feel, perhaps rightly, that at least some of the speech prefixes of Q2 show how Shakespeare thought of the character at each moment of the dialogue. Lady Capulet, for example, is variously designated in the speech prefixes of Q2 as *Wife, Lady,* and sometimes *Mother;* Capulet is occasionally referred to as *Father,* and Balthasar as *Peter;* the First Musician of our text (IV.v) is once called *Fidler* in Q2 and several times *Minstrel* or *Minstrels.* Other deviations (apart from obvious typographical errors) from Q2 are listed in the textual notes. There the adopted reading is given first, in italics, followed by a note in square brackets if the source of the reading is Q1; this is followed by the rejected reading in roman. Absence of a note in square brackets indicates that the adopted reading has been taken from some other source and represents guesswork at best. Apparently the editors of F as well as of Q3 and Q4 had no access to any authentic document.

In dealing with the troublesome stage direction at the end of I.iv, I have followed the solution adopted by H. R. Hoppe in his Crofts Classics edition (1947); and I have adopted the reading of "eyes' shot" for the customary "eyes shut" at III.ii.49 from the Pelican edition of John E. Hankins (Penguin, 1960), which presents a good argument for retaining the reading of Q2 with the addition of an apostrophe.

I.i.29 *in sense* [Q1] sense   34 *comes two* [Q1] comes   65 *swashing* washing   123 *drave* driue   150 *his* is   156 *sun* same   182 *well-seeming* [Q1] welseeing   205 *Bid a sick* [Q1] A sicke   205 *make* [Q1] makes   206 *Ah* [Q1] A

I.ii.32 *on* one   65–73 *Signior . . . Helena* [prose in Qq and F]   92 *fires* fier

I.iii.2–76 [Q2 prints Nurse's speeches in prose]   66, 67 *honor* [Q1] houre   99 *make it* [Q1] make

I.iv.7–8 *Nor . . . entrance* [added from Q1]   23 *Mercutio* Horatio   39 *done* [Q1] dum   42 *of this sir-reverence* [Q1] or saue you reuerence   45 *like* lights   47 *five* fine   53–91 *O . . . bodes* [verse from Q1; Q2 has prose]   57 *atomies* ottamie   63 *film* Philome   66 *maid* [Q1] man   113 *sail* [Q1] sute   114 s.d. *They . . . and* [Q2 combines with s.d. used here at beginning of I.v]

I.v.s.d. [Q2 adds "Enter Romeo"]   1, 4, 7, 12 *First Servingman . . . Second Servingman . . . First Servingman . . . First Servingman* [Q2 has "Ser.," "I.," "Ser.," and "Ser."]   97 *ready* [Q1] did readie   144 *What's this? What's this?* Whats tis? whats tis

II.i.9 *one* [Q1] on   10 *pronounce* [Q1] prouaunt   10 *dove* [Q1] day   12 *heir* [Q1] her   38 *et cetera* [Q1] or

II.ii.16 *do* to   20 *eyes* eye   45 *were* wene   83 *washed* washeth   99 *havior* [Q1] behauior   101 *more cunning* [Q1] coying   162 *than mine* then   167 *sweet* Neece   186 *Romeo* [Q1] Iu.   187–88 [between these lines Q2 has "The grey eyde morne smiles on the frowning night, / Checkring the Easterne Clouds with streaks of light, / And darknesse fleckted like a drunkard reeles, / From forth daies pathway, made by *Tytans* wheeles," lines nearly identical with those given to the Friar at II.iii.1–4; presumably Shakespeare first wrote the lines for Romeo, then decided to use them in Friar Lawrence's next speech, but neglected to delete the first version, and the printer mistakenly printed it]

II.iii.2 *Check'ring* Checking   3 *fleckèd* [Q1] fleckeld   74 *ring yet* [Q1] yet ringing

II.iv.18 *Benvolio* [Q1] Ro.   30 *fantasticoes* [Q1] phantacies   215 *Ah* A

II.v.11 *three* there

II.vi.27 *music's* musicke

III.i.2 *are* [Q1; Q2 omits]   91 s.d. *Tybalt . . . flies* [Q1; Q2 has "Away Tybalt"]   110 *soundly too. Your* soundly, to your   124 *Alive* [Q1] He gan   126 *eyed* [Q1] end   168 *agile* [Q1] aged   190 *hate's* [Q1] hearts   194 *I* It

III.ii.51 *determine of* determine   60 *one* on   72–73 [Q2 gives line 72 to Juliet, line 73 to Nurse]   76 *Dove-feathered* Rauenous douefeatherd   79 *damnèd* dimme

III.iii.s.d. *Enter Friar* [Q1] Enter Frier and Romeo   40 *But . . . banishèd* [in Q2 this line is preceded by one line, "This may flyes do, when I from this must flie," which is substantially the same as line 41, and by line 43, which is probably misplaced]   52 *Thou* [Q1] Then   61 *madmen* [Q1] mad man   73 s.d. *Knock* They knocke   75 s.d. *Knock* Slud knock   108 s.d. *He . . . away* [Q1; Q2 omits]   117 *lives* lies   143 *misbehaved* mishaued   162 s.d. *Nurse . . . again* [Q1; Q2 omits]   168 *disguised* disguise

III.v.13 *exhales* [Q1] exhale   36 s.d. *Enter Nurse* [Q1] Enter Madame and Nurse   42 s.d. *He goeth down* [Q1; Q2 omits]   54 *Juliet* Ro.   83 *pardon him* padon   140 *gives* giue   182 *trained* [Q1] liand

IV.i.7 *talked* talke   72 *slay* [Q1] stay   83 *chapless* chapels   85 *his shroud* his   98 *breath* [Q1] breast   100 *wanny* many   110 *In* Is   110 [after this line Q2 has "Be borne to buriall in thy kindreds graue"; presumably as soon as Shakespeare wrote these words he decided he could do better, and expressed the gist of the idea in the next two lines, but the canceled line was erroneously printed]   111 *shalt* shall   116 *waking* walking

IV.iii.49 *wake* walke   58 *Romeo, I drink* [after "Romeo" Q2 has "heeres drinke," which is probably a stage direction printed in error]   58 s.d. *She . . . curtains* [Q1; Q2 omits]

IV.iv.21 *faith* [Q1] father

IV.v.65 *cure* care   82 *fond* some   95 s.d. *casting . . . curtains* [Q1; Q2 omits]   101 *by* [Q1] my   101 *amended* amended. Exit omnes   101 s.d. *Peter* [Q2 has "Will Kemp," the name of the actor playing the role]   128 *grief* [Q1] griefes   129 *And . . . oppress* [Q1; Q2 omits]   135, 138 *Pretty* [Q1] Prates

V.i.11 s.d. *booted* [detail from Q1]   15 *fares my* [Q1] doth my Lady   24 *e'en* [Q1 "euen"] in   24 *defy* [Q1] denie   50 *And* An   76 *pay* [Q1] pray

V.iii.s.d. *with . . . water* [Q1; Q2 omits]   3 *yew* [Q1] young   21 s.d.
and Balthasar . . . iron [Q1; Q2 has "Enter Romeo and Peter," and
gives lines 40 and 43 to Peter instead of to Balthasar]   48 s.d.
Romeo . . . tomb [Q1; Q2 omits]   68 *conjurations* [Q1] commiration
71 *Page* [Q2 omits this speech prefix]   102 *fair* [Q2 follows with "I
will beleeue," presumably words that Shakespeare wrote, then re-
wrote in the next line, but neglected to delete]   108 *again. Here* [be-
tween these words Q2 has the following material, which Shakespeare
apparently neglected to delete: "come lye thou in my arme, / Heer's
to thy health, where ere thou tumblest in. / O true Appothecarie /
Thy drugs are quicke. Thus with a kisse I die. / Depart againe"]
137 *yew* yong   187 *too* too too   189 s.d. *Enter . . . wife* [Q2 places
after line 201, with "Enter Capels" at line 189]   190 *shrieked* [Q1]
shrike   199 *slaughtered* Slaughter   209 *more early* [Q1] now
earling

A NOTE ON THE SOURCE OF

Romeo and Juliet

The story of Romeo and Juliet was popular in Elizabethan times, and Shakespeare could have got his working outline of it from a number of places. Belleforest's *Histoires Tragiques* had a version, as did William Painter's *Palace of Pleasure;* and there had apparently been a play on the subject. Arthur Brooke, in an address "To the Reader" prefaced to his long narrative poem *The Tragicall Historye of Romeus and Juliet,* mentioned seeing "the same argument lately set foorth on stage"; but there is no evidence that Shakespeare worked from an older play or even that he consulted Belleforest or Painter, though he undoubtedly knew their works. All the evidence indicates that he worked directly from Brooke's poem, which Richard Tottell had printed in 1562 and Robert Robinson had reissued in 1587, shortly before the time that Shakespeare must have begun writing for the London stage.

Actually the story was popular, on the Continent at least, well before Elizabeth's time. Leaving out of account such obvious but distant analogues as the stories of Hero and Leander, Aeneas and Dido, Pyramus and Thisbe, and Troilus and Cressida, the first version of the story was one that appeared in Masuccio Salernitano's *Il Novellino* in 1476. This version had the clandestine lovers, the accommodating friar, the killing that led to the young man's banishment, the rival suitor, sleeping potion, thwarted messenger, and unhappy conclusion, but no suicides. It might have passed into oblivion had it not been for Luigi da Porto's *Istoria novellamente ritrovata di due Nobili*

Amanti (published *ca.* 1530), which laid the scene in Verona and identified the feuding families as Montecchi and Capelletti and the lovers as Romeo and Giulietta. Da Porto's story also named the friar Lorenzo and the slain man Thebaldo Capelletti and introduced the ball, the balcony scene, and the double suicide at the tomb. It was da Porto, moreover, who first named a minor character Marcuccio and gave him the icy hands that subsequent tellers of the tale regularly mentioned until Shakespeare discarded the detail and replaced it with a distinctive personality. Da Porto is also remembered for having Giulietta commit suicide by holding her breath—a detail which fortunately no one bothered to perpetuate.

Da Porto's tale was widely imitated both in Italy and in France, but the version of most importance to readers of Shakespeare was that of Matteo Bandello, who put the story into his *Novelle* (1554). Of all the versions before Shakespeare's, Bandello's is generally considered the best. It is a plain, straightforward narrative, unmarred by the sentimentality and moralizing that characterized the work of some of his adapters. In Bandello's story the masking appears; Peter is there (but as Romeo's servant), the Nurse has a significant part in the plot, and the rope ladder comes into play. Almost as important is the version of Pierre Boaistuau (1559), adapted from Bandello, which was included in Belleforest's *Histoires Tragiques*. Boaistuau made Romeo go to the ball in the hope of seeing his indifferent lady (the Rosaline of Shakespeare's play), worked out the business of the Capulets' restraint at discovering Romeo's presence, and developed the dilemma that Juliet finds herself in when she first hears of Tybalt's death; he also developed the character of the apothecary. All these things went into Painter's version (1567), which was a translation of Boaistuau, and into Brooke's, which was based on Boaistuau. The line of transmission from Masuccio to Shakespeare thus includes da Porto, Bandello, Boaistuau, and Brooke, in that order, with Painter standing unconsulted to one side. Shakespeare, however, used only Brooke directly and thus derived from the tradition only as much as Brooke passed on to him; but he borrowed freely from the great wealth of detail that Brooke himself had added.

Anyone interested in consulting Brooke's version for himself will find it in the first volume of Geoffrey Bullough's *Narrative and Dramatic Sources of Shakespeare* (London: Routledge and Kegan Paul, 1957). In spite of the tedious poulter's measure (iambic couplets in which the first line has twelve syllables and the second, fourteen) the poem is not entirely dull; and no other single source gave Shakespeare so much that was immediately useful. Readers should recognize at once the character and function of Benvolio (though Brooke neglected to give him a name), the Capulet that stormed at what he took to be his daughter's willful disobedience and threatened her with incarceration and endless misery, the garrulous, amoral Nurse and her conversations with the young lovers, and the needy apothecary. They will even find the clue to Mercutio's character (which Brooke did not develop) in the lines: "Even as a Lyon would emong the lambes be bolde,/ Such was emong the bashfull maydes, Mercutio to beholde." Numerous such hints, together with bits of business, suggestions for metaphors, and passages of dialogue, catch the eye as one scans Brooke's lines, not so much because they are arresting in themselves but because they call to mind the use Shakespeare has made of them. And if one gets safely past Brooke's "Address to the Reader," with its heavy-handed condemnation of lust, disobedience, and superstitious friars, one finds that Brooke too treated the lovers with sympathy and allowed his friar the best of intentions. In fact, Brooke, having discharged himself of his Protestant moralizing in the "Address," tended to make Fortune responsible for most things in the story; and Shakespeare, as we know, took Brooke's Fortune along with all the rest.

What Shakespeare did with Brooke's clean but relatively inert story was to add complication and focus, intensify it by drastic compression, and establish the intricate relationship of part to part in a texture of language that functions admirably as dialogue even as it creates the unity of a dramatic poem. In this transformation he made it possible for us to tolerate the Nurse, love Capulet, and pity the apothecary. He relieved the Friar of the tedium that Brooke had encumbered him with, and he changed Escalus into a man who genuinely suffers and commands sympathy. In bringing Tybalt to the ball and making him the discoverer of Romeo's presence there, he gave real point to the disastrous street fight in Act III; he also enlarged Paris' part in the story and ennobled his character, and he created Mercutio. More important, he made all three of these serve as foils to a Romeo who develops and matures in response to the challenges they present and who, before the end, has ironically become responsible for the deaths of all three. Shakespeare's real miracle, however, was Juliet, transformed from an adolescent arrogantly eager to outdo her elders to an appealing child-woman, barely fourteen, who learns to mix courage with her innocence, yet falls victim to a world that only briefly and unintentionally but fatally treats her as a plaything.

Commentaries

SAMUEL JOHNSON

from *The Plays of William Shakespeare*

This play is one of the most pleasing of our author's performances. The scenes are busy and various, the incidents numerous and important, the catastrophe irresistibly affecting, and the process of the action carried on with such probability, at least with such congruity to popular opinions, as tragedy requires.

Here is one of the few attempts of Shakespeare to exhibit the conversation of gentlemen, to represent the airy sprightliness of juvenile elegance. Mr. Dryden mentions a tradition, which might easily reach his time, of a declaration made by Shakespeare, that "he was obliged to kill Mercutio in the third act, lest he should have been killed by him." Yet he thinks him "no such formidable person, but that he might have lived through the play, and died in his bed," without danger to the poet. Dryden well knew, had he been in quest of truth, that, in a pointed sentence, more regard is commonly had to the words than the thought, and that it is very seldom to be rigorously understood. Mercutio's wit, gaiety, and courage, will always procure him friends that wish him a longer life; but his

From *The Works of Samuel Johnson, LL.D.* 9 vols. Oxford, 1825. This selection first appeared in *The Plays of William Shakespeare* (London, 1765).

death is not precipitated, he has lived out the time allotted him in the construction of the play; nor do I doubt the ability of Shakespeare to have continued his existence, though some of his sallies are, perhaps, out of the reach of Dryden; whose genius was not very fertile of merriment, nor ductile to humor, but acute, argumentative, comprehensive, and sublime.

The nurse is one of the characters in which the author delighted; he has, with great subtlety of distinction, drawn her at once loquacious and secret, obsequious and insolent, trusty and dishonest.

His comic scenes are happily wrought, but his pathetic strains are always polluted with some unexpected depravations. His persons, however distressed, have a conceit left them in their misery, a miserable conceit.

[1765]

SAMUEL TAYLOR COLERIDGE

from *The Lectures of 1811–1812, Lecture VII*

In a former lecture I endeavored to point out the union of the poet and the philosopher, or rather the warm embrace between them, in the *Venus and Adonis* and *Lucrece* of Shakespeare. From thence I passed on to *Love's Labor's Lost,* as the link between his character as a poet, and his art as a dramatist; and I showed that, although in that work the former was still predominant, yet that the germs of his subsequent dramatic power were easily discernible.

I will now, as I promised in my last, proceed to *Romeo and Juliet,* not because it is the earliest, or among the earliest of Shakespeare's works of that kind, but because in it are to be found specimens, in degree, of all the excellences which he afterwards displayed in his more perfect dramas, but differing. from them in being less forcibly evidenced, and less happily combined: all the parts are more or less present, but they are not united with the same harmony.

There are, however, in *Romeo and Juliet* passages where the poet's whole excellence is evinced, so that nothing superior to them can be met with in the productions of his after years. The main distinction between this play and others is, as I said, that the parts are less happily combined, or to borrow a phrase from the painter, the whole work is less in keeping. Grand portions are produced: we

From *Shakespearean Criticism* by Samuel Taylor Coleridge. 2nd ed., ed. Thomas Middleton Raysor. 2 vols. New York: E. P. Dutton and Company, Inc., 1960; London: J. M. Dent & Sons, Ltd., 1961. The exact text of Coleridge's lecture does not exist; what is given here is the transcript of a shorthand report taken by an auditor, J. P. Collier.

have limbs of giant growth; but the production, as a whole, in which each part gives delight for itself, and the whole, consisting of these delightful parts, communicates the highest intellectual pleasure and satisfaction, is the result of the application of judgment and taste. These are not to be attained but by painful study, and to the sacrifice of the stronger pleasures derived from the dazzling light which a man of genius throws over every circumstance, and where we are chiefly struck by vivid and distinct images. Taste is an attainment after a poet has been disciplined by experience and has added to genius that talent by which he knows what part of his genius he can make acceptable, and intelligible to the portion of mankind for which he writes.

In my mind it would be a hopeless symptom, as regards genius, if I found a young man with anything like perfect taste. In the earlier works of Shakespeare we have a profusion of double epithets, and sometimes even the coarsest terms are employed, if they convey a more vivid image; but by degrees the associations are connected with the image they are designed to impress, and the poet descends from the ideal into the real world so far as to conjoin both—to give a sphere of active operations to the ideal, and to elevate and refine the real.

In *Romeo and Juliet* the principal characters may be divided into two classes: in one class passion—the passion of love—is drawn and drawn truly, as well as beautifully; but the persons are not individualized farther than as the actor appears on the stage. It is a very just description and development of love, without giving, if I may so express myself, the philosophical history of it—without showing how the man became acted upon by that particular passion, but leading it through all the incidents of the drama and rendering it predominant.

Tybalt is, in himself, a commonplace personage. And here allow me to remark upon a great distinction between Shakespeare and all who have written in imitation of him. I know no character in his plays, (unless indeed Pistol be an exception) which can be called the mere portrait of an individual: while the reader feels all the satisfaction arising from individuality, yet that very individual is a sort of class character, and this circumstance renders Shakespeare the poet of all ages.

Tybalt is a man abandoned to his passions—with all the pride of family, only because he thought it belonged to him as a member of that family, and valuing himself highly, simply because he does not care for death. This indifference to death is perhaps more common than any other feeling: men are apt to flatter themselves extravagantly, merely because they possess a quality which it is a disgrace not to have, but which a wise man never puts forward, but when it is necessary.

Jeremy Taylor in one part of his voluminous works, speaking of a great man, says that he was naturally a coward, as indeed most men are, knowing the value of life, but the power of his reason enabled him, when required, to conduct himself with uniform courage and hardihood. The good bishop, perhaps, had in his mind a story, told by one of the ancients, of a Philosopher and a Coxcomb, on board the same ship during a storm: the Coxcomb reviled the Philosopher for betraying marks of fear: "Why are you so frightened? I am not afraid of being drowned: I do not care a farthing for my life."— "You are perfectly right," said the Philosopher, "for your life is not worth a farthing."

Shakespeare never takes pains to make his characters win your esteem, but leaves it to the general command of the passions and to poetic justice. It is most beautiful to observe, in *Romeo and Juliet,* that the characters principally engaged in the incidents are preserved innocent from all that could lower them in our opinion, while the rest of the personages, deserving little interest in themselves, derive it from being instrumental in those situations in which the more important personages develop their thoughts and passions.

Look at Capulet—a worthy, noble-minded old man of high rank, with all the impatience that is likely to accompany it. It is delightful to see all the sensibilities of our nature so exquisitely called forth; as if the poet had the hundred arms of the polypus, and had thrown them out

in all directions to catch the predominant feeling. We may
see in Capulet the manner in which anger seizes hold of
everything that comes in its way, in order to express itself,
as in the lines where he reproves Tybalt for his fierceness
of behavior, which led him to wish to insult a Montague,
and disturb the merriment.

> Go to, go to;
> You are a saucy boy. Is't so, indeed?
> This trick may chance to scath you;—I know what.
> You must contrary me! marry, 'tis time.—
> Well said, my hearts!—You are a princox: go:
> Be quiet or—More light, more light!—For shame!
> I'll make you quiet.—What! cheerly, my hearts!
>
> (I.v.84–90)

The line

> This trick may chance to scath you;—I know what,

was an allusion to the legacy Tybalt might expect; and
then, seeing the lights burn dimly, Capulet turns his anger
against the servants. Thus we see that no one passion is
so predominant, but that it includes all the parts of the
character, and the reader never has a mere abstract of a
passion, as of wrath or ambition, but the whole man is
presented to him—the one predominant passion acting, if
I may so say, as the leader of the band to the rest.

It could not be expected that the poet should introduce
such a character as Hamlet into every play; but even in
those personages, which are subordinate to a hero so
eminently philosophical, the passion is at least rendered
instructive, and induces the reader to look with a keener
eye and a finer judgment into human nature.

Shakespeare has this advantage over all other dramatists
—that he has availed himself of his psychological genius
to develop all the minutiae of the human heart: showing
us the thing that, to common observers, he seems solely
intent upon, he makes visible what we should not otherwise have seen: just as, after looking at distant objects
through a telescope, when we behold them subsequently

with the naked eye, we see them with greater distinctness, and in more detail, than we should otherwise have done.

Mercutio is one of our poet's truly Shakespearean characters; for throughout his plays, but especially in those of the highest order, it is plain that the personages were drawn rather from meditation than from observation, or to speak correctly, more from observation, the child of meditation. It is comparatively easy for a man to go about the world, as if with a pocketbook in his hand, carefully noting down what he sees and hears: by practice he acquires considerable facility in representing what he has observed, himself frequently unconscious of its worth or its bearings. This is entirely different from the observation of a mind, which, having formed a theory and a system upon its own nature, remarks all things that are examples of its truth, confirming it in that truth and, above all, enabling it to convey the truths of philosophy, as mere effects derived from, what we may call, the outward watchings of life.

Hence it is that Shakespeare's favorite characters are full of such lively intellect. Mercutio is a man possessing all the elements of a poet: the whole world was, as it were, subject to his law of association. Whenever he wishes to impress anything, all things become his servants for the purpose: all things tell the same tale, and sound in unison. This faculty, moreover, is combined with the manners and feelings of a perfect gentleman, himself utterly unconscious of his powers. By his loss it was contrived that the whole catastrophe of the tragedy should be brought about: it endears him to Romeo and gives to the death of Mercutio an importance which it could not otherwise have acquired.

I say this in answer to an observation, I think by Dryden (to which indeed Dr. Johnson has fully replied), that Shakespeare having carried the part of Mercutio as far as he could, till his genius was exhausted, had killed him in the third act, to get him out of the way. What shallow nonsense! As I have remarked, upon the death of Mercutio the whole catastrophe depends; it is produced by it. The scene in which it occurs serves to show how indifference to any subject but one, and aversion to activity on the part of

Romeo, may be overcome and roused to the most resolute and determined conduct. Had not Mercutio been rendered so amiable and so interesting, we could not have felt so strongly the necessity for Romeo's interference, connecting it immediately, and passionately, with the future fortunes of the lover and his mistress.

But what am I to say of the Nurse? We have been told that her character is the mere fruit of observation—that it is like Swift's "Polite Conversation," certainly the most stupendous work of human memory, and of unceasingly active attention to what passes around us, upon record. The Nurse in *Romeo and Juliet* has sometimes been compared to a portrait by Gerard Dow, in which every hair was so exquisitely painted, that it would bear the test of the microscope. Now, I appeal confidently to my hearers whether the closest observation of the manners of one or two old nurses would have enabled Shakespeare to draw this character of admirable generalization? Surely not. Let any man conjure up in his mind all the qualities and peculiarities that can possibly belong to a nurse, and he will find them in Shakespeare's picture of the old woman: nothing is omitted. This effect is not produced by mere observation. The great prerogative of genius (and Shakespeare felt and availed himself of it) is now to swell itself to the dignity of a god, and now to subdue and keep dormant some part of that lofty nature, and to descend even to the lowest character—to become everything, in fact, but the vicious.

Thus, in the Nurse you have all the garrulity of old age, and all its fondness; for the affection of old age is one of the greatest consolations of humanity. I have often thought what a melancholy world this would be without children, and what an inhuman world without the aged.

You have also in the Nurse the arrogance of ignorance, with the pride of meanness at being connected with a great family. You have the grossness, too, which that situation never removes, though it sometimes suspends it; and, arising from that grossness, the little low vices attendant upon it, which, indeed, in such minds are scarcely vices.— Romeo at one time was the most delightful and excellent young man, and the Nurse all willingness to assist him; but her disposition soon turns in favor of Paris, for whom she professes precisely the same admiration. How wonderfully are these low peculiarities contrasted with a young and pure mind, educated under different circumstances!

Another point ought to be mentioned as characteristic of the ignorance of the Nurse: it is, that in all her recollections, she assists herself by the remembrance of visual circumstances. The great difference, in this respect, between the cultivated and the uncultivated mind is this—that the cultivated mind will be found to recall the past by certain regular trains of cause and effect; whereas, with the uncultivated mind, the past is recalled wholly by coincident images or facts which happened at the same time. This position is fully exemplified in the following passages put into the mouth of the Nurse:

> Even or odd, of all days in the year,
> Come Lammas eve at night shall she be fourteen.
> Susan and she—God rest all Christian souls!—
> Were of an age.—Well, Susan is with God;
> She was too good for me. But, as I said,
> On Lammas eve at night shall she be fourteen;
> That shall she, marry: I remember it well.
> 'Tis since the earthquake now eleven years;
> And she was wean'd,—I never shall forget it,—
> Of all the days of the year, upon that day;
> For I had then laid wormwood to my dug,
> Sitting in the sun under the dove-house wall:
> My lord and you were then at Mantua.—
> Nay, I do bear a brain:—but, as I said,
> When it did taste the wormwood on the nipple
> Of my dug, and felt it bitter, pretty fool,
> To see it tetchy, and fall out with the dug!
> Shake, quoth the dove-house: 'twas no need, I trow,
> To bid me trudge.
> And since that time it is eleven years;
> For then she could stand alone.
>
> (I.iii.16–36)

She afterwards goes on with similar visual impressions,

so true to the character. More is here brought into one portrait than could have been ascertained by one man's mere observation, and without the introduction of a single incongruous point. . . .

Another remark I may make upon *Romeo and Juliet* is, that in this tragedy the poet is not, as I have hinted, entirely blended with the dramatist—at least, not in the degree to be afterwards noticed in *Lear, Hamlet, Othello,* or *Macbeth.* Capulet and Montague not unfrequently talk a language only belonging to the poet, and not so characteristic of, and peculiar to, the passions of persons in the situations in which they are placed—a mistake, or rather an indistinctness, which many of our later dramatists have carried through the whole of their productions.

When I read the song of Deborah, I never think that she is a poet, although I think the song itself a sublime poem: it is as simple a dithyrambic production as exists in any language; but it is the proper and characteristic effusion of a woman highly elevated by triumph, by the natural hatred of oppressors, and resulting from a bitter sense of wrong: it is a song of exultation on deliverance from these evils, a deliverance accomplished by herself. When she exclaims, "The inhabitants of the villages ceased, they ceased in Israel, until that I, Deborah, arose, that I arose a mother in Israel," it is poetry in the highest sense: we have no reason, however, to suppose that if she had not been agitated by passion, and animated by victory, she would have been able so to express herself; or that if she had been placed in different circumstances, she would have used such language of truth and passion. We are to remember that Shakespeare, not placed under circumstances of excitement, and only wrought upon by his own vivid and vigorous imagination, writes a language that invariably, and intuitively becomes the condition and position of each character.

On the other hand, there is a language not descriptive of passion, not uttered under the influence of it, which is at the same time poetic, and shows a high and active fancy, as when Capulet says to Paris,

Such comfort as do lusty young men feel,
When well-apparell'd April on the heel
Of limping winter treads, even such delight
Among fresh female buds, shall you this night
Inherit at my house.

(I.ii.26–30)

Here the poet may be said to speak, rather than the dramatist; and it would be easy to adduce other passages from this play, where Shakespeare, for a moment forgetting the character, utters his own words in his own person.

In my mind, what have often been censured as Shakespeare's conceits are completely justifiable, as belonging to the state, age, or feeling of the individual. Sometimes, when they cannot be vindicated on these grounds, they may well be excused by the taste of his own and of the preceding age; as for instance, in Romeo's speech,

Here's much to do with hate, but more with love:—
Why then, O brawling love! O loving hate!
O anything, of nothing first created!
O heavy lightness! serious vanity!
Misshapen chaos of well-seeming forms!
Feather of lead, bright smoke, cold fire, sick health!
Still-waking sleep, that is not what it is!

(I.i.178–84)

I dare not pronounce such passages as these to be absolutely unnatural, not merely because I consider the author a much better judge than I can be, but because I can understand and allow for an effort of the mind, when it would describe what it cannot satisfy itself with the description of, to reconcile opposites and qualify contradictions, leaving a middle state of mind more strictly appropriate to the imagination than any other, when it is, as it were, hovering between images. As soon as it is fixed on one image, it becomes understanding; but while it is unfixed and wavering between them, attaching itself permanently to none, it is imagination. . . .

It remains for me to speak of the hero and heroine, of

Romeo and Juliet themselves; and I shall do so with unaffected diffidence, not merely on account of the delicacy,
but of the great importance of the subject. I feel that it is
impossible to defend Shakespeare from the most cruel of
all charges—that he is an immoral writer—without enter-
ing fully into his mode of portraying female characters,
and of displaying the passion of love. It seems to me that
he has done both with greater perfection than any other
writer of the known world, perhaps with the single exception of Milton in his delineation of Eve. . . .

Shakespeare has described this passion in various states
and stages, beginning, as was most natural, with love in
the young. Does he open his play by making Romeo and
Juliet in love at first sight—at the first glimpse, as any
ordinary thinker would do? Certainly not: he knew what
he was about, and how he was to accomplish what he was
about: he was to develop the whole passion, and he
commences with the first elements—that sense of imperfection, that yearning to combine itself with something
lovely. Romeo became enamored of the idea he had
formed in his own mind, and then, as it were, christened
the first real being of the contrary sex as endowed with the
perfections he desired. He appears to be in love with
Rosaline; but, in truth, he is in love only with his own
idea. He felt that necessity of being beloved which no
noble mind can be without. Then our poet, our poet who
so well knew human nature, introduces Romeo to Juliet,
and makes it not only a violent, but a permanent love—
a point for which Shakespeare has been ridiculed by the
ignorant and unthinking. Romeo is first represented in a
state most susceptible of love, and then, seeing Juliet, he
took and retained the infection.

This brings me to observe upon a characteristic of
Shakespeare, which belongs to a man of profound thought
and high genius. It has been too much the custom, when
anything that happened in his dramas could not easily be
explained by the few words the poet has employed, to pass
it idly over, and to say that it is beyond our reach, and
beyond the power of philosophy—a sort of terra incognita
for discoverers—a great ocean to be hereafter explored.

Others have treated such passages as hints and glimpses of something now nonexistent, as the sacred fragments of an ancient and ruined temple, all the portions of which are beautiful, although their particular relation to each other is unknown. Shakespeare knew the human mind, and its most minute and intimate workings, and he never introduces a word, or a thought, in vain or out of place: if we do not understand him, it is our own fault or the fault of copyists and typographers; but study, and the possession of some small stock of the knowledge by which he worked, will enable us often to detect and explain his meaning. He never wrote at random, or hit upon points of character and conduct by chance; and the smallest fragment of his mind not unfrequently gives a clue to a most perfect, regular, and consistent whole.

As I may not have another opportunity, the introduction of Friar Lawrence into this tragedy enables me to remark upon the different manner in which Shakespeare has treated the priestly character, as compared with other writers. In Beaumont and Fletcher priests are represented as a vulgar mockery; and, as in others of their dramatic personages, the errors of a few are mistaken for the demeanor of the many: but in Shakespeare they always carry with them our love and respect. He made no injurious abstracts: he took no copies from the worst parts of our nature; and, like the rest, his characters of priests are truly drawn from the general body.

H. B. CHARLTON

from *Shakespearian Tragedy*

In their general structure and idea, the three tragedies so far reviewed were in the current dramatic tradition of their day. But *Romeo and Juliet* is a departure, a comprehensive experiment. It links the English stage to the Renaissance tragedy which by precept and by practice Cinthio[1] in the middle of the sixteenth century had established in Italy.

Cinthio's principles were in the main an adaptation of Seneca's, or rather of what he took to be Seneca's purposes, to the immediate needs of Cinthio's contemporary theatre. His own object he declared to be *"servire l'età, a gli spettatori."* Tragedy must grip its audience. It must therefore reflect a range of experience and base itself on a system of values which are felt by its audience to be real. Many of his proposals are the direct outcome of this general principle, and one or two of them are especially pertinent to our argument. For instance, tragedy must no longer rely mainly for its material on ancient mythology nor on accredited history; for these depict a world which may have lost urgent contact with a modern audience's sense of life. The best plots for modern tragedy will be

---

[1] See H. B. Charlton, *Senecan Tradition in Renaissance Tragedy,* first published in 1921 as an introduction to *The Poetical Works of Sir William Alexander* (Manchester University Press and Scottish Texts Society) and reissued separately by the Manchester University Press in 1946.

From *Shakespearian Tragedy* by H. B. Charlton. London and New York: Cambridge University Press, 1948. Reprinted by permission of Cambridge University Press.

found in modern fiction. For modern fiction is the mythology of today. It is the corpus of story through which the world appears as it seems to be to living men; it mirrors accepted codes of conduct, displays the particular manner of contemporary consciousness, and adopts the current assumptions of human values. Let the dramatist, therefore, draw his plots from the novelists. An inevitable consequence followed from this. There is nothing in which the outlook on life adopted by the modern world is more different from that of the ancient classical world than in its apprehension of the human and spiritual significance of the love of man for woman. Love had become for the modern world its most engrossing interest and often its supreme experience. Modern fiction turns almost exclusively on love. So when dramatists took their tales from the novelists, they took love over as the main theme of their plays. Seven of Cinthio's nine plays borrow their plots from novels (most of them from his own series, the *Hecatommithi*); the other two are "classical," but are two of the great classical love stories, *Dido* and *Cleopatra*. Jason de Nores, a much more conservatively Aristotelian expositor than his contemporary Cinthio, to exemplify the form which the most perfect tragedy could take, constructs the plot for it from one of Boccaccio's tales.

Whether by direct influence or by mere force of circumstance, Cinthio's practice prevailed. Sixteeth-century tragedy found rich material in the novels. But the traditionalists were perpetually reminding the innovators that tragedy always had had and always must have an historical hero. *"In tragoedia reges, principes, ex urbibus, arcibus, castris,"* Scaliger, the Parnassian legislator, announced. No one would accept a hero as great unless his memory were preserved in the historian's pages. *"C'est l'histoire qui persuade avec empire,"* as Corneille put it. Shakespeare, an eager and humble apprentice, naturally followed traditional custom. *Titus Andronicus, Richard III,* and *Richard II* belong in the main to the conventional pattern. They deal with historical material. Their heroes are of high rank and potent in determining the destiny of nations. The plot is never mainly a lovers' story, though a love intrigue intrudes sporadically here and there within the major theme. But somehow the prescriptions had not produced the expected result. There was something unsatisfying in these plays as divinations of man's tragic lot. And so the conventions were jettisoned in *Romeo and Juliet*.

Shakespeare was casting in fresh directions to find the universality, the momentousness, and above all the inevitability of all-compelling tragedy. In particular, he was experimenting with a new propelling force, a new final sanction as the determinant energy, the *ultima ratio* of tragedy's inner world; and though *Romeo and Juliet* is set in a modern Christian country, with church and priest and full ecclesiastical institution, the whole universe of God's justice, vengeance, and providence is discarded and rejected from the directing forces of the play's dramatic movement. In its place, there is a theatrical resuscitation of the half-barbarian, half-Roman deities of Fate and Fortune.

The plot of *Romeo and Juliet* is pure fiction. Shakespeare took it from Arthur Broke's poem, *The Tragicall Historie of Romeus and Juliet* (1562). Shakespeare knew from Broke's title page that the tale was taken from an Italian novelist, "written first in Italian by Bandell." He knew, too, what sort of novels Bandello wrote, for Painter had retold them in his *Palace of Pleasure* (1567). They were clear fictions. Moreover the hero and the heroine, Romeo and Juliet, had none of the pomp of historic circumstance about them; they were socially of the minor aristocracy who were to stock Shakespeare's comedies, and their only political significance was an adventitious role in the civic disturbance of a small city-state. Romeo and Juliet were in effect just a boy and a girl in a novel; and as such they had no claim to the world's attention except through their passion and their fate.

To choose such folk as these for tragic heroes was aesthetically well-nigh an anarchist's gesture; and the dramatist provided a sort of program-prologue to prompt the audience to see the play from the right point of view. In this playbill the dramatist draws special attention to two features of his story. First, Verona was being torn by

a terrible, bloodthirsty feud which no human endeavor
had been able to settle; this was the direct cause of the
death of the lovers, and but for those deaths it never would
have been healed. Second, the course of the young lovers'
lives is from the outset governed by a malignant destiny;
fatal, star-crossed, death-marked, they are doomed to
piteous destruction.

The intent of this emphasis is clear. The tale will end
with the death of two ravishingly attractive young folk;
and the dramatist must exonerate himself from all complicity in their murder, lest he be found guilty of pandering
to a liking for a human shambles. He disowns responsibility and throws it on Destiny, Fate. The device is well
warranted in the tragic tradition, and especially in its
Senecan models. But whether, in fact, it succeeds is a
matter for further consideration. The invocation of Fate
is strengthened by the second feature scored heavily in
the prologue, the feud. The feud is, so to speak, the means
by which Fate acts. The feud is to provide the sense of
immediate, and Fate that of ultimate, inevitability. For it
may happen that, however the dramatist deploys his
imaginative suggestions, he may fail to summon up a Fate
sufficiently compelling to force itself upon the audience as
unquestioned shaper of the tragic end. In such circumstance Romeo's and Juliet's death would be by mere
chance, a gratuitous intervention by a dramatist exercising
his homicidal proclivities for the joy of his audience. Hence
the feud has a further function. It will be the dramatist's
last plea for exculpation or for mercy; and it will allow
his audience to absolve him or to forgive him without loss
of its own "philanthropy"; for through death came the
healing of the feud, and with it, the removal of the threat
to so many other lives.

It becomes, therefore, of critical importance to watch
Shakespeare's handling of these two motives, Fate and
Feud, to see how he fits them to fulfill their function, and
to ask how far in fact they are adequate to the role they
must perforce play. Both Fate and Feud, although absent
as motives from the earliest European form of the Romeo
and Juliet story, had grown variously in the successive

tellings of the tale before it came to Broke.[2] The general trend had been to magnify the virulence of the feud, and, even more notably, to swell the sententious apostrophizing of Fate's malignity. Broke, for instance, misses no opportunity for such sententiousness. Longer or shorter, there are at least fifteen passages in his poem where the malignity of Fate is his conventionally poetic theme. "Froward fortune," "fortune's cruel will," "wavering fortune," "tickel fortune," "when fortune list to strike," "false fortune cast for her, poore wretch, a myschiefe newe to brewe," "dame fortune did assent," "with piteous plaint, fierce fortune doth he blame," "till Attropos shall cut my fatall thread of lyfe," "though cruel fortune be so much my dedly foe," "the blyndfyld goddesse that with frowning face doth fraye, and from theyr seate the mighty kinges throwes downe with hedlong sway," "He cryed out, with open mouth, against the starres above, The fatall sisters three, he said, had done him wrong"—so, again and again, does Broke bring in

> The diversenes, and eke the accidents so straunge,
> Of frayle unconstant Fortune, that delyteth still in chaunge.[3]

Romeo cries aloud

> Against the restles starres, in rolling skyes that raunge,
> Against the fatall sisters three, and Fortune full of chaunge.[4]

There are more elaborate set speeches on the same theme:

> For Fortune chaungeth more, than fickel fantasie;
> In nothing Fortune constant is, save in unconstancie.
> Her hasty ronning wheele, is of a restles coorse,
> That turnes the clymers hedlong downe, from better to the
>　　woorse,

[2] For differences between the many pre-Shakespearian versions, see H. B. Charlton, *Romeo and Juliet as an Experimental Tragedy* (British Academy Shakespeare Lecture, 1939) and "France as Chaperone of Romeo and Juliet" in *Studies in French presented to M. K. Pope*, Manchester University Press (1939).

[3] Broke, *Romeus and Juliet* (Hazlitt's Shakespeare's Library, Vol. I, 1875), p. 142.

[4] *Ibid.*, p. 151.

And those that are beneth, she heaveth up agayne.[5]

So when Shakespeare took up the story, Broke had already sought to drench it in fatality. But since Shakespeare was a dramatist, he could not handle Fate and Feud as could a narrative poet. His feud will enter, not descriptively, but as action; and for fate he must depend on the sentiments of his characters and on an atmosphere generated by the sweep of the action. The feud may be deferred for a moment to watch Shakespeare's handling of Fate.

His most frequent device is to adapt what Broke's practice had been; instead of letting his persons declaim formally, as Broke's do, against the inconstancy of Fortune, he endows them with dramatic premonitions. Setting out for Capulet's ball, Romeo is suddenly sad:

> my mind misgives
> Some consequence, yet hanging in the stars,
> Shall bitterly begin his fearful date
> With this night's revels; and expire the term
> Of a despised life, clos'd in my breast,
> By some vile forfeit of untimely death:
> But he that hath the steerage of my course
> Direct my sail!
>
> (I.iv.106–13)

As the lovers first declare their passion, Juliet begs Romeo not to swear, as if an oath might be an evil omen:

> I have no joy of this contract tonight:
> It is too rash, too unadvised, too sudden;
> Too like the lightning, which doth cease to be
> Ere one can say "It lightens."
>
> (II.ii.117–20)

Romeo, involved in the fatal fight, cries "O, I am fortune's fool!" (III. i. 138). Looking down from her window at Romeo as he goes into exile, Juliet murmurs

---

[5] *Ibid.,* p. 147. See also pp. 97, 115.

> O God, I have an ill-divining soul!
> Methinks I see thee, now thou art below,
> As one dead in the bottom of a tomb.
>
> (III.v.54–56)

With dramatic irony Juliet implores her parents to defer her marriage with Paris:

> Or, if you do not, make the bridal bed
> In that dim monument where Tybalt lies.
>
> (III.v.202–03)

Besides these promptings of impending doom there are premonitions of a less direct kind. The friar fears the violence of the lover's passion:

> These violent delights have violent ends
> And in their triumph die, like fire and powder,
> Which as they kiss consume.
>
> (II.vi.9–11)

Another source of omen in the play is the presaging of dreams; for from the beginning of time, "the world of sleep, the realm of wild reality" has brought dreams which look like heralds of eternity and speak like Sybils of the future. There is much dreaming in *Romeo and Juliet*. Mercutio may mock at dreams as children of an idle brain, begot of nothing but vain fantasy. But when Romeo says he "dream'd a dream tonight," Mercutio's famous flight of fancy recalls the universal belief in dreams as foreshadowings of the future. Again Romeo dreams; this time, "I dreamt my lady came and found me dead." (V. i. 6). As his man Balthasar waits outside Juliet's tomb, he dreams that his master and another are fighting and the audience knows how accurately the dream mirrors the true facts.

But Shakespeare not only hangs omens thickly round his play. He gives to the action itself a quality apt to conjure the sense of relentless doom. It springs mainly from his compression of the time over which the story stretches. In all earlier versions there is a much longer lapse. Romeo's wooing is prolonged over weeks before the secret wedding; then, after the wedding, there is an interval of three or four months before the slaying of Tybalt; and Romeo's exile lasts from Easter until a short time before mid-September when the marriage with Paris was at first planned to take place. But in Shakespeare all this is pressed into three or four days. The world seems for a moment to be caught up in the fierce play of furies reveling in some mad supernatural game.

But before asking whether the sense of an all-controlling Fate is made strong enough to fulfill its tragic purpose let us turn to the feud. Here Shakespeare's difficulties are even greater. Italian novelists of the quattro- or cinquecento, throwing their story back through two or three generations, might expect their readers easily to accept a fierce vendetta. But the Verona which Shakespeare depicts is a highly civilized world, with an intellectual and artistic culture and an implied social attainment altogether alien from the sort of society in which a feud is a more or less natural manifestation of enmity. The border country of civilization is the home of feuds, a region where social organization is still of the clan, where the head of the family-clan is a strong despot, and where law has not progressed beyond the sort of wild justice of which one instrument is the feud.

> For ere I cross the border fells,
> The tane of us shall die

It was well-nigh impossible for Shakespeare to fit the blood lust of a border feud into the social setting of his Verona. The heads of the rival houses are not at all the fierce chieftains who rule with ruthless despotism. When old Capulet, in fireside gown, bustles to the scene of the fray and calls for his sword, his wife tells him bluntly that it is a crutch which an old man such as he should want, and not a weapon. Montague, too, spits a little verbal fire, but his wife plucks him by the arm and tells him to calm down: "thou shalt not stir one foot to seek a foe." Indeed, these old men are almost comic figures, and especially

Capulet. His querulous fussiness, his casual bonhomie, his almost senile humor, and his childish irascibility hardly make him the pattern of a clan chieftain. Even his domestics put him in his place:

> Go, you cotquean, go,
> Get you to bed; faith, you'll be sick tomorrow
> For this night's watching,
>
> (IV.iv.6–8)

the Nurse tells him; and the picture is filled in by his wife's reminder that she has put a stop to his "mouse-hunting." There is of course the prince's word that

> Three civil brawls, bred of an airy word,
> By thee, old Capulet, and Montague,
> Have thrice disturb'd the quiet of our streets.
>
> (I.i.92–94)

But these brawls bred of an airy word are no manifestations of a really ungovernable feud. When Montague and Capulet are bound by the prince to keep the peace, old Capulet himself says

> 'tis not hard, I think,
> For men so old as we to keep the peace.
>
> (I.ii.2–3)

and there is a general feeling that the old quarrel has run its course. Paris, suitor to Juliet, says it is a pity that the Capulets and the Montagues have lived at odds so long. And Benvolio, a relative of the Montagues, is a consistent peacemaker. He tries to suppress a brawl amongst the rival retainers and invites Tybalt, a Capulet, to assist him in the work. Later he begs his friends to avoid trouble by keeping out of the way of the Capulets, for it is the season of hot blood:

> I pray thee, good Mercutio, let's retire:
> The day is hot, the Capulets abroad,
> And if we meet, we shall not scape a brawl;

For now, these hot days, is the mad blood stirring.

(III.i.1–4)

When the hot-blooded Mercutio does incite Tybalt to a quarrel it is again Benvolio who tries to preserve the peace:

> We talk here in the public haunt of men:
> Either withdraw unto some private place,
> And reason coldly of your grievances,
> Or else depart.

(III.i.51–54)

Hence the jest of Mercutio's famous description of Benvolio as an inveterate quarreler, thirsting for the slightest excuse to draw sword.

Moreover, the rival houses have mutual friends. Mercutio, Montague Romeo's close acquaintance, is an invited guest at the Capulets' ball. Stranger still, so is Romeo's cruel lady, Rosaline, who in the invitation is addressed as Capulet's cousin. It is odd that Romeo's love for her, since she was a Capulet, had given him no qualms on the score of the feud. When Romeo is persuaded to go gate-crashing to the ball because Rosaline will be there, there is no talk at all of its being a hazardous undertaking. Safety will require, if even so much, no more than a mask.[6] On the way to the ball, as talk is running gaily, there is still no mention of danger involved. Indeed, the feud is almost a dead letter so far. The son of the Montague does not know what the Capulet daughter looks like, nor she what he is like. The traditional hatred survives only in one or two high-spirited, hot-blooded scions on either side, and in the kitchen folk. Tybalt alone resents Romeo's presence at the ball, yet it is easy for all to recognize him; and because Tybalt feels Romeo's coming to be an

6 In the earlier versions the mask is not a precaution for safety. Shakespeare, taking it partly as such, has to realize how utterly ineffective it is. Romeo is soon known:

> This, by his voice, should be a Montague!
> Fetch me my rapier, boy. What dares the slave
> Come hither, cover'd with an antic face,
> To fleer and scorn at our solemnity?   (I. v. 56–59)

insult, he seeks him out next day to challenge him, so
providing the immediate occasion of the new outburst.
Naturally, once blood is roused again, and murder done,
the ancient rancor springs up with new life. Even Lady
Capulet has comically Machiavellian plans for having
Romeo poisoned in Mantua. But prior to this the evidences
of the feud are so unsubstantial that the forebodings of
Romeo and Juliet, discovering each other's name, seem
prompted more by fate than feud. There will, of course,
be family difficulties; but the friar marries them without a
hesitating qualm, feeling that such a union is bound to be
accepted eventually by the parents, who will thus be
brought to amity.

The most remarkable episode, however, is still to be
named. When Tybalt discovers Romeo at the ball, in-
furiated he rushes to Capulet with the news. But Capulet,
in his festive mood, is pleasantly interested, saying that
Romeo is reputed to be good-looking and quite a pleasant
boy. He tells Tybalt to calm himself, to remember his
manners, and to treat Romeo properly:

> Content thee, gentle coz, let him alone;
> He bears him like a portly gentleman;
> And, to say truth, Verona brags of him
> To be a virtuous and well govern'd youth:
> I would not for the wealth of all the town
> Here in my house do him disparagement:
> Therefore be patient, take no note of him:
> It is my will, the which if thou respect,
> Show a fair presence and put off these frowns,
> An ill-beseeming semblance for a feast.
>
> (I.v.67–76)

When Tybalt is reluctant, old Capulet is annoyed and
testily tells him to stop being a saucy youngster:

> He shall be endured:
> What, goodman boy! I say, he shall: go to.
> Am I the master here or you? Go to.
> You'll not endure him! God shall mend my soul!
> You'll make a mutiny among my guests

You will set cock-a-hoop. You'll be the man!
   . . . Go to, go to;
You are a saucy boy: is't so indeed?
This trick may chance to scathe you, I know what:
You must contrary me! marry, 'tis time.
Well said, my hearts! You are a princox; go.
         (I.v.78–88)

This is a scene which sticks in the memory; for here the dramatist, unencumbered by a story, is interpolating a lively scene in his own kind, a vignette of two very amusing people in an amusing situation. But it is unfortunate for the feud that this episode takes so well. For clearly old Capulet is unwilling to let the feud interrupt a dance; and a quarrel which is of less moment than a galliard is being appeased at an extravagant price, if the price is the death of two such delightful creatures as Romeo and Juliet;

        their parents' rage,
Which, but their children's end, naught could remove,
        (Prologue, 10–11)

loses all its plausibility. A feud like this will not serve as the bribe it was meant to be; it is no atonement for the death of the lovers. Nor, indeed, is it coherent and impressive enough as part of the plot to propel the sweep of necessity in the sequence of events. If the tragedy is to march relentlessly to its end, leaving no flaw in the sense of inevitability which it seeks to prompt, it clearly must depend for that indispensable tragic impression not on its feud, but on its scattered suggestions of doom and of malignant fate. And, as has been seen, Shakespeare harps frequently on this theme.

But how far can a Roman sense of Fate be made real for a modern audience? It is no mere matter of exciting thought to "wander through eternity" in the wake of the mystery which surrounds the human lot. Mystery must take on positive shape, and half-lose itself in dread figures controlling human life in their malice. The forms and the phrases by which these powers had been invoked were a

traditional part in the inheritance of the Senecan drama
which came to sixteenth-century Europe. Fortuna, Fatum,
Fata, Parcae: all were firmly established in its *dramatis
personae*. Moreover their role in Virgilian theocracy was
familiar to all with but a little Latin:

> Qua visa est fortuna pati Parcaeque sinebant
> Cedere res Latio, Turnum et tua moenia texi;
> Nunc iuvenem imparibus video concurrere fatis,
> Parcarumque dies et vis inimica propinquat.[7]

For Roman here indeed were the shapers of destiny, the
ultimate ἀνάγκη which compels human fate, whether as the
μοιρα of individual lot, or the εἱμαρμένη of a world order.
Horace himself linked Fortuna in closest companionship
with Necessitas: *"te semper anteit serva Necessitas,"* he
writes in his prayer to Fortuna.[8] It was a note which re-
verberated through Senecan stoicism.

But with what conviction could a sixteenth-century
spectator take over these ancient figures? Even the human
beings of an old mythology may lose their compelling
power; "what's Hecuba to him, or he to Hecuba?" But the
gods are in a much worse case; pagan, they had faded
before the God of the Christians: *Vicisti, Galilæe!* Fate
was no longer a deity strong enough to carry the responsibility of a tragic universe; at most, it could intervene casually as pure luck, and bad luck as a motive turns tragedy
to mere chance. It lacks entirely the ultimate tragic ἀνάγκη.
It fails to provide the indispensable inevitability.

Is then Shakespeare's *Romeo and Juliet* an unsuccessful
experiment? To say so may seem not only profane but
foolish. In its own day, as the dog's-eared Bodley Folio
shows, and ever since, it has been one of Shakespeare's
most preferred plays. It is indeed rich in spells of its own.
But as a pattern of the idea of tragedy, it is a failure. Even
Shakespeare appears to have felt that, as an experiment,
it had disappointed him. At all events, he abandoned
tragedy for the next few years and gave himself to history

7 *Aeneid* XII. 147.
8 *Odes* I. xxxv.

and to comedy; and even afterwards, he fought shy of the simple theme of love, and of the love of anybody less than a great political figure as the main matter for his tragedies.

Nevertheless it is obvious that neither sadism nor masochism is remotely conscious in our appreciation of *Romeo and Juliet,* nor is our "philanthropy" offended by it. But the achievement is due to the magic of Shakespeare's poetic genius and to the intermittent force of his dramatic power rather than to his grasp of the foundations of tragedy.

There is no need here to follow the meetings of Romeo and Juliet through the play, and to recall the spell of Shakespeare's poetry as it transports us along the rushing stream of the lovers' passion, from its sudden outbreak to its consummation in death. Romeo seals his "dateless bargain to engrossing death," choosing shipwreck on the dashing rocks to secure peace for his "sea-sick weary bark." Juliet has but a word: "I'll be brief. O happy dagger!" There is need for nothing beyond this. Shakespeare, divining their naked passion, lifts them above the world and out of life by the mere force of it. It is the sheer might of poetry. Dramatically, however, he has subsidiary resources. He has Mercutio and the Nurse.

Shakespeare's Mercutio has the gay poise and the rippling wit of the man of the world. By temperament he is irrepressible and merry; his charm is infectious. His speech runs freely between fancies of exquisite delicacy and the coarser fringe of worldly humor; and he has the sensitiveness of sympathetic fellowship. Such a man, if any at all, might have understood the depth of Romeo's love for Juliet. But the camaraderie and the worldly *savoir-faire* of Mercutio give him no inkling of the nature of Romeo's passion. The love of Romeo and Juliet is beyond the ken of their friends; it belongs to a world which is not their world; and so the passing of Romeo and Juliet is not as other deaths are in their impact on our sentiments.

Similarly, too, the Nurse. She is Shakespeare's greatest debt to Broke, in whose poem she plays a curiously unexpected and yet incongruously entertaining part. She is the one great addition which Broke made to the saga. She is garrulous, worldly, coarse, vulgar, and babblingly given to reminiscence stuffed with native animal humor and self-assurance. Shakespeare gladly borrowed her, and so gave his Juliet for her most intimate domestic companion a gross worldly creature who talks much of love and never means anything beyond sensuality. Like Romeo's, Juliet's love is completely unintelligible to the people in her familiar circle. To her nurse, love is animal lust. To her father, who has been a "mouse-hunter" in his time, and to her mother, it is merely a social institution, a worldly arrangement in a very worldly world. This earth, it would seem, has no place for passion like Romeo's and Juliet's. And so, stirred to sympathy by Shakespeare's poetic power, we tolerate, perhaps even approve, their death. At least for the moment.

But tragedy lives not only for its own moment, nor by long "suspensions of disbelief." There is the inevitable afterthought and all its "obstinate questionings." Our sentiments were but momentarily gratified. And finally our deeper consciousness protests. Shakespeare has but conquered us by a trick: the experiment carries him no nearer to the heart of tragedy.

JOHN RUSSELL BROWN

S. Franco Zeffirelli's "Romeo and Juliet"

An editorial in *Theatre Notebook* spoke of "revelation,"
The Observer of "revelation, even perhaps a revolution,"
and *Theatre World* of excitement, "unity of presentation,"
and a "reality which lifted one inescapably back to medieval Italy."[1] These are examples of the enthusiastic
reception which has kept Franco Zeffirelli's production of
Romeo and Juliet in the repertory of a London or touring
company of the Old Vic from 4 October 1960, into 1962,
bringing them a greater success than they have enjoyed for
more than a decade. Yet on the morning after its firstnight,
the critic of *The Times* spoke coldly of the performances,
and in *The Sunday Times* Harold Hobson described a
failure: to his disenchanted view, Romeo was "well-
spoken" but "pasty-faced and sulky," Juliet flapped "her
arms about like a demented marionette." After its season
in London these conflicting reactions seem less remarkable: it was a production of unique and consistent achievement which exchanged a number of conventional virtues
for others which are not often found in our presentations
of Shakespeare. And it was effected with such intelligence,
sympathy, and authority that we can now take stock and
ask how important these unusual virtues are for this play
and, perhaps, for others.

From *Shakespeare Survey 15* (1962). Reprinted by permission of Cambridge University Press.

[1] *Theatre Notebook*, XV (1961), *The Observer* (9 October 1960);
Theatre World (November 1960).

The break with custom was clearest in Zeffirelli's visual presentation of Romeo. Audiences have come to expect a dark handsomeness, reminiscent of Sir Laurence Olivier in the production of 1935. A white shirt is usually open at the neck; a dark wig accentuates a tall, noble brow; the eyes are made up to appear large and deep. The pose chosen for official photographs usually suggests a lonely, haughty, and brooding mind. With some additional swagger from the cloak Motley designed for him, Richard Johnson's Romeo at Stratford-upon-Avon in 1958 was in this tradition. Another recognizable but less common strain is the poetic: this is graceful, fluent, light. Michel Bernardy's Romeo for Saint-Denis's Strasbourg company in 1955 exemplified it, looking like some "herald Mercury." Both these traditions Zeffirelli broke. John Stride, his Romeo, wore no velvet; he had no wig, no cloak, no ornament; his shirt did not open at the neck. One of his costumes, devised by Peter Hall (the designer, not the director), seemed to be made of tweed, and none of them imposed grandiloquent postures; they were comfortable, hard-wearing, familiar clothes in grays and grayish-blues. In them, this Romeo could sit, squat, run, or stroll; he could run his hand through his hair or look insignificant among a crowd. He was so little the gilded youth that it seemed odd that he should have a personal servant. Clearly, this director had paid less attention than usual to the opening words of the Prologue: "Two households, both alike in dignity"; but in recompense he had avoided the meaningless gloss of "fancy dress" which many other Romeos assume with their splendid clothes. John Stride seemed to be English rather than Italianate, lively rather than sensuous; and he looked more convincingly in his teens than other actors of the part who have been equally young in fact.

To varying degrees all the young people in the play, except Paris, shared these qualities. Perhaps the Capulets were more richly dressed than the Montagues, but all the youth of Verona were at ease. Running and sauntering, they were immediately recognizable as unaffected teenagers; they ate apples and threw them, splashed each other with water, mocked, laughed, shouted; they became serious, sulked, were puzzled; they misunderstood confidently and expressed affection freely. Much of this behavior has been seen before in Peter Hall's productions of *A Midsummer Night's Dream* and *The Two Gentlemen* at Stratford-upon-Avon,[2] but besides dispensing with the magnificent clothes that sat incongruously on Hall's Lysander or Silvia, Zeffirelli did not condescend towards his young lovers and did not underestimate them. He gave prominence to a sense of wonder, gentleness, strong affection, clear emotion, and, sometimes, fine sentiment, as well as to high spirits and casual behavior. His characters were exciting and affecting as less responsive heroines and heroes could never be.

For after the first visual surprise there were others. Despite the prodigality of the director's invention, the stage business seemed to spring from the words spoken, often lending them, in return, immediacy, zest or delicacy. So the unpompous behavior could catch the audience's interest for the characters and for the old story. In the balcony scene after Juliet (Miss Judi Dench) had been called away, there was a still silence on her return before she dared speak again or Romeo dared to come out of hiding: this was given meaning by Romeo's preceding soliloquy:

> I am afeard,
> Being in night, all this is but a dream,
> Too flattering-sweet to be substantial.
>
> (II.ii.139–41)

And by illustrating their mutual sense of awe and fear, their response to the seemingly precarious nature of their new-found reality which at this time needs each other's presence to be substantiated, the still silence gave added force to the memory of Romeo's words. It also helped to prepare the audience for the direction and urgency of Juliet's following speech:

> If that thy bent of love be honorable,
> Thy purpose marriage, send me word tomorrow. . . .

2 Reviewed in *Shakespeare Survey*, XIII (1960) and XIV (1961).

Words and stage business together drew the audience into
the dramatic illusion. Such should be the aim of all directors of plays, but Zeffirelli has been unusual among our
contemporaries in unifying Shakespeare's words and an
inventive, youthful and apparently spontaneous action.
Again, as the lovers leave the stage with the Friar to be
married, Romeo walked backwards so that he continued
to face Juliet who was supported on the Friar's arm:
Romeo was "bewitched by the charm of looks" (II. Prol. 6)
rapt in

> . . . the imagined happiness that both
> Receive in either by this dear encounter.
> (II.vi.28–29)

So the stage business took its cue from the words spoken,
and centered Romeo's interest, without respect to absurdity
or other concerns, on his delight in love. As they met
adversity and danger, phrases like "Stand not amazed"
(III. i. 136), " 'Tis torture" (III. iii. 29), "Blubbering
and weeping" (III. iii. 87) were all directly and convincingly related to the action, and consequently they were far
more compelling than is customary in productions which
deliberately court a sumptuous setting and exotic mood.

The street "brawls" were realized in the same way. The
fight between Mercutio and Tybalt had a mixture of daring
and mockery which reflected the exaggeration of the text:

Consort! what, dost thou make us minstrels? an thou make
minstrels of us, look to hear nothing but discords: here's my
fiddlestick; here's that shall make you dance. 'Zounds, consort!
(III.i.47–50)

Since few people in a modern audience can judge its fine
points, the conventional duel usually appears either elegant
and correct, or dangerous, or sometimes impassioned; it
can hardly reflect the tone of this passage. Yet Zeffirelli
made the fight high-spirited, like the words. Mercutio,
gaining possession of both swords, used one as a whetstone
for the other before handing Tybalt's back—stopping to

wipe its handle with mocking ostentation. With such
preparation, Romeo could respond to Mercutio's sour jests
after he is wounded as casually as the text demands—
"Courage, man; the hurt cannot be much"—without appearing callow; the dying man's protestations could be
taken as the holding up of an elaborate jest. Enacting the
mood of the text in this way did not devalue the scene:
the bragging turned to earnest all the more effectively with
the suddenly involved and simple words of Romeo, "I
thought all for the best" (line 106).

Visually, Zeffirelli's presentation of the young characters
was remarkable, but not very original: he had gone further
and was more consistent in a development already common—in less subtle and responsible hands, it is all too
common. The greatest innovation of his production lay
in unifying words and stage business, in making the actors'
speech as lively and fluent as their physical action. The
result was that the dialogue did not appear the effect of
study and care, but the natural idiom of the characters in
the particular situations. It is a long time since Shakespeare's text has been so enfranchised. Juliet's "I have
forgot why I did call thee back" is often answered with
rhetorical neatness, or passionate emphasis, or fanciful
humor, in Romeo's "Let me stand here till thou remember
it" (II. ii. 171–72), but in this production the reply was
frank and happy, appropriate to the quick sensations of
the situation and suggesting a mutual response; the literary
finesse of the text was not used to draw attention to itself
but to give form and pressure to the dramatic moment. Or
again, the interchange between the Friar and Romeo:

> *Friar.* . . . wast thou with Rosaline?
> *Romeo.* With Rosaline, my ghostly father? no;
> I have forgot that name, and that name's woe.
>
> (II.iii.44–46)

was transformed by making Romeo blurt out "I have forgot
that name" as a sudden realization, a thought which had,
at that instant, come to him for the first time: it was still
an antithesis to the Friar's expectation, as a literary

analysis of the speech could show, but its sudden clarity was represented and accentuated by the manner in which it was spoken.

Some critics complained that this treatment of the dialogue destroyed the "poetry" of the play. But it would probably be truer to say that the poetry was rendered in an unfamiliar way. Zeffirelli has directed many operas, and turning to a Shakespeare production he ensured that many speeches were tuned with musical exactness. Changes of tempo, pitch, and volume were used to strong dramatic effect. For example, when Romeo called "Peace, peace" at the climax of the Queen Mab speech, Mercutio's "True" followed quickly and flatly, and then, changing the key, "I talk of dreams . . ." was low and quiet, rapt in mood. This director knows more about musical speech than most of those working in our theaters today. There were, however, some notable lapses: Mercutio's speech and Juliet's potion soliloquy lost their cumulative effects because they were broken by too much stage business (Juliet was made to writhe about in a red spotlight); the moments of incantatory stillness, which can have, in T. S. Eliot's words, a "winged validity" beyond their immediate dramatic impulse, were surrendered for livelier effects; and the actors seldom delighted in the "concord of sweet sounds." But Zeffirelli's animated style of speech was appropriate to much of the dialogue of the young characters in the play: in its new dramatic life the "poetry" showed its bravery, *élan,* gentleness. By making it sound like the natural idiom of the lovers and their companions, the director was restoring many of the original tones, the original freshness. In *Much Ado About Nothing,* Benedick says that Claudio was "wont to speak plain and to the purpose, like an honest man and a soldier," but being turned lover he is "turned orthography; his words are a very fantastical banquet, just so many strange dishes" (II. iii). Romeo is such a lover: meeting with Mercutio after the balcony scene his verbal wit runs "the wild-goose chase" and he is told: "now art thou what thou art, by art as well as by nature" (II. iv. 94–95). The "art" of much of the poetry in this play was surely intended to sound like a delighted and energetic response to immediate sensations, and in regaining this impression the actors responded in an appropriate way to the conscious artifice of their text. Their speaking reflected many of its moods, mixing humor with concern (as in Juliet's "Swear not by the moon"), mockery with envy, passion with fear and hesitation. The metrical basis of the speech was sometimes insecure, but its color and movement were often wonderfully accurate. Individual actors and actresses have achieved this dramatic life in Shakespearean roles at the present day—Sir Laurence Olivier and Miss Dorothy Tutin are the most gifted and unfailing of them—but here the same quality was sustained through whole scenes. The director had treated wit, rhetoric and "poetry" as an integral part of his production.

His success was chiefly with the young characters in the earlier part of the play. The first signs of merely routine handling were in the figures of authority. The Prince was given customary emphasis by two attendants with halberds, a voluminous gown and, by the standards of this production, rich accouterments. On his first entry he stood right up-center, and his words were accompanied by a muffled, rolling drum off-stage. But he lacked dramatic life comparable with that of the figures around him: the stage devices had added only an undefined impressiveness. This might be judged appropriate for his early appearance, but on his return after the death of Tybalt, when he stood downstage center, he still seemed out of touch with the other characters, for these hitherto agile and fluently organized figures immediately became fixed in postures at either side. In the last scene where the Prince finds himself implicated in the general sorrow and guilt ("for winking at your discords"), he stood unmoving, high above the heads of everyone else on the stage, and necessarily spoke in the earlier lifeless and formal manner. The director did attempt a more animated Friar, but here the business he invented seemed inapposite and occasionally impertinent: in the middle of his first speech a bell sounded off stage and he stopped to kneel and cross himself, and when Juliet met Romeo at his cell he stepped between them to effect a comic collision involving all three figures—a kind of humor wholly different from that quieter kind written into the lines he speaks—and this stage trick was repeated before the end of the short scene. In the last act, at the tomb, the Friar had such little relevance to the dramatic situation that he did not re-enter after he had left Juliet alone with Romeo's body: his speeches and all reference to him were cut.

While Zeffirelli had created an animating style for the story of the young lovers, he had not found a means of comparable liveliness to represent the authoritative figures which Shakespeare had made the center of important scenes. In this, the production was like many others which have been seen in England recently: Sir Tyrone Guthrie's treatment of the King of France in *All's Well*, Peter Hall's of Priam in *Troilus*, and Tony Richardson's of the Duke of Venice in *Othello*, all shown at Stratford in recent years, are examples of the same malaise. Even when it was Romeo and Juliet who assumed new dignity and authority in confronting catastrophe, this director seemed unsure of touch. Juliet's "Is there no pity sitting in the clouds. . . ?" (III. v. 198) was said hurriedly, sitting on the floor, as if she needed no strength of mind to frame and speak this question. (One may contrast Alan Webb's dignified and affecting delivery of the comparable, "O heavens, can you hear a good man groan, And not relent, or not compassion him?" from Peter Brook's production of *Titus Andronicus*.) Juliet's concluding line in this scene, with its authoritative and calm phrasing, "If all else fail, myself have power to die," was said lightly on the point of running from the stage. Similarly, Romeo's stature in the final scene was belittled by failing to show his authority and compassion before the dead bodies of the other young men, as Shakespeare's text ensures: his description of Paris as "One writ with me in sour misfortune's book" and:

> Tybalt, liest thou there in thy bloody sheet?
> O, what more favor can I do to thee,
> Than with that hand that cut thy youth in twain
> To sunder his that was thine enemy?
> Forgive me, cousin!

were both excised from the text used for this production, and no such effect was attempted.

Important moments of grief also seemed underplayed. The distraction, frustration, and fear of the young lovers were well represented with nervous intensity; the fault here was that the cries and groans and other physical reactions were sometimes at odds with the technical demands of long speeches with elaborate syntax and rhetoric. It was the more general and more considered grief that seemed hollow. The mourning for Juliet when she is discovered as if dead was staged formally like the authoritative scenes, and anonymous servants were introduced mechanically, two at a time, to extend the tableau and so attempt to effect an impression of climax. This indeed is one old-fashioned way of responding to the formal nature of the verse. Elsewhere it might serve; but in this production it was in glaring contrast with the minutely and freshly motivated stage business of adjacent scenes. The dramatic illusion previously established was lost in this presentation of general sorrow and was replaced with something that bore little or no resemblance to it. Romeo's address to the Apothecary showed the failure to represent a more considered grief. This is a speech of peculiar difficulty, for it must manifest complex reactions. In a vigorous handling, Zeffirelli concentrated on its agitation, so that his Romeo repeatedly struck and browbeat the "caitiff wretch." Here the difficulty was that this manner could not present consideration and compassion, responses that are implicit in:

> The world is not thy friend nor the world's law;
> The world affords no law to make thee rich; . . .

> There is thy gold, worse poison to men's souls,
> Doing more murders in this loathsome world,
> Than these poor compounds that thou mayst not sell . . .

> Farewell: buy food, and get thyself in flesh.

> (V.i.72–84)

And the long and detailed description of the apothecary's shop and wares issued strangely from the mind of this

Romeo, given over to turbulence and spite. The scene should surely be directed in a way that can show how grief *and* resolution have entered deeply into Romeo's soul, making him precise, understanding, compassionate, sharp, subtle, and even cynical: it is a complex moment that cannot be presented by a simple pursuit of energetic expression.

The still moments of general or deliberate grief were, like the figures of authority, unsatisfactory. The concluding scene indicated how far Zeffirelli, despite his sympathetic handling of almost all of the earlier acts, failed to respond to Shakespeare's text in these matters. He cut a hundred and twenty consecutive lines, those from the last of Juliet's to the Prince's "Where be these enemies? . . . ." The outcry of the people, the "ambiguities," the concern to find the "head" and "true descent" of the calamity, the general suspicion in which the Prince at last finds himself implicated along with the others, the call for "patience," the demand for "rigor of severest law," were all sacrificed. The main reason for this was not shortage of time, for the scene was then extended by much interpolated silent business: anonymous servants, embraced in pairs, symmetrically placed as a statuesque expression of general grief; mechanically, without being ordered to do so, they moved the bodies of Romeo and Juliet to the catafalque; in a slow procession, accompanied by singing off stage, the supposedly reconciled families departed with composed neatness at opposite sides of the tomb, without a look at the dead bodies and without recognition of each other; Benvolio and the Nurse were then reintroduced to take silent farewells of the bodies; and, finally, to swelling music, the lights faded with impressive slowness until the curtain fell. The ending had been refashioned as a solemn, exotically illuminated dumb-show. In comparison with the animated interplay of words and action that had preceded it, this spectacle seemed empty and meaningless. The conclusion of a production that had gripped and moved its audience was pretentious, sentimental, and vague.

Again it must be admitted that the discrepancy was not unexpected. Professional producers in recent years have all cut something from the last scene of *Romeo and Juliet*. Glen Byam Shaw, directing at Stratford-upon-Avon in 1954 and 1958, cut the dialogue between the Friar and Balthazar as the former approached the tomb, cut lines on the entry of the watch, delayed the Prince's entry, so that he had no need to repeat his question, and eliminated some of his orders; he also cut a few lines of the Friar's explanation and the whole of the depositions of Balthazar and Paris's page. The Stratford production of 1945 cut the Friar's last speech from forty lines to six; that of 1941 omitted the Friar altogether after he had left Juliet; and Peter Brook's production of 1947 deleted everything after Juliet's last words and, then, simply brought on the Chorus to conclude with a few of the Prince's last lines (and yet on this occasion there was time enough in the course of the play for introducing a Negro servant, an Arab, a carpet seller, a "man with a drum" and various other extra attractions).[3]

Directors working in the English theater do not respond to Shakespeare's presentation of authority and responsibility and of understanding, compassionate grief. This is surely a loss. The Prince's acknowledgment of complicity is Shakespeare's addition to the story as he found it in Arthur Brooke's narrative poem, *The Tragical History of Romeus and Juliet*. Moreover we know that Shakespeare was deeply concerned with the ways in which responsibility is learnt in adversity. The theme recurs at important crises in plays throughout his career: it is found when Richard the Second is imprisoned and when Henry the Fifth prays before Agincourt, and later, when Lear, Pericles, Cymbeline, Leontes, and Prospero become suppliants. Such a climax in *Romeo and Juliet* needs the development of the preceding hundred and twenty lines which Zeffirelli cut. And these lines have important dramatic interests to present on their own account. Compared with Arthur Brooke, who gave Juliet two long speeches immediately before her death, and with Otway, Cibber, and Garrick, who revised the play in the seventeenth and eighteenth

---

[3] The promptbooks of these productions are in the library of the Royal Shakespeare Theatre, Stratford-upon-Avon.

centuries and invented final speeches for the heroine, Shakespeare has hustled her last moments; he allowed her only the briefest possible utterances and brought the busy watchmen on stage immediately afterwards. Shakespeare gave time and words and action at this important culmination of the tragedy to the crowded stage as one after another of the characters kneel as "parties of suspicion" and as the two families stand silently listening. The Friar's long speech is so tightly written that it is difficult for a director to do anything but keep it almost intact or cut it out entirely; its very texture shows that it cannot represent a slackening of interest in the dramatist but rather a determination to show the manifold ways in which small, overconfident human decisions had worked together with some kind of destiny, that "greater power than we can contradict." Shakespeare's complicated and highly-worked last movement of the tragedy suggests that, however powerful destiny may seem, man and a Prince among men react to catastrophe with a sifting of responsibility and a demand for justice:

> Go hence, to have more talk of these sad things;
> Some shall be pardon'd, and some punished.

Zeffirelli's change to dignified dumb-shows of grief could not endow these words with the socially responsible, seemingly endless particularity of Shakespeare's full text. To present *Romeo and Juliet* satisfactorily it is necessary to find a style which can sustain the dramatic life of the entire last scene and of those earlier moments of authority and responsibility and of compassionate, understanding grief which prepare for this conclusion.

In part the shortcomings of this production may have been due to a lack of sympathy, for several of the less successful passages are known to be capable of lively presentation. In part it was probably due to a weakness in the metrical control of speech, for most of these moments involve sustained utterance or counterpointed phrases. It may also be bound up with the timing of the production as a whole.

At the very end the director used a slow pace in order to make the invented conclusion impressive, but this was after he had hurried some speeches which demand time to give the impression of consideration and after he had cut much from the second half of the play: III. iv and IV. iv were cut completely, the beginning of IV. ii, the musicians from IV. v, the first twenty-three lines of the important scene of Romeo in Mantua. It looks as if the earlier acts had been given too easy a rein. Discounting two intervals, the performance lasted two hours and fifty minutes: the first part, up to the end of II. ii, took an hour; the second part, up to the end of III. i, took forty minutes; and this left but an hour and ten minutes for most of Act III and the whole of Acts IV and V. It may well be that Zeffirelli purposely tried to speed up Acts III, IV, and V, sensing that the tempo had become too slack.

The beginning was slow in order to establish characters and atmosphere. For example, Romeo's first entrance was long and silent accompanied by shouting and laughter off stage; it showed his solitary, self-absorbed nature at the cost of narrative pressure. To introduce Mercutio with Benvolio for II. iv, time was taken to show them lounging in the street and encountering two casual passers-by who had left the stage before the first of Shakespeare's words had been spoken. After the Prince had pronounced judgment for the death of Tybalt, the stage emptied very slowly until only the Chorus was left and then he closed the scene by slowly walking the full depth of the deserted stage and, again slowly, lifting his hands in a gesture of despair. Some of the long pauses were made in order to enforce the lively manner of speech and action, but the style of acting was not the chief cause of slowness: that was rather the scenic realism. Twice a curtain rose to show the stage covered with smoke giving a hazy impression and to singing or calling and a whole crowd of stage-dressing supernumeraries. Two sets of curtains were used within the proscenium so that the scenery could be changed on every possible occasion, even if to disclose merely "another part of the streets" or "another room in Capulet's house." Some of the changes marvelously mirrored the change of mood implicit in the text: the most effective was to Juliet's bedroom with pale blue walls and a tall bed furnished with the same blue and white, making these colors dominant for the first time and giving a sense of space, femininity, and domestic peace. But all too many scene-changes were trivial in effect, one being only more or less commodious than the other or cumbersomely providing a large and by no means essential property, like the desk for Friar Lawrence placed before an all but meaningless backdrop.

The audience and critics generally admired the settings which were designed by Zeffirelli himself—though their mechanism and scenic realism were often old-fashioned in contrast to the style of acting. But on reflection we may question their usefulness and tact. With a simpler, but not necessarily less evocative or less changeable setting, the new, alert style of action and speaking might have made an even greater impact and the "realism" center more in the human behavior on which the story and the tragedy depends. By the same means, the tempo could have been more brisk. This would have answered the motif of "sudden haste" which is found in Shakespeare's text repeatedly, and with insistence:

It is too rash, too unadvised, too sudden: Too like the lightning. . . . on a sudden one hath wounded me, That's by me wounded. . . . Tybalt, that an hour Hath been my kinsman. . . . let Romeo hence in haste. . . . Hie to your chamber. . . . Hie you, make haste . . . hie hence, be gone, away! . . . Come, stir, stir, stir! . . . Uncomfortable time, why camest thou now . . .? . . . O mischief, thou art swift. . . . Stay not to question . . . then I'll be brief.

Such phrases are found in almost every scene after the first few and are not without significance. The pace, or momentum, of events can help to represent the "star-crossed" elements of the love story and so enable Romeo and Juliet to appear to be fighting with growing urgency against an increasingly complex concatenation of misfortunes, against a narrative logic that seems to emanate from "inauspicious stars" beyond man's control. The speedier over-all tempo which a simpler setting would have permitted could have aided this element of the tragedy.

And, to return to the earlier and even more important point, a simpler setting with a brisker pace would have allowed the director to give the breathing time which is necessary in Acts III, IV, and V for presenting the theme of responsibility and the deeper understanding which men learn through this catastrophe. The young characters of this production were so compellingly alive that the loss of the full play is the more unfortunate. It would be a pity if Zeffirelli's unity of speech and action, his enfranchisement of the elaborate dialogue as the natural idiom of the characters of the play, were to be associated in the public's mind with a tragedy which seemed to have lost its momentum and lifelike qualities halfway through performance.

Suggested References

The number of possible references is vast and grows alarmingly. (The *Shakespeare Quarterly* devotes a substantial part of one issue each year to a list of the previous year's work, and *Shakespeare Survey*—an annual publication—includes a substantial review of recent scholarship, as well as an occasional essay surveying a few decades of scholarship on a chosen topic.) Though no works are indispensable, those listed below have been found helpful.

1. Shakespeare's Times

Byrne, M. St. Clare. *Elizabethan Life in Town and Country*. Rev. ed. New York: Barnes & Noble, Inc., 1961. Chapters on manners, beliefs, education, etc., with illustrations.

Craig, Hardin. *The Enchanted Glass: the Elizabethan Mind in Literature*. New York and London: Oxford University Press, 1936. The Elizabethan intellectual climate.

Joseph, B. L. *Shakespeare's Eden: The Commonwealth of England 1558–1629*. New York: Barnes & Noble, Inc., 1971. An account of the social, political, economic, and cultural life of England.

Nicoll, Allardyce (ed.). *The Elizabethans*. London: Cambridge University Press, 1957. An anthology of Elizabethan writings, especially valuable for its illustrations from paintings, title pages, etc.

Shakespeare's England. 2 vols. Oxford: The Clarendon Press, 1916. A large collection of scholarly essays on a wide variety of topics (e.g., astrology, costume, gardening, horsemanship), with special attention to Shakespeare's references to these topics.

Tillyard, E. M. W. *The Elizabethan World Picture.* London: Chatto & Windus, 1943; New York: The Macmillan Company, 1944. A brief account of some Elizabethan ideas of the universe.

Wilson, John Dover (ed.). *Life in Shakespeare's England.* 2nd ed. New York: The Macmillan Company, 1913. An anthology of Elizabethan writings on the countryside, superstition, education, the court, etc.

2. Shakespeare

Barnet, Sylvan. *A Short Guide to Shakespeare.* New York: Harcourt Brace Jovanovich, Inc., 1974. An introduction to all of the works and to the traditions behind them.

Bentley, Gerald E. *Shakespeare: A Biographical Handbook.* New Haven, Conn.: Yale University Press, 1961. The facts about Shakespeare, with virtually no conjecture intermingled.

Bradby, Anne (ed.). *Shakespeare Criticism, 1919–1935.* London: Oxford University Press, 1936. A small anthology of excellent essays on the plays.

Bush, Geoffrey Douglas. *Shakespeare and the Natural Condition.* Cambridge, Mass.: Harvard University Press; London: Oxford University Press, 1956. A short, sensitive account of Shakespeare's view of "Nature," touching most of the works.

Chambers, E. K. *William Shakespeare: A Study of Facts and Problems.* 2 vols. London: Oxford University Press, 1930. An invaluable, detailed reference work; not for the casual reader.

Chute, Marchette. *Shakespeare of London.* New York: E. P. Dutton & Co., Inc., 1949. A readable biography fused with portraits of Stratford and London life.

Clemen, Wolfgang H. *The Development of Shakespeare's Imagery.* Cambridge, Mass.: Harvard University Press, 1951. (Originally published in German, 1936.) A temperate account of a subject often abused.

Craig, Hardin. *An Interpretation of Shakespeare.* Columbia, Missouri: Lucas Brothers, 1948. A scholar's book designed for the layman. Comments on all the works.

Dean, Leonard F. (ed.). *Shakespeare: Modern Essays in Criticism.* New York: Oxford University Press, 1957.

Mostly mid-twentieth-century critical studies, covering Shakespeare's artistry.

Granville-Barker, Harley. *Prefaces to Shakespeare*. 2 vols. Princeton, N. J.: Princeton University Press, 1946–47. Essays on ten plays by a scholarly man of the theater.

Harbage, Alfred. *As They Liked It*. New York: The Macmillan Company, 1947. A sensitive, long essay on Shakespeare, morality, and the audience's expectations.

———. *William Shakespeare: A Reader's Guide*. New York: Farrar, Straus, 1963. Extensive comments, scene by scene, on fourteen plays.

Ridler, Anne Bradby (ed.). *Shakespeare Criticism, 1935–1960*. New York and London: Oxford University Press, 1963. An excellent continuation of the anthology edited earlier by Miss Bradby (see above).

Schoenbaum, S. *Shakespeare's Lives*. Oxford: Clarendon Press, 1970. A review of the evidence, and an examination of many biographies, including those by Baconians and other heretics.

———. *William Shakespeare: A Compact Documentary Life*. New York: Oxford University Press, 1977. A readable presentation of all that the documents tell us about Shakespeare.

Smith, D. Nichol (ed.). *Shakespeare Criticism*. New York: Oxford University Press, 1916. A selection of criticism from 1623 to 1840, ranging from Ben Jonson to Thomas Carlyle.

Spencer, Theodore. *Shakespeare and the Nature of Man*. New York: The Macmillan Company, 1942. Shakespeare's plays in relation to Elizabethan thought.

Stoll, Elmer Edgar. *Shakespeare and Other Masters*. Cambridge, Mass.: Harvard University Press; London: Oxford University Press, 1940. Essays on tragedy, comedy, and aspects of dramaturgy, with special reference to some of Shakespeare's plays.

Traversi, D. A. *An Approach to Shakespeare*. Rev. ed. New York: Doubleday & Co., Inc., 1956. An analysis of the plays, beginning with words, images, and themes, rather than with characters.

Van Doren, Mark. *Shakespeare*. New York: Henry Holt & Company, Inc., 1939. Brief, perceptive readings of all of the plays.

Whitaker, Virgil K. *Shakespeare's Use of Learning*. San Marino, Calif.: Huntington Library, 1953. A study of the relation of Shakespeare's reading to his development as a dramatist.

3. Shakespeare's Theater

Adams, John Cranford. *The Globe Playhouse*. Rev. ed. New York: Barnes & Noble, Inc., 1961. A detailed conjecture about the physical characteristics of the theater Shakespeare often wrote for.

Beckerman, Bernard. *Shakespeare at the Globe, 1599–1609*. New York: The Macmillan Company, 1962. On the playhouse and on Elizabethan dramaturgy, acting, and staging.

Chambers, E. K. *The Elizabethan Stage*. 4 vols. New York: Oxford University Press, 1923. Reprinted with corrections, 1945. A valuable reference work on theaters, theatrical companies, and staging at court.

Gurr, Andrew. *The Shakespearean Stage 1574–1642*. Cambridge: Cambridge University Press, 1970. On the acting companies, the actors, the playhouses, the stages, and the audiences.

Harbage, Alfred. *Shakespeare's Audience*. New York: Columbia University Press; London: Oxford University Press, 1941. A study of the size and nature of the theatrical public.

Hodges, C. Walter. *The Globe Restored*. London: Ernest Benn, Ltd., 1953; New York: Coward-McCann, Inc., 1954. A well-illustrated and readable attempt to reconstruct the Globe Theatre.

Kernodle, George R. *From Art to Theatre: Form and Convention in the Renaissance*. Chicago: University of Chicago Press, 1944. Pioneering and stimulating work on the symbolic and cultural meanings of theater construction.

Nagler, A. M. *Shakespeare's Stage*. Tr. by Ralph Manheim. New Haven, Conn.: Yale University Press, 1958. An excellent brief introduction to the physical aspect of the playhouse.

Smith, Irwin. *Shakespeare's Globe Playhouse*. New York: Charles Scribner's Son's, 1957. Chiefly indebted to J. C.

Adams' controversial book, with additional material and scale drawings for model-builders.

Venezky, Alice S. *Pageantry on the Shakespearean Stage.* New York: Twayne Publishers, Inc., 1951. An examination of spectacle in Elizabethan drama.

4. Miscellaneous Reference Works

Abbott, E. A. *A Shakespearean Grammar.* New edition. New York: The Macmillan Company, 1877. An examination of differences between Elizabethan and modern grammar.

Berman, Ronald. *A Reader's Guide to Shakespeare's Plays,* rev. ed. Glenview, Ill.: Scott, Foresman and Company, 1973. A short bibliography of the chief articles and books on each play.

Bullough, Geoffrey. *Narrative and Dramatic Source of Shakespeare.* 4 vols. Vols. 5 and 6 in preparation. New York: Columbia University Press; London: Routledge & Kegan Paul, Ltd., 1957–. A collection of many of the books Shakespeare drew upon.

Campbell, Oscar James, and Edward G. Quinn. *The Reader's Encyclopedia of Shakespeare.* New York: Thomas Y. Crowell Co., 1966. More than 2,700 entries, from a few sentences to a few pages on everything related to Shakespeare.

Greg, W. W. *The Shakespeare First Folio.* New York and London: Oxford University Press, 1955. A detailed yet readable history of the first collection (1623) of Shakespeare's plays.

Kökeritz, Helge. *Shakespeare's Names.* New Haven, Conn.: Yale University Press, 1959; London: Oxford University Press, 1960. A guide to the pronunciation of some 1,800 names appearing in Shakespeare.

————. *Shakespeare's Pronunciation.* New Haven, Conn.: Yale University Press; London: Oxford University Press, 1953. Contains much information about puns and rhymes.

Linthicum, Marie C. *Costume in the Drama of Shakespeare and His Contemporaries.* New York and London: Oxford University Press, 1936. On the fabrics and dress of the age and references to them in the plays.

Muir, Kenneth. *Shakespeare's Sources*. London: Methuen & Co., Ltd., 1957. The first volume on the comedies and tragedies, attempts to ascertain what books were Shakespeare's sources, and what use he made of them.

Onions, C. T. *A Shakespeare Glossary*. London: Oxford University Press, 1911; 2nd ed., rev., with enlarged addenda, 1953. Definition of words (or senses of words) now obsolete.

Partridge, Eric. *Shakespeare's Bawdy*. Rev. ed. New York: E. P. Dutton & Co., Inc.; London: Routledge & Kegan Paul, Ltd., 1955. A glossary of bawdy words and phrases.

Shakespeare Quarterly. See headnote to Suggested References.

Shakespeare Survey. See headnote to Suggested References.

Smith, Gordon Ross. *A Classified Shakespeare Bibliography 1936–1958*. University Park, Pa.: Pennsylvania State University Press, 1963. A list of some 20,000 items on Shakespeare.

Spevack, Marvin. *The Harvard Concordance to Shakespeare*. Cambridge, Mass.: Harvard University Press, 1973. An index to Shakespeare's words.

Wells, Stanley, ed. *Shakespeare: Select Bibliographies*. London: Oxford University Press, 1973. Seventeen essays surveying scholarship and criticism of Shakespeare's life, work, and theater.

5. *Romeo and Juliet*

Brooke, Nicholas. *Shakespeare's Early Tragedies*. London: Methuen & Co., 1968.

Champion, Larry S. *Shakespeare's Tragic Perspective*. Athens, Georgia: University of Georgia Press, 1976.

Colie, Rosalie. *Shakespeare's Living Art*. Princeton: Princeton University Press, 1974.

Hamilton, A. C. *The Early Shakespeare* San Marino, Cal.: The Huntington Library, 1967.

Hoppe, Harry R. *The Bad Quarto of "Romeo and Juliet." A Bibliography and Textual Study*. Ithaca, New York: Cornell University Press; London: Oxford University Press, 1948.

Hosley, Richard (ed.). *The Tragedy of Romeo and Juliet*. New Haven: Yale University Press, 1954.

Knight, G. Wilson. *Principles of Shakespearian Production With Especial Reference to the Tragedies.* Baltimore: Pelican Books, 1949, pp. 39–40, 84–90.

Lawlor, John. *"Romeo and Juliet." Stratford-upon-Avon Studies 3: Early Shakespeare,* ed. John Russell Brown and Bernard Harris. New York: St Martin's Press, 1961, pp. 123–45; London: Edward Arnold (Publishers) Ltd., 1961.

Levin, Harry. "Form and Formality in *Romeo and Juliet," Shakespeare Quarterly,* 11 (1960), 3–11.

Mahood, M. M. *Shakespeare's Word Play.* London: Methuen & Co., Ltd., 1957, pp. 56–72.

Myers, Henry Alonzo. *Tragedy: A View of Life.* Ithaca, N.Y.: Cornell University Press, 1956. Contains " 'Romeo and Juliet' and 'A Midsummer Night's Dream': Tragedy and Comedy," reprinted in Signet Classic *A Midsummer Night's Dream,* ed. Wolfgang Clemen, 1963.

Moore, Olin H. *The Legend of Romeo and Juliet.* Columbus, Ohio. Ohio State University Press, 1950.

Spurgeon, Caroline F. E. *Leading Motives in the Imagery of Shakespeare's Tragedies.* Shakespeare Association Lecture for 1930, pp. 1–17.

Stoll, Elmer Edgar. *Shakespeare's Young Lovers.* London: Oxford University Press, 1937, pp. 1–44.

Vyvyan, John. *Shakespeare and the Rose of Love.* London: Chatto & Windus, Ltd., 1960, pp. 136–86; New York: Barnes & Noble, Inc., 1960.

The SIGNET CLASSIC Shakespeare

(0451)

- [ ] **ALL'S WELL THAT ENDS WELL, Sylvan Barnet,** ed., Tufts University. (516575—$1.95)
- [ ] **ANTONY AND CLEOPATRA, Barbara Everett,** ed., Cambridge University. (517725—$2.25)
- [ ] **AS YOU LIKE IT, Albert Gilman,** ed., Boston University. (516672—$1.95)
- [ ] **THE COMEDY OF ERRORS, Harry Levin,** ed., Harvard. (517423—$2.25)
- [ ] **CORIOLANUS, Reuben Brower,** ed., Harvard. (518446—$2.50)*
- [ ] **CYMBELINE, Richard Hosley,** ed., University of Arizona. (512685—$1.50)
- [ ] **HAMLET, Edward Hubler,** ed., Princeton University. (517636—$1.95)
- [ ] **HENRY IV, Part I, Maynard Mack,** ed., Yale. (515358—$1.95)
- [ ] **HENRY IV, Part II, Norman H. Holland,** ed., M.I.T. (517229—$2.50)
- [ ] **HENRY V, John Russell Brown,** ed., University of Birmingham. (515757—$1.95)
- [ ] **HENRY VI, Part I, Lawrence V. Ryan,** ed., Stanford. (517059—$3.50)
- [ ] **HENRY VI, Part II, Arthur Freeman,** ed. (515234—$2.95)
- [ ] **HENRY VI, Part III, Milton Crane,** ed. (513231—$1.95)
- [ ] **HENRY VIII, Samuel Schoenbaum,** ed., Northwestern University. (512464—$1.50)
- [ ] **JULIUS CAESAR, William and Barbara Rosen,** eds., University of Connecticut. (514300—$1.75)
- [ ] **KING JOHN, William H. Matchett,** ed., University of Washington. (513991—$1.95)
- [ ] **KING LEAR, Russel Fraser,** ed., Princeton University. (517687—$2.25)
- [ ] **LOVE'S LABOR LOST, John Arthos,** ed., University of Michigan. (517733—$2.50)

*Price in Canada is $2.95

𝒞

The SIGNET CLASSIC Shakespeare

Buy them at your local

bookstore or use coupon

on next page for ordering.

ℂ

World Drama from SIGNET CLASSIC

(0451)

☐ **TARTUFFE and OTHER PLAYS by Molière.** Translated, with an Introduction by Donald M. Fame. Includes *The Ridiculous Précieuses, The School for Husbands, The School for Wives, Don Juan, The Versailles Impromptu,* and *The Critique of The School for Wives.* (515668—$2.95)

☐ **THE MISANTHROPE and OTHER PLAYS by Molière.** Translated, with an Introduction by Donald M. Fame. Includes *The Doctor in Spite of Himself, The Miser, The Would-Be Gentleman, The Mischievious Machinations of Scapin, The Learned Women,* and *The Imaginary Invalid.* (517210—$3.50)

☐ **CHEKHOV: THE MAJOR PLAYS by Anton Chekhov.** *Ivanov, The Sea Gull, Uncle Vanya, The Three Sisters* and *The Cherry Orchard.* New translation by Ann Dunnigan. Foreword by Robert Brustein. (517679—$2.95)

☐ **IBSEN: FOUR MAJOR PLAYS, Volume I, by Henrik Ibsen.** *The Master Builder, A Doll's House, Hedda Gabler,* and *The Wild Duck.* New translation with Foreword by Rolf Fjelde. (513975—$2.25)

☐ **IBSEN: FOUR MAJOR PLAYS, Volume II, by Henrik Ibsen.** *Ghosts, An Enemy of the People, The Lady from the Sea,* and *John Gabriel Borkman.* New translation by Rolf Fjelde. (516559—$2.50)

☐ **PLAYS by George Bernard Shaw,** Introduction by Eric Bentley. *Man and Superman, Candida, Arms and the Man,* and *Mrs. Warren's Profession.* (517865—$3.95)

☐ **PYGMALION and MY FAIR LADY.** George Bernard Shaw's brilliant romantic play and the internationally acclaimed musical adaptation by Alan Jay Lerner, together in one special edition. (517601—$2.50)

Buy them at your local bookstore or use this convenient coupon for ordering.
THE NEW AMERICAN LIBRARY, INC.,
P.O. Box 999, Bergenfield, New Jersey 07621
Please send me the books I have checked above. I am enclosing $_____
(please add $1.00 to this order to cover postage and handling). Send check or money order—no cash or C.O.D.'s. Prices and numbers are subject to change without notice.
Name_____
Address_____
City _____ State _____ Zip Code _____
Allow 4-6 weeks for delivery.
This offer is subject to withdrawal without notice.